Ghosts and Other A

© David H

Foreword

Aberration is such a good word. The dictionary definition says it is 'a departure from what is normal, usual, or expected, typically an unwelcome one'. Most of my stories contain such things. These tales are fictional, and for entertainment purposes only (as all the paranormal TV programmes state), but that doesn't mean that they COULDN'T actually happen, does it? Many of the stories are based on my own theories on ghosts, the afterlife and other supernatural occurrences. Some are meant as cautionary tales against using the paranormal and occult as a plaything. This book is a follow-on from my previous book 'Mysteria - An anthology of spooky and mysterious tales'. It is meant to be enjoyed in a quiet room when you are all alone. A room where the light throws certain corners into darkness. It is in those corners that the demons and anomalies in my book dwell - there.....and in your nightmares.

Closing the Gates

It was the last day and the last shift in the old engineering factory. After 120 years the company was closing its doors. The work had largely moved away. They once made parts and tools for local industry, but due to a combination of foreign imports and a declining home manufacturing market, the company decided to call it a day and wind up proceedings. The last shift finished and all the workers said their goodbyes. Everyone met in the canteen for a final get-together. Tears were shed and the continuation of friendships was vowed. Soon the doors closed for business for the very last time. Only one person remained. Tony, the night watchman.

Tony had once been a fitter at the very same factory. He started as an apprentice at the age of fifteen. He worked through until his retirement then took the part time job as night watchman. In truth, he didn't know what to do with himself. His wife had died some years previously and the nights were lonely without her. 'What better job for someone in that position' he had thought to himself.

The place always felt a little eerie at night, but tonight had an extra significance. It also felt dead. It felt like patrolling the empty shell of a giant corpse. A dinosaur that had finally succumbed to its inevitable demise. Some of the machines had already been removed, and the marks upon the floor where they had once stood felt like a dagger in his heart. He knew every machine in the factory, and the name of every person who had worked at it since his first days. The big old milling machine where so many cast iron castings had been machined was gone. The thick, black dust from the castings still littered the floor. A graphite grey fine powder that came off them. He remembered old Bob who could make the machine sing. A real craftsman. Working to tolerances of a thousandth of an inch on a regular basis. His face covered in the dust, so that when he took off his mask, you could see the contrast between the filth on his forehead and the clean face beneath.

Bob had retired about twenty years previously and had since died. He attended his meagre funeral on one overcast afternoon in December. He could still remember how he always addressed him with the greeting 'Now young man, how are you on this fine morning?' Out of the blue, it all became too much for him and he began to sob like a child. The significance sat heavily on his shoulders. He wasn't too worried about himself, but his grandson had a young family and was now out of work. As for himself, well he had no idea what he would do. It was then that he heard a familiar laugh behind him, followed by the words 'Now young man, whatever is the matter?' He swivelled on his heels and was confronted by old Bob.

Tony closed his eyes and shook his head, whilst saying to himself 'This isn't real. Get a grip'. He had seen someone do it in a film. It didn't work in the film, and it didn't work now either. When he opened his eyes, Bob was still standing there. 'Have you gone bloody daft lad. Standing there wafting your head around?' Bob asked.

'Is it really you, Bob....is it?' Tony asked him. 'Well it's not bloody Father Christmas is it?', Bob replied.

Tony didn't know whether to laugh or cry at the remark. In the end he did a weird combination of the both.

'Have you come to have a last look round the old place, Bob?' Tony asked. 'Last look be buggered, they don't kill a million memories just by closing the doors' he replied. Bob waved his hand and told Tony to take a look. There they all were. All the old workmen of his childhood. Tony knew every face in there and the names of their wives and husbands, and every one of their children. Where Bob stood, the silhouette of his huge old milling machine appeared. Bob hit the start button and the old machine throbbed into life as he machined the face of a cast iron component.

When Tony looked around, all the machines were working. The clattering noise that accompanied the sound of heavy industry. A voice hailed him impatiently 'Don't just stand there you lazy little bugger, go and help Alf drill out them castings'. It was his old foreman. Gerry. Tony immediately said 'Yes Mr Walsh', but his voice sounded different. It sounded young. He looked and he was wearing his blue engineers overalls. He had slipped back in time. He was back in the nineteen fifties again. Tony knew that this couldn't be happening, but it was. He knew he wasn't dreaming as all the sights, smells and noises assailed his senses. He could actually touch his overalls and the flat cap upon his head. 'Maybe I'm dead' Tony said to himself. 'Not yet, but you bloody well might be if you don't get a move on lazy-bones' Gerry said.

Thus, in this blissful scene from his past, Tony continued to be the teenager he had once been. After a while all the machines were shut down one by one and all the old employees gathered around him. It was Bob who spoke up first. He looked Tony in the face and smiled, then said 'This old place had earned its place in history and we carry each piece of it in our hearts. We were never happier than when we were here. You don't close down a family, lad. It isn't possible'.

Gerry then joined the conversation. He said 'When your time is ready, this place, this factory, these people, will all be here. No more worries about overseas imports or a shrinking market. Over on this side, we have enough orders for a million years'. Then he heard Billy Pearson, the shop steward speak up. 'Aye, no rest for us buggers. Still enough work to kill a donkey' he said, to the laughter of all the workers. Bob continued the conversation by saying 'We will have to be leaving soon. Why don't you go and say hello to your Jean. You remember where her machine is don't you?' 'She's there. She's really there?' Tony said excitedly. 'Aye, she is lad. Best get a move on. Women don't like to be kept waiting.

Tony saw his Jean again. Although they couldn't kiss or touch, they could, and did renew their love for each other. Tony asked Jean 'Did you all come back to say goodbye to the old place?' She smiled at him and answered 'No love. We came because you asked us to'.

Logbarr Lake

'There's a bear in the woods,' the old man said.

Chris smiled sweetly at him and said, 'Thanks for the tip-off. I will keep an eye out for it'.

The old man shrugged his shoulders and said, 'Well, it's your funeral'.

Chris knew that bears hadn't been in the wild in Scotland for hundreds of years. He had called in at The Tourist Board kiosk and picked up one of those 'Places of Interest' booklets. No one there warned him that an escaped bear from a zoo or a circus was on the loose. He just put it down to the old man being 'a little confused'. He thought no more of it.

The plan was to do a little wild fishing. Inside the forest there were small lakes and tarns. These were remote and very seldom fished. He would camp up beside these lakes and fish during the day. It was his first holiday since he had been 'ill'. Chris suffered with severe depression. This was the first time in ages that he had felt like venturing out. He followed the maps and checked his positions regularly with his hand held GPS. Soon he reached the first of his beloved lakes.

The brooding forest cast a dark shadow across the water on the far bank. It was so still and calm that the trees were perfectly mirrored on the glass-like surface of the lake. The water lilies and reeds were being nudged. A sure sign that fish were feeding. They would have to wait. First he must set up camp. Within minutes the tent was pitched and a small fire was burning in an enclosure of rocks that he had gathered. His kettle was hissing merrily on a stand above the fire. He made himself a cup of tea and started to set up a rod.

Many people would feel vulnerable and frightened alone in a forest. Not Chris - he adored it! 'It's the towns and cities that are the real jungles,' he would often say. He never felt quite safe walking home at night through the city. Although Chris was ex-military and knew how to handle himself, he hated feeling on edge. The last time he had felt so alert was during his final tour of duty. It had left him with a healthy mistrust of doorways and dark alleyways. The forest easily betrayed any advancing threat. The crackle of dry twigs underfoot. The peaceful silence, broken only by birdsong and the droning of insects. Only in places like this could he relax.

Chris managed to land a couple of wild brown trout. These were now grilling over the open fire. These would make a splendid lunch. The sun was beating down and the dragonflies played catch-as-catch-can over the surface of the lake in their mating ritual. A buzzard screamed somewhere high above the trees and a water vole swam lazily across the lake's surface. This was meat and drink to Chris. It just didn't get any better than this! Soon it would be nightfall. Chris busied himself in gathering fuel for the fire. Tomorrow he would de-camp and move on to his next destination. Apart from the charred remains of his fire, Chris prided himself in leaving every place that he camped at, as he originally found it.

Shortly before night fell, Chris set out his perimeter wires. These were a set of trip-lines that ran through a series of looped spikes that terminated in an electric alarm gadget. If someone walked through the wires, it pulled a pin from the alarm box and the alarm would sound. It gave him an extra layer of security. He wasn't expecting any unwelcome visitors, but if they arrived, then he would be ready for them. It would also warn him if any foxes strayed into the perimeter that had been attracted by the smell of his food larder that hung from the branch of a tree close by his tent. He had also set up a night vision camera to capture short videos of any animals that approached camp. He would often capture lovely short clips of deer and foxes on trips like these. With everything in place, Chris settled down for the night.

It would be around 2 am when Chris was woken by the sound of someone singing close by. Within seconds he was out of the tent, his hunting knife in hand. Sitting on the ground by the fire was the old man. The one who had warned him about bears. He was singing 'Teddy Bear's Picnic' whilst idly poking at the ashes of the fire with a stick and smiling.

'Just what I need. A screaming nutter disturbing my sleep,' Chris mumbled to himself. 'What do you want?' he asked. At the same time wondering why he hadn't tripped the alarm.

'Just a warm by your fire and to help you,' the old man answered.

'Help me with what?' Chris asked.

'The bear, of course,' the old man said, whilst nodding towards the far bank.

Chris looked and could hardly believe what he saw. It looked like a shimmering hologram of a bear. Not just a bear, but an abnormally huge one. This bear must have been ten feet tall.

'You can put your knife away young man. It will be little help to you,' the old man said.

Chris let out a small and panicked laugh and said, 'I'll just hang on to it, if it's all the same to you'.

'Now do you believe me about the bears?' the old man asked.

Chris told the old man that he was indeed seeing something but, as yet, he hadn't decided what it was. He wondered if this was some kind of elaborate hoax that was perpetrated on tourists to bring a little notoriety to the area. Probably some kind of projected image. A hologram of some kind. Then he saw the bear enter the water. It seemed to be swimming towards them. If that's a hologram, then how come it's disturbing the surface of the lake? Chris thought to himself. Fear and panic had now been channelled automatically in his mind. He had clicked immediately into combat mode. He readied himself for the approach of the creature.

Chris moved so that the fire was between him and the creature. It emerged slowly from the water and slumped to the ground. Its breathing was laboured and slow.

The old man gently caressed the bear's head and it licked his hand as would a puppy. 'She means no harm' the old man said. 'We will be gone soon'. The old man then told Chris a fantastical tale. One that to this very day he hasn't told a soul. 'Did you check your map and look what this lake is called?' the old man asked Chris.

Chris said that he had. 'It's called Logbarr Lake isn't it?'

The old man smiled and said that it was, but it was once called Lagu Bera. The old words for Lake of the Bear. He went on to tell Chris that there was once an ancient race of people who had imprisoned a great bear in a cave. They had taunted it and weakened it. It was to be the son of the chieftain who would despatch the bear in combat as a rite of passage. The old bear was released from the cave, but instead of attacking or trying to escape, it lay upon the ground in front of the young man. He was touched with remorse for the pitiful state of this wondrous creature. He called for water and food and brought it to the bear. It ate hungrily. From thenceforth, the two of them were inseparable. He became known as Chieftain of the Bear Clan. He proved invincible in battle and became a great and wise leader. On his deathbed, the old bear never strayed from his side. When the chieftain died, the bear swam out to the centre of the lake and drowned itself. On the anniversary of the chieftain's death, the ghost of the bear was seen to emerge from the lake and lie down beside where his master had died.

'I'm the last one. The land of the line' the old man said. 'The last to honour the ritual'. As he said these words, the figure of the bear slowly faded away. At that, the old man began to cry. 'I have been given just months to live. The story will die with me,' he said.

Chris was still reeling from everything that had just happened. The old man took a medallion from his pocket. It was an old, battered silver coin. It had words that Chris found unfamiliar. It bore a figure of a bear and a crown on the reverse side.

'I want you to have this, young man,' he said.

Chris knew better than to argue. He accepted the coin graciously and shook the hand of the old man.

Every year Chris visited Logbarr Lake, and every year he waited by the lake side to welcome the bear. He never suffered another day of depression after that. At last he had found a fellow warrior. Someone he could truly identify with.

At last - Chris belonged.

The Whisperings

The storm rolled in with inky blackness. It glowered down oppressively, leaving Finn brooding in expectation. It posed like a smirking bully that was about to do something unspeakable, then move on without a care. 'Time I was inside,' Finn thought to himself. He pulled his coat tighter around his gaunt frame and headed home. 'Hah, home indeed!' he thought, and with good reason. It had felt so far away from home as to feel as if the word was a complete travesty. Home was somewhere you felt safe. Somewhere that you felt cosy and warm. That old pile was far from that.

It was an old hill farm that he had brought back from the brink of destruction. The heathland held no interest for him as a commercial venture, but the house seemed ideal. Ideal to allow him the peace to write. On summer's days, the house was a joy. He could open the window and hear sheep bleating on the hills, and the melancholic piping of the curlew. During summertime his writing was filled with colour and warmth, but this wasn't summer, it was deepest winter.

Of late, his publisher had begun to worry a little. Finn's writings had taken on a dark and almost Gothic feel to them. His fans had fallen in love with his rustic tales of country life. His delicious descriptions of the love-filled characters of his local village. His new stuff was different. Behind every phrase there seemed to lie a tinge of malice and foreboding. The jolly postman. Once a jovial and ruddy-faced bringer of good tidings, had become a skulking character. Someone he seemed to see as a viper in the nest. A disseminator of gossip. A tittle-tattle of the worst kind. The once jovial characters in the village had now become curtain-twitchers. They seemed to whisper in corners and exclude him. Every time that Finn heard laughter, it felt as if it was him that they were laughing at.

Finn now avoided the village pub, and indeed the village in its entirety. Instead he preferred to drive an extra five miles to shop in anonymity in the nearest big town. He used the excuse that everything was cheaper and just as fresh, but he didn't even fool himself. It was pure bloody-mindedness. He didn't want to give 'those people' his money or support. Finn was slipping slowly and inexorably into a pit of loneliness and despondency. It was at this time that he started to see the dark figure.

The first time Finn saw the figure, it was just a small, black silhouette on the distant horizon. The figure always stood perfectly still and always facing towards him as if watching him. Occasionally, he would see the figure lift its arms as if bringing something up to its face. He could only assume it must be a pair of binoculars. 'So, the little shits are spying on me now are they?' he mumbled under his breath. It both exhilarated and frightened him in equal proportions. An affirmation (in his eyes) that his suspicions about the villagers were true, but also a deep-seated fear of what they may have in store for him. Of late, and as if buoyed by its own arrogance. The figure had started to move closer and closer towards him on every sighting.

Finn had now started to only venture out at daybreak, or at dusk. He had bought himself a pair of Alsatians. He had searched long and hard to find a pair that were both trained and also quite large for the breed standard. They became his constant companions. He would also venture out with a double-barrelled, 12 bore shotgun tucked underneath his arm. He became the sort of figure that it would be dangerous to meet. He had become unstable.

The telephone rang on Finn's desk. The two Alsatians were instantly alerted and sat by his side. Finn tentatively lifted the receiver and said 'Hello?' The voice that greeted him was his publishers. 'Finn old fella. How is it going?' he asked. 'It's going OK, why do you ask?' Finn replied. His publisher said that he wanted to come over and have a chat with him, and would later that afternoon be okay? Finn hesitated for a while before saying 'Yes, that will be fine. It will be good to see a friendly face,' before pausing and adding the words, 'For a change'.

'Is everything okay?' his publisher asked.

Finn just laughed it off and said, 'Oh, it's just my dour mood. It gets lonely up here. Just me and the bloody curlews'.

It was just after two-thirty in the afternoon when Finn's publisher knocked on his door. He was immediately taken aback by the noise that greeted him. First the two Alsatian's huge, booming barks, and the sound of their bodies banging against the door in their frenzy to get at him. Then next Finn's voice shouting out his orders 'Rebel, Spartan, get here NOW.... Sit'. Finn opened his door a little and peeped through the gap, before opening it wide and saying 'Tom, dear old friend, so good to see you, come on in'. He then hugged him, and said 'Take no notice of my two boys here. Their bark is worse than their bite'. Tom smiled in reply, but also noticed that neither dog averted their gaze from him for even a split second.

'So lovely to see you. For what reason do I owe this wonderful visitation?' Finn asked.

Tom shuffled a little uneasily in his seat, before asking 'Is everything okay Finn?'

'Of course. Why do you ask?' Finn replied.

Tom then mentioned that his writings had 'lost a little of their warmth'.

Finn then went on to tell him about how the villagers had started to shun him and gossip behind his back. He also mentioned the dark figure with the binoculars. 'I put their shitty little village on the map. I put money in their grubby little hands by bringing tourists' Finn said. 'Perhaps that's why they despise me now. Everyone now knows about their sordid little goings-on', he said.

Tom asked Finn if he had asked the villagers if this was the case, but Finn just dismissed it with a sarcastic laugh, and the words 'Do you think the snidey little in-breds would admit it?'. 'I have even had my mail diverted to a P.O. box' Finn added. 'I don't trust that red-faced little pariah that brings the mail'.

Tom said his goodbyes and made his excuse to leave, by saying 'I don't want to be driving down country lanes in the dark'. Tom was worried. Even more worried now that he realised that the detective that he had hired to keep an eye on Finn had been spotted. He had become increasingly worried about the tone of his writings and sent out the private investigator to watch Finn and allay any fears that he had. He would dismiss the investigator the next day as his worst fears had been proven to be true. Finn was indeed 'not himself'. The appearance of the detective would only make things worse.

Tom made discreet enquiries in the village about Finn. He started off at the Post Office and General Store. Apart from the pub, this was the daytime hub of village activity. He asked how the tourist trade was going.

Sandra, the postmistress looked at him and said 'What tourist trade?'

He then mentioned that Finn had said that the tourist trade had picked up after the publication of his books.

Sandra laughed a little then said 'Well, we all suspected it was us he used as the characters in his book, but he set the village in a county on the other side of the country. So how could we GET any tourist trade?'

'Good point' Tom said.

Sandra went on to tell him that the village had slowly changed over the decades. Instead of four or five small farms dotted around, there were now just two large farms that were owned by a land agent. She also said that three quarters of the houses in the village were occupied by outsiders, or used just as holiday homes. 'It's just a quaint little dormitory village now,' she said, and then smiled softly.

Tom apologised for his intrusiveness.

Sandra said 'Tell him that he is welcome here and that no one wants to know his business. We keep ourselves to ourselves.'

Tom noticed that Finn's writings had become more and more nonsensical. He began talking about 'The Black Man'. He was some kind of demonic figure that had started to appear at the foot of his bed. Finn said that he was some kind of occult figure. A demon of some kind. He began to write about hearing incantations at night, even though his dogs never made a murmur. He also told him that he had started to sleep with his shotgun, and kept it loaded and beneath the bedsheets with him.

Eventually, Finn's writings stopped entirely. A week later, Tom heard from the police that Finn's body had been found on the moors with his shotgun beside him. He was semi-naked and had put the barrel of the shotgun beneath his chin and pulled the trigger. An obvious suicide. His Alsatians had been with him at the time. When they found him, his body had been horribly mutilated as if animals had been feeding on him. It was suspected that the dogs had done it.

The funeral service was held back in his home town. The villagers were glad of this, as they didn't want the publicity, or indeed the 'tragedy tourists' that would come sniffing around the moors. Tom knew that Finn would rest in peace in his family plot beside his mum and dad.

On the same day, in one of the barns at one of the farms, a handful of the old villagers sat around a coal brazier. They were drinking a toast and laughing. One of them said 'To a good harvest. A toast to our mother goddess Gaia. May she bless our crops by our sacrifice'. On the brazier, a piece of meat was sizzling. It was being tended to by Sandra, the postmistress. 'It's ready now. Let's eat' she said. It was a human heart. It was Finn's heart!

Four Merlins

It took them around an hour to climb up to the top of the hill. It was a remote spot to start with, but there was quite a bit left to see of the old Lancaster bomber. All seven occupants were killed, and the eldest was just twenty three. They had been limping home from a mission when the fog came down. They never even saw the hilltop that took their lives. The occasion was even more auspicious as it was the anniversary of the crash. It was seventy two years to the day.

Ken and Tony were making a sort of pilgrimage. They weren't thrill seekers or disaster tourists, they had decided to go to each crash site that they could find and say a prayer. They would also lay a single red rose at each spot they visited.

They were both ex-servicemen themselves, but had been fortunate enough to come through it all unscathed. Tony read 'The Airman's Prayer' and Ken followed it with the famous verse from 'The Fallen' by Laurence Binyon. The verse that starts with 'They shall not grow old, as we that are left grow old'. The two men then held a minute's silence. As usually happened, a single tear ran down Tony's cheek. He remembered comrades and brothers that were no longer alive. The atmosphere felt alive and thick with the spirits of these poor airmen. It was a chilling and a sombre place. They both silently prayed that their passing was mercifully swift.

Ken and Tony each took a photograph on their phones for their blog and made their way back down the hill. It wasn't a moment too soon. Black clouds were gathering on the horizon. They were relieved to reach the safety of the little country inn at which they were staying for the night. 'Did you find it then?' the landlord asked. Ken nodded. He was still a little too moved to speak. The landlord brought over two whiskies and placed them before them both, and said 'On the house'. They both drank the health of the landlord. He too was moved by their pilgrimage to pay their respects.

The morning after, over breakfast, Ken told Tony that he had experienced the strangest dream. He told him that he heard the sound of the four Merlin engines of a Lancaster bomber. It flew so low over his bedroom that it made the window pane rattle. Shortly after this there was a loud thud. 'It was a really vivid dream. I woke up sweating,' he said.

Tony was absolutely speechless. He himself had experienced the very same dream. At that moment, the landlord came across carrying two plates of 'The full Monty'. Two hearty full English breakfasts. He looked rather sheepish and hovered around the table before finally speaking. 'This might sound daft, but did either of you happen to hear anything last night. A low flying aircraft?' he said.

Both men simultaneously said, 'Yes, I did'.

'It happens every year', he said. 'Keep it to yourselves, though. I don't want those lads to become a sideshow.'

When Ken got home he examined the pictures on his phone, then rang Tony in a state of some excitement. Tony answered the phone and Ken blurted out the words 'I think I have taken a picture of their ghosts.'

Tony said that he had similar anomalies on his pictures too. There was no doubt about it. On two of the pictures you could see seven faint silhouettes. They only posted the ones that DIDN'T have the silhouettes onto the blog. They wanted this to be kept as a strict secret.

It was now a year later. Ken and Tony had decided to re-visit the crash site, but this time they would stay out on the moorland by the crash site. The crash was reported to have happened at one-fifteen in the morning. They would park up and make their way on foot up the hillside by torchlight. They wouldn't stay for long. Just long enough to see if it would happen again.

They made themselves comfortable against the remnants of a dry stone wall some twenty yards from the crash scene. It was a still and clear night. They could see the twinkling lights of the town below. It looked like a pretty little model village. Suddenly, everywhere went completely black. There was a full moon, and they could see the village below bathed in moonlight. 'A power cut do you think?' Ken asked. Then Tony pointed to the skies and said 'Look up there'. There they saw the unmistakeable outline of a Lancaster bomber. Both men were mesmerised by the vision. Neither of them was frightened, merely enthralled. 'That's strange, he looks well high enough to clear the hill' Tony said. It was then that they saw the silhouette of another aircraft. Tony knew this plane well from his childhood. He had an old world war two plane-spotters guide to the shape and outlines of flying aircraft. 'It's a Hurricane' Tony said 'but what is he doing'. They looked on in horror as the Hurricane cut across the Lancaster diagonally and opened fire, and they saw bits flying off the Lancaster and the starboard wing finally detaching itself. The plane slammed into the hillside. Within a second or two, all the lights in the village came back on. The scene was as before. No burning wreckage, just the icy stillness of the moor at night.

It was Ken who spotted them first. 'Look, there are people walking towards us. Perhaps it's the police wondering what we are up to,' he said. As the men approached, they both realised that these were the spirits of the airmen. Both men sat in awe and trepidation as to what was about to befall them. The spirit of a young airman approached them whilst the others stood a little way back. They could see by his uniform that he would have been the captain of the crew. The spirit spoke up. 'Thank you for taking the trouble to come here, and thank you for the prayers in our honour,' he said.

The two men merely nodded. They were just too shocked to

speak.

'I'm free now, do you see?' the captain said. 'We are all free. Free to cross over.' The spirit then went on to explain that he had been blamed for his bad airmanship and captaincy. 'They said the navigator hadn't read and plotted our course properly and I was at the wrong height. They also said it was a foggy night over the hills, it wasn't. It was how you saw it tonight with a full moon'.

The Hurricane pilot had reported that he had shot down a Dornier that had been returning from a bombing mission and must have drifted off course. He was completely blameless as the night sky had been thick with them. The Lancaster had hit shore at a different position, and although it was on course for home, it wasn't in an expected position. It was a 'wrong place, wrong time' type of incident.

The young airmen went on to tell them that they had met and made their peace with the Hurricane pilot. He himself had been shot down and killed a few months afterwards. He told Ken and Tony that it was the injustice of the lie that had been fettering them to the crash site. 'Now that someone knows what happened, we can move on. Thank you, gentlemen. Now if you will forgive us, we will take our leave of you'. At that, a strange glow began and a tunnel of light opened up. They saw the outlines of the young men walking towards it. The last thing they heard was their laughter at some joke or other. Just before they faded away, a Hurricane flew over them and did a victory roll before soaring upwards and disappearing.

The sound of the Lancaster was never again heard over the rooftops of the old pub.

Alien Abduction

He was awakened from his sleep by the light being switched on in the room. He opened his eyes and was dazzled by the strip light above him. He looked around and he found himself inside a small, oblong shaped room with white walls. He tried to rise, but found that he was fastened to the bed. He had absolutely no idea who he was, or indeed, where he was. Panic gripped him and he struggled to try and free himself. Almost immediately, three men in white laboratory coats entered the room.

'Don't struggle. You will only hurt your wrists,' one of the white coated men said in a deadpan, emotionless voice. 'Can you tell us your name?' he went on to ask.

The man just went on to say 'Help...help me. Where am I?....WHO am I?'

The three white coated men then began to discuss him as if he wasn't there. 'What he did was impossible. He is either alien in origin or using extremely advanced technology,' one of the white coats said. He then turned to the man and asked 'Do you have any recollection at all of the last forty-eight hours?'

'I have no recollection of absolutely ANYTHING. ARE YOU LISTENING TO ME?' the man yelled in reply.

'We are taking you to another room where you will be more comfortable. Once there we can unbuckle the restraints,' the white coat said.

He was wheeled along a corridor. As he looked up, he felt almost hypnotized by the strip lights in the ceiling at monotonously regular intervals as they passed him by. Eventually they entered a room. They unbuckled the restraints and allowed him to sit up. As he sat up and looked around, he found himself inside a room. There were pictures on the wall of someone's family. A comfortable looking bed, a desk and chair with a laptop on top, and a window looking out towards a forest. 'I'm afraid we are going to have to keep you detained in here until you regain your memory. It's for your own safety' one of the white coats said. 'And ours too' he heard another white coat mumble under his breath. They unfastened all the restraints and let him stand up. 'Make yourself comfortable' one of the white coats said, then they all left the room. He heard the key turn in the door.

He noticed that the room had small CCTV cameras. One over the door and one in the far corner of the room. He was in a state of rising panic. Somehow he felt some kind of training kicking in that helped him control the panic. 'OK, let's just assess what we know,' he said to himself. Apart from the basic intelligence he possessed and the ability to read (and therefore probably to write), he knew very little else. It was as if his entire life had started an hour earlier. He walked over to the laptop and pressed the power button. It sprang into life. On the desk was a small shaving mirror. It suddenly occurred to him that he had absolutely no idea what he even looked like. He looked in the mirror and was quite pleasantly surprised. A handsome, well-defined, tanned face looked back at him. His angular and strong jaw sported a very stylish amount of designer stubble. 'Well, you aren't ugly. That's a big plus' he said to himself. By this time the laptop had powered up. The background wallpaper on the desktop was of himself and a beautiful woman. They were holding the hands of a small boy who was between them. They were complete strangers to him. He suddenly began to cry. This was all too much. He had a wife and child, and if the photo was anything to go by, they all loved each other.

He checked to see if he had internet access. To his surprise he did. 'Well, I can't be much of a threat,' he thought to himself. He went to check his email. Half a dozen or so emails came into his inbox. They were addressed to Jeremy Morton-Jones. 'That must be me' he mumbled to himself, before going on to think, 'It sounds a bit posh'. None of the emails made any sense. From what he gleaned from them, he worked at some kind of research centre. Just then, he heard the door being unlocked. Someone dressed as an army officer, accompanied by one of the white coats, entered the room and said 'We need to ask you a few questions, Jeremy'. Then went on to say 'I assume you have figured out it is your name by now?'.

Jeremy nodded and said, 'So it would seem.'

'Please answer these questions carefully and precisely. Do you remember what happened yesterday evening?' the officer said.

Jeremy told him that he was scared beyond all reason, and if he remembered a damn thing, be it good or bad, he would be overjoyed to discuss it.

The white coat said to the officer 'We believe him to be telling the truth'.

'Well, let me fill you in,' the officer said. He then went on to tell him what had happened.

He told him that he was a civilian scientist attached to a unit that researched supposed UFO sightings. He was in the forest taking soil samples after there had been a sighting of an alien craft having landed, when, as if from nowhere, a beam of light came down and lifted him off the ground by some six feet. He went on to tell him that it held him there, suspended in mid air for some twenty seconds or so, before bringing him gently down to earth. 'You then moved from your position in the forest and over to the army vehicle some fifty yards away' the officer told him. 'Nothing unusual in that you might think, but you did it in less than a second'. 'Me??' Jeremy said, whilst wondering it this was some kind of test, or a wind-up. What the officer went on to tell him was beyond all belief.

'It seems the aliens gave you a few more little gifts,' the

officer said. He went on to tell him that he flipped an army lorry over as if it was an empty cardboard box. One soldier panicked and took a shot at him and he had some kind of force field that deflected the bullet, which went on to hit another soldier in the knee. He also told him that he then actually flew. 'How can a man raise himself off the ground like bloody Superman, then fly straight through a chain-link fence without even leaving a hole in it?' he said. 'You then entered the missile silos and brought the whole base offline. Again, you flew through a three feet thick steel blast door.' he told him.

He was told that he then came back out of the missile silo and collapsed upon the ground. 'We tried to lift you, but you weighed that much that we couldn't budge you. You were still glowing,' the officer said. Apparently, it took over half an hour until he had regained normal human weight. 'We ran a few blood tests, and your DNA was like nothing we have ever seen,' he added. Jeremy was asked to roll up his sleeve, and the white coat took more blood samples. They then left.

All kinds of things were now running through Jeremy's mind, as he desperately struggled to make some kind of sense of the whole crazy story. He began to wonder if he still possessed any of these gifts. He picked up a corner of the desk and could barely lift it. He tried to walk through the door like some kind of pantomime ghost, but he just walked straight into it. 'Well it seems I am not Superman any more,' he thought to himself.

A little while later, one of the white coats came in to tell him that his blood samples were now perfectly normal again. He also told him that his wife had been informed and would be coming round to see him.

'Do you think my memory will ever come back?' Jeremy asked.

The white coat told him that they had no idea.

Later that evening, a well dressed, attractive woman walked

in through the door. Jeremy recognised her from the picture on his laptop. Her face was tear-stained as she ran towards him, and she fell sobbing against his shoulder. 'Do you really have no idea who I am, darling?' she said between sobs. Jeremy shook his head. 'It's me darling, your little Fi-Fi, your wife Fiona' she said.

'I half recognise your face. I think it must be coming back to me. I do love you,' Jeremy said in reply. All of this was complete lies.

'They say it's OK to come home,' Fiona said, before adding, 'We live inside the barracks in the soldiers' houses anyway. It's not like you can run away,' she added.

That night, Jeremy returned home. 'We had better start as we mean to go on. We will be sleeping together' Fiona said resolutely.

A gorgeous woman was insisting that he take her to bed. Jeremy certainly wasn't about to complain. They spent a passionate time together. To Jeremy it felt like the first time all over again.

Over the following weeks, she slowly started filling in the gaps in his knowledge. He still didn't remember a thing about his former life. All knowledge of his former occupation had also been erased from his memory, but he was on sickness pay, so this wasn't a financial issue. They began to fall in love all over again. His son was away at boarding school, so he had been spared all of the trauma.

Fiona announced that they seemed to be happy with his progress and had given them permission to drive down to Cornwall for a romantic weekend 'Just like we did on our honeymoon,' she said. Then remembered that he wouldn't have a clue what on earth she was talking about.

The following day they packed a few belongings and headed off. They had rented a secluded little cottage well off the beaten track. It overlooked the sea. On arrival, Fiona told Jeremy to have a walk into the village and see if any of it looked familiar. It was a beautiful day, so he happily obliged.

He had a very pleasant walk around a little fishing harbour. He licked at an ice cream cone that he had bought whilst he rambled around aimlessly, looking into the shop windows of the touristy shops. After about an hour he returned to the cottage. As he opened the door, the officer who had interrogated him was inside. 'Hello Jerry, just dropped by to see how you are doing. Making sure everything is OK,' the officer said.

Jeremy smiled and told him that he was doing just fine. They sat around the old farmhouse table and had a cup of tea.

It was a beautiful evening, and Fiona suggested that they all go for a ramble along the cliffs towards the old smuggler's cove. 'It's beautiful scenery, and the sea birds are just fabulous,' Fiona said, so off they went.

As they were walking along the cliff path, the officer said, 'Here is as good as anywhere.' Then he pulled a hand gun out of his pocket. 'Does he remember anything?' he asked Fiona.

'Not a thing,' she replied, whilst wearing a smug, self-satisfied grin.

'I suppose it's only fair we tell him,' the officer said. He went on to tell Jeremy that he had been part of an experiment. They had developed a new and powerful psychotropic drug that altered a person's whole psyche. It tapped into the raw and savage side of the state of mind and turned the person into an unfeeling killer. 'Sorry to spin stories about little green men,' the officer said, 'But it is far more believable at times than the truth.' He went on to tell him that they had to wipe his mind after the experiment had ended, as they couldn't have the public finding out the truth. 'Oh, and Fiona, she is just a field agent. You aren't married,' he said.

'So, are you going to shoot me now?' Jeremy said, barely

concealing the absolute terror he was feeling.

His so-called wife, Fiona said, 'Shhh, darling. Don't be silly.' She moved towards him with arms outstretched as if to comfort him in her embrace. Instead she pushed him firmly in the middle of his chest.

Jeremy tumbled over the cliff's edge to his death on the jagged rocks below. Shall I run to the village screaming now and tell them my husband has accidentally fallen off the cliffs?' Fiona said, then laughed heartily.

The officer smiled and said 'You really are one callous bitch.' Then joined her in her laughter.

The Old Railway Platform

The story takes place in 1962, just before the Beeching report, and the closure of many of the branch lines and smaller stations on the rail network.

Paul left his friend's house around 9:45 pm to catch the train home. The little village station was around a mile away from his friend's house. He had brought a torch to light his way along the dark country lanes. As he approached the little station, he was struck by its quaintness. This was the first time he had travelled to meet his friend since he had moved in to his new cottage. The outside of the station still had the old enamel advertising signs, advertising now defunct brands of tobacco and cigarettes - plus one advertising *Winalot*. He obviously hadn't taken notice when he got off the train a few hours earlier. He had been too busy studying the directions that his friend had sent to him.

    As he entered the station, it really did feel like stepping into a museum. No electric lights, just the yellowish glow of the gas lamps. In the grate glowed the remnants of a coal fire. The smell of the gas light and the coal fire, combined with the stale tobacco odour, and the sulphurous smell from the steam locomotives gave the room an aroma that was unique to these little branch lines. His train was due in approximately ten minutes. He sat on one of the benches and took out a paperback book from his pocket. The light was so poor that after ten minutes or so, he gave it up as his eyes grew tired with trying to read in the gloomy gaslight. He wandered out onto the platform and took a look around. The platform had similar advertising signs, and a cigarette machine selling Black Cat cigarettes. Paul smiled as he saw the price of the cigarettes. They were just a shilling for a pack of ten. He could see that there seemed to be some packets inside the machine, so he took out a shilling and inserted it in the slot. 'They will be worth it as a collector's item if the machine lets me have them,' he thought to himself. He pulled open the drawer and there were his cigarettes. He sniffed at the packet and then opened them. They looked fine, so he lit one up. They were perfect. He bought two more packets. His usual brand back home cost him half a crown for ten.

The breeze started to blow, and the willow and alder trees across the line hissed at him as the leaves rattled in the wind. It felt as if they were trying to whisper some dark secret to him. He began to feel the true isolation of the little station. He went back inside to get some warmth from the fire in the waiting room. He glanced at his watch. There were still five more minutes before his train was due.

Paul noticed that the windows still had their old wartime blackout curtains up. They were drawn closed. This gave the room an even more dismal feel. 'They must think there's still a bloody war on,' he thought to himself. Just then, someone who he assumed was the station master entered the waiting room. 'No more trains at this time of night young man,' he announced.

'Since when? - there's supposed to be one due in five minutes according to the chap I bought the tickets off,' Paul said.

'Well, there isn't now,' the station master said. He then went on to say, 'Can I see your identity card please?'

Paul laughed and said, 'We haven't needed those since 1952. Has no one told you the war is over, grandad?'

The station master said, 'OK, don't say I didn't warn you.' He then went into his office and phoned the police.

Paul chuckled to himself and wondered what the police would make of him. He began to wonder if he was a little senile, and seeing he wasn't doing much harm out here in the sticks, they let him continue with the job out of kindness. Two minutes later, two police officers entered the room. They marched straight up to him and one of them said, 'Can I see your identity card please?'

Paul waited for him to break out into a grin and explain about the station master, and to tell him that he was always doing this, but they didn't.

'I'll ask you one last time. Can I see your identity card?' the policeman said.

Paul told them he didn't have one. The police officer then read him his rights and fastened a pair of handcuffs on his wrists.

As they marched him through the door, Paul expected to see a police car parked outside, but there wasn't. 'The police station is just in the village. Don't give us any trouble or you'll get this' one of the policeman said, whist waving his truncheon menacingly under his nose. They frog-marched Paul along the road.

They were about to walk past his friend's house when he said. 'My friend John lives there. He can vouch for me. He will tell you who I am'.

The two police officers burst out laughing and said 'Who do you think put us up to it?' He then saw John standing in the window with tears of laughter streaming down his face.

Very soon they were all inside John's house. Paul threatened him with dire revenge, but this just made John laugh even more. 'This is Tony and Geoff. They are in the local am-dram. They are playing a pair of police officers, so I thought that I would 'borrow' them for a prank' John said, then offered Paul a glass of scotch.

'So who is the old station master?' Paul asked.

'That actually IS the station master. He will do anything for a half bottle of scotch' John answered.

They all agreed that it was a very well thought-out ruse. 'You can stay the night. I'll make you up a bed in the spare room' John said, before offering round the scotch again.

Just then, a knock came at John's door. John opened the door and the station master was standing there. He looked somewhat distressed. 'Please tell me that your friend didn't actually get on that train?' he asked.

'No, he is in here drinking whisky. Why do you ask?'

'Oh thank god, thank god,' the station master said.

John invited him inside and asked him whatever the matter was, and why he was so upset. 'The train. The signals. Something must have happened. It met the express train to Edinburgh in the tunnel. A huge fireball. Dozens killed and injured.

Paul was visibly shaken. He took his packet of Black Cat cigarettes out of his pocket and lit one up. 'I haven't seen those in donkey's years,' the station master said.

'Yes you have,' Paul said. 'I bought them out of the cigarette machine on the platform'.

The station master said, 'That cigarette machine was taken away back in 1952. I know that as a fact, because after then, I had to remember to pick them up at the newsagents before going to work'.

'OK, the gag is now over. I saw them there alongside all the old enamel signs,' Paul said.

'There's only one person here having a joke, and that's you,' the station master said.

John drew Paul to one side and said to him, 'There's just been a terrible rail accident, and one you could well have been part of. The man is naturally upset. What does it matter who is right?'

Paul nodded in answer.

An hour or so later, John and Paul were walking the station master back to his cottage. He wasn't used to drinking whisky and had partaken a little too much. They steadied him as he walked along. Once at his cottage they made sure he was safely inside and under the tender care of his wife when they turned to head off back.

'Look John, please just humour me. I want to see if the station really does have those enamel advertising signs outside it. Come back and look with me....please' Paul said.

'Well, if it makes you get some sleep tonight, I suppose it's worth it,' John said 'But you will feel really stupid when you see that there aren't any.

When they turned the corner in the road and John saw the station, he stopped dead in his tracks 'But...it just doesn't look like that,' he said.

'I told you,' Paul said.

John told him that he catches the train to work every morning from the station, and this just isn't how it looks. 'Come and look at the platform,' Paul said.

The station was locked, so they climbed over the small perimeter fence and were soon on the platform. John wandered along with a total look of bemusement upon his face. 'I'm telling you now, this just isn't how this station looks,' he said.

'Well, it bloody does now,' Paul said. Then he pointed out the cigarette machine. 'Go on, stick a bob in it, it works,' he went on to say.

John took a shilling out of his pocket, inserted it into the machine and then pulled open the drawer. 'There we are, ghost ciggies,' Paul said sarcastically.

Paul and John then heard the sound of footsteps walking along the platform, but no one was there. Then, as if emerging out of a fog, or a hole in time and space, a man appeared some ten yards away from them. He stopped and lit a cigarette. The flare from the match lit up his face so that they could briefly see his features. 'Oh my god, it's my Dad,' Paul said.

'But...your Dad is dead. We went to his funeral together,' John said.

Paul just nodded. The man walked towards them both. 'Hello Son,' he said.

Paul just stared at him open mouthed. John seemed to be frozen in sheer terror. His Dad smiled and took another drag on his cigarette, then said, 'Take this as a warning son. Don't get on that train.'

Paul was shaken into wakefulness by the old station master. 'You were fast asleep. You've missed your train,' he said.

Paul realised that he had just had the most vivid dream of his life. He glanced at his watch and saw that his train had left some five minutes earlier. 'There will be no more until seven o'clock in the morning,' the station master said.

Paul gathered his thoughts and his belongings and trudged the mile or so back to John's house. 'Can I sleep on your couch, I fell asleep and missed my train,' he said to John as he opened the door. He was beckoned inside.

The next morning he headed back to the little station, but there was a notice pinned to the door. 'No trains today due to major accident. Line closed,' it said.

The station master appeared beside him and said, 'Someone is looking after you, young man. Just think, if you hadn't fallen asleep, you would have been on that train.'

Can You Smell Flowers?

Did you ever get that feeling that you are not alone? It's a common enough feeling, and most of us just shrug it off, or put it down to an over-active imagination. Aidan was used to working alone, so it became particularly irksome that he had developed this unwanted malady. This weird feeling had been hanging around his shoulders for around a month or so. He couldn't remember when it actually started, but it was definitely upon him.

Aidan was a web designer. His office was above a haberdasher's shop on the high street. Visitors would press a button on an intercom to speak to him, then enter through an adjacent door and climb the stairs to visit him. This day he had an appointment with Jenna. She made jewellery for prestigious clients and desired a website to match. She pressed the buzzer and Aidan welcomed her into his humble little office. 'Would you like a coffee?' he asked.

'Oh god yes, I haven't had my caffeine hit yet,' Jenna replied, whilst sporting a warm smile.

As they were sipping their coffee and discussing the website, straight out-of-the-blue, Jenna said, 'How do you put up with him?'

'How do I put up with who?' Aidan asked.

Jenna smiled and apologised. 'Sorry, I am clairvoyant. You might think it all tosh and mumbo-jumbo, but there's a young man who walks around the room in an agitated manner.'

Aidan's expression must have been comical to behold, because Jenna began to chuckle.

'Well that's a conversation stopper - do tell me more,' Aidan said.

'Sorry, I just felt I had to mention him. He knows I can see him and he just won't go away.'

Aidan then volunteered the information that for a month or so, he too had felt a presence.

Jenna told him that this young man had been alive just previous to the outbreak of world war one. He and his wife once occupied the room and ran the shop below. He told her that he and his wife died in 1912. 'It seems his wife passed first, and then him. It was tuberculosis,' Jenna said. She carried on relaying back snippets of information as she received them. She told Aidan that he had a son, and then a grandson, and now further down the line he had a great, great grandson. 'Apparently, he is the last of the line, and that seems to be his issue,' Jenna said.

They put all of it aside and carried on discussing the website. Aidan put forward a set of proposals and Jenna said that she would like to go ahead with them. Once business had been concluded, Jenna asked if she might come back and try and get to the bottom of what troubled his spooky co-habitant.

Aidan was single, and Jenna was a very attractive woman of a similar age. He didn't find her company a problem in the very least. 'Sure, why not' Aidan said. They agreed to meet back at his office the following evening.

The next day arrived and Aidan had gone for the 'casual but very smart' look, and had been very particular about his personal appearance. He also added a subtle amount of his most expensive aftershave and had moisturised! Across town, Jenna had done something very similar. They met outside Aidan's office at seven thirty precisely. Aidan opened the door and they entered his office.

'I've brought something along with me for you to wear. I find it helps,' Jenna said; then handed him a small box. Inside it he found a small crucifix and chain. 'I knocked it up this afternoon. You don't have to wear it. In fact, sell it if you like.'

It's 18 carat gold'. Aidan said. 'It's beautiful, and thank you so, so much. I wouldn't dream of selling it. I will treasure it.' Then he kissed her cheek.

Jenna flushed a little; then giggled like a schoolgirl and said, 'Glad you like it. Always a good thing to have a bit of protection.'

Jenna dragged two chairs into the middle of the room. Then she switched off the main light, just leaving a desktop lamp on Aidan's desk still lit.

'What happens now? Do we light candles and then you go off into a trance or something?' Aidan said.

Jenna rolled her eyes and smiled softly back at him, before saying 'No, we are just fine as we are, and I will be fully conscious throughout'. She sat quietly for a few minutes. 'I asked him for his name, but he says he doesn't want to reveal it just yet,' she said.

In his mind, Aidan began to wonder if this was the usual flim-flam and mediumship cop out. Then she told him that the shop was once a small grocer's shop. 'They weren't rich. It wasn't a rich neighbourhood, and they always had people owing them money, but they lived adequately' she told him.

'He is asking you if you know a George McDonald?' Jenna said.

Aidan told her that he knew a George McDonald, and in fact he knew two. Both his father and grandfather went by that name.

'My god, this man is telling me that he is one of your ancestors,' Jenna said. She then went on to tell him that this man claimed to be his great, great grandfather. She laughed and said 'Bet you can't guess what his Christian name is?'

Aidan rolled his eyes and said. 'I'm wondering if it's George?'

Jenna chuckled and said 'BINGO - hey you must be psychic too!'

'Yeah, yeah,' Aidan said, before going on to say, 'I have a

middle name.'

'Well, we don't have to ask what it is do we?' Jenna said.

They both laughed. 'I knew there was a reason I picked this particular shop from all the others on the market,' Aidan said. 'It almost felt as if something was guiding me here.'

'Tell him I will feel a lot less creeped out now I know it's family here with me'.

'You can tell him yourself, you know. He heard you and is smiling,' Jenna said.

Aidan felt strangely relaxed and at peace with the whole thing. 'You said he was worried about me. Not bad news is it?' he asked.

Jenna then began to blush. 'Oh, this is so embarrassing,' she said.

Aidan looked at her with an amused look on his face. 'Tell me' he said.

Jenna buried her face in her hands to hide her blushes and said 'He's been talking to my Nan.'

Apparently the two spirits had been talking and had discussed that they both had ancestors who were both successful at what they did, but never socialised because of business and lack of time, and indeed a lack of courage to just go out to the places where they might meet someone. 'So, the old buggers have been matchmaking?' Aidan said.

Jenna laughed and said, 'It seems so, and my gran asked me to ask the young man if he wouldn't mind keeping a civil tongue in his head,'

Aidan laughed and said, 'Sorry gran' and then blew a kiss into the air.

'I'm really sorry about this. I feel so embarrassed,' Jenna said.

Aidan looked straight into her eyes and said, 'I'm not sorry. I'm not sorry in the least'. He then reached across and held her hand and said, 'I rather hoped to ask you out anyway.'

She laughed a little and said, 'I did wonder. The aftershave and all that'. Jenna leaned over towards Aidan and gently kissed him on the lips. 'And there's your answer,' she said.

The grandparents on the other side of the veil smiled at each other, and the spirit of George said, in his lilting Scottish highlands tone, 'I think this calls for a wee dram.' The two then slowly faded into a small and singular point of light.

'Can you smell flowers?' Aiden asked.

'Yes, they are carnations. They were Nan's favourites,' Jenna answered.

Then they kissed one more time.

The Madness

'You are not real. You are NOT real. You are all in my mind. Why am I doing this to myself?' Over and over again he said it to the figure in the corner of the room. The figure of a man he had killed in battle over twenty years previously. 'I know you are not real, because I saw the massive hole in the back of your head where the bullet made its exit.'

John, or Jacko as everyone called him, had been visited by this figure for the past month. He took it as being the late onset of PTSD, but somehow he thought he knew himself better. Maybe it is. What other explanation is there? he thought. That was until he found two spent shell cases on the little set of drawers where the figure had been standing. Jacko recognised them immediately as the same calibre he had used during his army career.

The next night, Jacko waited around for the figure to return. Tonight it would be sorted. 'Just like last time. It's me or you, and you are already dead, so let's hear what your problem is?' Jacko said to an empty room. He had already come to terms with all that stuff. It was a war. Soldiers fight and soldiers die. It could just as easily have been him, and luckily it wasn't. The man that he shot was a sniper. He had been playing cat and mouse for over an hour with him. Spotting where the sounds were coming from. Finally he found him. His head was framed perfectly in his rifle sights. A smooth pull of the trigger and he saw the man's head being knocked to one side and him dropping out of sight. All he felt at the time was a sense of achievement as this man had taken out at least four of his platoon.

Right on cue, the figure of the man appeared. 'What do you want?' Jacko asked.

The figure didn't answer. He merely looked back with vacant

eyes and an expression that was bathed in pain and regret. 'Are you deaf as well as dead? I asked you. What do you want?'

Still there was no answer.

'If you want an apology from me for killing you, I can tell you now, you are wasting your time. If we were to go back to then, and your head was in my rifle sights again, I would STILL pull the trigger and still be glad I did,' Jacko said.

The figure nodded as a sign that he understood the words. The ghost (if such he was) and Jacko sat and looked at each other for what felt like an eternity. Slowly the figure faded away and was gone. Jacko wondered if that would be that, but that is when he saw the small, black and white photograph on the set of drawers. It was a picture of a little boy of around five years old. Out of nowhere, tears began to course down Jacko's cheeks. Something told him that this was this man's son. He thought about his daughter who would be around that age when all the madness happened. He wondered how she would have fared not to have her daddy around. How she would have felt had he not have been there to walk her down the aisle. 'I feel sorry for your little boy, and I hope he has grown to be a fine young man, but what I did had to be done,' Jacko said. This time he said it in a tone of compassion.

The figure didn't return the next night, or for several nights afterwards. Jacko relaxed and put the whole episode out of his mind. Then, out of the blue, there he was again. Still with a melancholic expression.

'Was that a picture of your son?' Jacko asked. The figure nodded. 'He looks like a fine young boy' Jacko said. For the first time ever, the figure smiled. Jacko then addressed the figure.

'Look, we were soldiers, and we were fighting in a war that neither of us started, and probably neither of us wanted to be in. I joined the army before we went to war with your country. I did my duty, as did you. I lost four good friends due to your actions.

I can tell you this much though. Although I felt a certain reward in the fact that my actions stopped you killing anyone else, I didn't enjoy killing you. In fact, you were the first. When it was all over I cried like a child.'

The expression on the figure's face was one of desolation and sadness.

'We cannot rewrite history. I would kindly ask you not to return. If you are after an apology, or for me to admit some kind of guilt and ask for your forgiveness, it will never happen.'

The figure nodded solemnly. Then something remarkable happened. Jacko's four colleagues who had been killed by the man also appeared in the room.

'How goes it Jacko you old bastard?' one of the figures said.

Jacko recognised him as his mate, Mick.

'Can't complain you old git. At least I'm not dead like you. Clumsy bastard!' Jacko replied.

Mick burst out into his usual robust laughter. It was squaddie humour, and something the two men were more than familiar with. It was the same humour that carried them through and stopped them going insane. It was a coping mechanism.

'This is not what you think, Jacko.' Mick said.

'What is it then?' he asked.

It was at this moment that the enemy soldier stood up and spoke for the very first time. 'I am not looking for an apology from you. Neither am I trying to make you feel pity for me. You did your duty as I did mine. It is I that am here to apologise to you. I feel no pain any more, except that in my heart. We were linked in a moment of history. The pain in my heart is linked to the pain in your mind. I want this to stop. I want to move on and be at peace, but I need you to be at peace too. You cannot blame yourself for surviving when your friends didn't, and there is no blame in the bullet that killed me. The blame, the true blame, lies in those that started the madness.'

After the speech, all the figures faded away. On the set of drawers was another photograph. It was of five smiling, tanned soldiers at the peak of their prime. On the back was written one single word, 'Inseparable.'

The strongest bonds are those that are forged through adversity. There can be no more potent adversity than that of war. These men were all brothers in the truest sense. They were there for each other after death as in life. On the other side of the veil there are no enemies. Anyone who walks in the light is bathed in love. Jacko never again saw the visitor. He knew that they would all be reunited on the other side in the strongest bond of all. That of eternal love and peace.

The Lodge in the Woods

Ever since he was a young lad, Stephen avoided the wood by the river. As a boy, he had been badly frightened there. He had been chasing after a young boy who had been trespassing on his father's land. He meant him no real harm; he just enjoyed the chase. He finally penned him in between some thick hawthorn bushes and the river. To his astonishment, the boy merely smiled, then slowly faded away, right in front of his eyes. He was only nine at the time, and it terrified him. Now the land belonged to him since his father had passed a few years earlier, and he had an idea that he wanted to pursue.

In the wood and the surrounding two fields were the remnants of an abandoned village. All that was left were the overgrown outlines of where the houses had once stood. The story that went with the village had been a shameful occurrence in his family's history.

It was back in the 1600's and the plague came to the little village of Sarnford. Sir Richard, the owner of the village and all the land that surrounded it, acted swiftly. He didn't want the plague to spread to his manor house and to his family, so he posted notices on the outskirts which forbade anyone to leave the village. To make sure of this, he employed thugs with dogs and weapons to patrol it. This became an excuse to settle some old scores. Some of the thugs entered the village and dragged off a few of the men to outside the village. There they were viciously beaten to death, or had the dogs set upon them. The village was decimated, most with the plague, some through starvation, as no food was allowed to enter the village, and some by the hired thugs. The pitiful handful that remained fled the village once the plague had passed and the sanctions had been lifted. To a man and a woman, they cursed their Lord, Richard and the thugs that carried out his orders. It had been known as an unlucky place ever since.

Stephen thought it an ideal location to build a fishing lodge, as the adjoining river was a top class trout river. He could build accommodation there and charge people to stay there and fish the river. He had the plans agreed by the local council and an architect drew up the plans. He approached two local firms, but seemingly both were 'busy'. In truth, the locals had long memories, and the abandoned village was to them a kind of unofficial monument to the deceased villagers. It was also a reminder of what those that were supposedly their betters did. To them it seemed sacrilegious.

Eventually, a firm of building contractors a couple of hundred miles away took on the job. From the very first day things went wrong with alarming regularity. A security firm had been hired to keep an eye on the building materials and the machinery at the site. On the first night, two men had been frightened so badly that they flatly refused to go back there, preferring to hand in their notices instead. He sent other men there. Some with many years experience. But none of them liked the job.

Freak accidents also seemed to plague the build. None of them proved fatal, but they all resulted with men spending time in casualty and having time off work. It ran on for weeks longer than planned, and proved far more expensive than budgeted for, but eventually the lodge was built. It was built to the most luxurious specifications. It even had a sauna and a hot tub. Stephen sent out invitations to local businessmen and selected council members to spend an all expenses paid fishing weekend at the lodge as his personal guest. It was said locally that you knew that you had arrived if your name was on the exclusive, ten person, VIP list.

Everyone was brought by chauffeur to the fishing lodge, and

a champagne buffet had been laid on. Everyone was shown to their rooms, and in each room was a box of expensive, hand-made chocolates and a bottle of vintage port. The champagne buffet was in full swing and everyone was enjoying the party immensely. Then one of the guests said, 'Oh my god, what on earth is that revolting smell?'

Soon, all the guests were complaining and some of them were gagging at the smell. 'It smells like rotting flesh and raw sewage,' one man said. He went to open the door, but it wouldn't budge. 'Stephen, what the bloody hell is going on here? Unlock this door AT ONCE!' he said.

Stephen informed him that the door wasn't locked, and to prove the fact, he turned the key in the door. First to lock it, then secondly, to unlock it again. Nothing made any difference. The door just wouldn't budge. The same thing happened with all the windows. Although none of them were locked, including the patio doors, none would budge. In desperation, Stephen picked up a large bronze bust and hurled it at one of the windows. It merely bounced off it without even leaving a mark. It was then that someone spotted the burning torches coming through the woods.

'Thank god, someone is coming to our rescue,' one of the female guests said. It was then that they heard the snarling and baying dogs. Stephen's blood ran cold. He knew that these were no rescuers.

Soon, figures began to assemble at the windows. Their faces were skeletal, with the remains of rotting flesh still partially covering their features. Their eyes had long since been eaten by decay, but from their dark cavernous eye sockets a bluish-green light emanated. One figure held up a tarnished and tattered piece of paper against the window. It read:

'By order of Lord Richard, none shall leave this village on pain of death. Any dissenters and miscreants shall forfeit their lives upon leaving the confines of this village.'

One guest began to laugh and applaud. 'Oh well done Stephen old chap. This is a first rate prank. This must have cost an extraordinary amount of money' he said.

'You think this is a fucking prank?' Stephen replied.

'Now, now old man. Language. Ladies present and all that,' the guest grumpily retorted.

Stephen merely pushed him aside and approached the figure holding up the notice against the window. 'These people are innocent. I am the descendant of Lord Richard. Punish me, but let these people go' Stephen implored.

At this, the doors burst open and a voice bellowed 'LEAVE THIS PLACE....NOW!!'

The guests needed no second invitation, almost trampling each other underfoot to vacate the place. All except Stephen. A force had paralysed him and he was rooted, statue-like, in his position by the window.

After the last guest had left, the lodge seemed to evaporate, brick by brick, as night and day rapidly rotated in seconds, as if someone was turning back the days in mere seconds. Briefly, Stephen caught a glimpse of the two security guards. 'Help me,' he mouthed at them, but no sound would come forth. The two security guards fled in flight, as if they had seen a ghost. To them, back then, they had.

With each daily rotation, Stephen felt the hunger pangs and the dreadful, dreadful thirst of dehydration. The weight was also falling off him at an alarming rate.

The guests had fled to the hall and had called the police to inform them of the night's events. When the police arrived, they found the fishing lodge completely intact. The lights were on and the doors were wide open. Inside, the place stank. On inspection, the tables that contained the once luxurious buffet, now held trays of rotting and putrefying food. It looked as if it had been there for months. Amongst all this, and beside the window, they discovered the skeletal remains of Stephen.

Angels

Jack had lit a small fire of twigs and small bits of branches in the middle of a ring of stones that he had gathered together. He was on a path by the edge of a mixed forest. The mossy grass was the perfect place to pitch the tent and make camp for the night. It would be dark in an hour or so. He had gathered enough fuel to last him until he crawled into his sleeping bag and went to sleep. He was around seven miles from the nearest village, and that was one of those 'one pub and a post office' type places. He didn't mind this in the least. Jack knew that towns and cities were far more dangerous places to be. He loved being alone in the wilds of the British countryside.

Jack knew this area quite well. He had been walking these hills and fells for many years. It was his father who first took him. That was thirty years previously. His dad was no longer alive. It was at least a year after his father's death before Jack ventured out again. The memories were just too painful.

Jack placed his camping kettle over the flames on a small wire stand, and waited for the cheerful whistle as the kettle boiled. That is when he heard the sound of breaking twigs. He turned around expecting to see a deer or other wild animal, when to his surprise, he saw a man in what looked like a military uniform.

'I'm sorry, I didn't mean to startle you. I seem to be lost' he said. As he approached the camp fire, Jack could see that he was wearing an RAF uniform. Jack knew that there was an RAF base around eight miles to the west, and informed the man of that. He assumed he had set out to walk there and had lost his bearings.

'Fancy a cup of tea?' Jack asked.

'God, I could bloody murder one,' the young airman replied.

Jack laughed and said, 'Well, sit yourself down on the grass. The kettle has just boiled.'

'Are you due there tonight?' Jack asked, feeling somewhat worried that the young man would be up on a charge.

'No, tomorrow will be just fine,' he answered, then sipped at his tea.

Although Jack liked his own company, he was also the sociable type, and seeing that this chap was out in the middle of nowhere, he asked him if he would like to sleep by the fire. He told him that he would rig up a shelter from the fly sheet of the tent. Although Jack was the sociable type, sharing his somewhat cramped and cozy tent with another man, was something that he didn't relish.

'That is extremely kind of you. Are you sure you don't mind?' the airman asked.

'Not a problem at all. Can't leave you out here in the wilds can we?' Jack replied. It was mid summer and a warm and hazy evening, so he knew the man would be okay.

'I was about to ask, but thought it a little cheeky,' the airman said.

Jack told him that it was no bother at all. He said that he could put his jacket over himself to keep out the cold. 'The grass is soft and springy. It's like sleeping on a mattress' Jack said.

The two men chatted amiably for around an hour or so. They discovered that they both shared a love of the outdoors. The airman was also a fell walker, and also did a bit of climbing. Jack then pulled out a small hip flask that contained whisky, and asked the airman if he fancied a nightcap. The airman grinned widely, and said, 'Do bears shit in the woods?'

Jack poured a drop into each of their tea mugs. 'Good health to you,' the airman said.

'To you as well,' Jack replied.

Both men then turned in for the night.

'I hope you get a good night's sleep,' Jack said.

'I'm absolutely knackered, and that tot of whisky helped. I'll be asleep in no time,' the airman replied.

Both men wished each other good night, and both went to sleep.

Jack awoke around six o'clock in the morning. He wondered how his airman friend had fared the night. He unzipped the tent expecting to see the airman there. Instead he saw just his jacket beneath the makeshift shelter. 'Oh well, he must have fancied an early start to get back to base' Jack said to himself. 'I could have made him a bit of breakfast and a brew. Put some fire into his belly' he went on to say.

It was then that he heard the sound of men talking. It was somewhere just around a bend in the path. Jack wondered what on earth was going on. He could also hear the sound of heavy machinery. He put on his boots and his jacket and went off to investigate. As he turned the corner, the sight that greeted him astounded him. The place was milling with soldiers. In the trees he could see something that looked like wreckage. As he came closer, he was amazed to see that it was the fuselage of a world war two Hurricane. The propeller blades were bent out of shape, and there was a small impact crater where the aircraft had hit the ground, before bouncing off into the trees. Jack's immediate thought was that he had stumbled into a film set of some kind, and that some irate security officer would be advancing upon him and asking him what the hell he thought he was doing, but no one at all seemed to notice him. Jack stared in fascination at the bizarre scene, before he was distracted by someone from behind saying, 'Bit of a sodding mess isn't it?'

He turned to find the young airman behind him, but this time he was in full world war two flying kit. 'I have no idea what happened. The engine just cut out and I could see the trees below. I picked what looked like a clearing and headed for it,' the airman said.

Jack turned to the airman and said, 'Is this some kind of elaborate wind-up? That is a world war two Hurricane. Unless you are some kind of member of a historic aircraft team and have crashed accidentally, this is all madness'.

The young airman smiled and said, 'You haven't figured it out yet, have you?'

'Figured what out?' Jack said, somewhat irritably.

The young airman then told him his story.

He had been involved in a skirmish and had been badly shot up. He was limping his way back to base when the engine began coughing and spluttering. He tried to land in the clearing but hit the ground hard and rammed it into the trees. He had dislocated his shoulder and broken his forearm in the collision. He managed to scramble clear and staggered off towards where he thought the base was. He spent several hours walking around in circles in a semi daze. He lay down under some overhanging trees and tried to get some rest. The place he lay was exactly where Jack had been camping. That is where he died of hypothermia and shock. It was two days later before his body was discovered.

'You broke the circle. I have been wandering around looking for shelter for seventy years, and you broke the circle,' the airman said. 'My spirit couldn't rest until someone broke the circle. You gave me shelter, hot tea, a tot of whisky and a warm bed for the night. Thank you'.

Jack was about to say, 'It would be what any decent human being would do,' but he never got the chance. The airman, the whole crash site and the soldiers just faded away before his eyes. Jack shuddered and wondered if it had all been real.

He slipped his hands into his coat pockets to keep them warm. It was then that he felt something in the right hand pocket. He took it out to find in was a set of RAF wings. It was what was known as a 'sweethearts badge'. He had probably meant to give it to his wife or girlfriend but had never got around to it. It was the airman's way of saying thank you for releasing his spirit from its earth-bound purgatory. It was then he heard the airman's voice for one last time.

He said, 'Every angel earns his wings. We have both earned ours.' He then heard the unmistakable sound of a Rolls Royce Merlin engine, and a Hurricane flew majestically above the tree tops. As it banked upwards towards the sun, it did a victory roll and disappeared. They had indeed both earned their wings.

Last Breath

It was always the same. Always unexpected and almost subliminal. At first a very gentle and almost inaudible sobbing, which gradually grew clearer. Then those awful words spoken in abject terror. Spoken almost between tears and sobs. 'No, please don't. I didn't mean to do it.' Then the sound of a key turning in a lock - then silence. The attic room should have been a very useful room. It was well lit by two windows and afforded a beautiful view across the bay. The trouble is, no one would stay in there for any length of time. It had been redecorated and was bright and clean, but everyone hated it.

No one else but Shannon ever heard the cries. She had even stopped mentioning it. It became one of those 'mummy is off on one again' type things. Shannon had inherited certain gifts and intuitive skills from her mother and grandmother. It was something she didn't publicise, as her own family thought the whole idea absurd, and she didn't want her views causing them any embarrassment. Everything would have carried on in exactly the same manner, until one day her daughter Jessica experienced something that turned her into a blubbering wreck.

Shannon was asleep. It would be around two o'clock in the morning. Her bedroom door burst open and her hysterical daughter burst into the room.

'Oh my god, Jess, whatever is the matter?' her mother asked.

Jess then told her that she had been awoken by a sound in her bedroom. It was the sound of someone wheezing as they breathed. She opened her eyes and saw a small and very pale looking boy. He kept putting something to his mouth and breathing in. By the way Jess described it, it sounded like an asthma inhaler. She calmed down her hysterical daughter and told her that she could sleep in her bed that night.

The next day was a Saturday. Over breakfast, Shannon and Jess discussed the previous night's incident. 'All this time I poked fun at you for this kind of thing, mum,' Jess said.

Shannon told her that it was only in her teens that she became aware of her 'intuitions' as she referred to them. 'Maybe it's a thing that only comes with puberty?' Shannon idly remarked.

This made Jess bristle a little, and she said, 'I started my periods over a year and a half ago. For goodness sake mum, I'm nearly fourteen.'

Shannon smiled, and said, 'I know, darling. Quite the young lady'. This both placated and mildly irritated Jess.

The tension between them was broken when Shannon said, 'I believe that attic room is at the centre of all this. That is where I hear the sobbing. Tonight we will put down our camping mattresses and sleeping bags and we will sleep in there.'

Jess was aghast at the whole idea. 'Are you SERIOUS?' she asked.

Shannon told her that she was absolutely serious. She went on to say, 'He is a frightened and very unhappy little boy. He means us no harm. He wants our help.' She then went on to say 'If that was you, and you were the little spirit, wouldn't you want someone to help?'

Jess started to cry. 'Yes, yes of course I would, but I am frightened of ghosts. What if I freak out?' she asked.

Shannon then told her a pearl of wisdom that had been passed on from her grandma. 'It isn't the dead that you need to fear, but the living. If the dead visit you then they need to be listened to. That is all that they ask, just that you listen.' Shannon then went on to tell her that she too had caught glimpses of the little boy from time to time.

Jess got as far as saying 'Why didn't you...' before she

stopped herself.

'Say something?' Shannon asked.

Jess just giggled. No more needed to be discussed on that subject.

That night, both Shannon and Jess made their impromptu beds in the attic room. Neither felt in the least bit tired, such was their apprehension at what may lie ahead. Shannon had lit a few candles and had placed them around the room. 'We can't leave the light on as it makes it difficult for them to come through' she said. Jess remarked on how pretty the room looked by candle-light. Both were treating it almost as an adventure and a 'girl's night' - until Jess said, 'I can hear music'.

Drifting up from downstairs was the sound of the Beatle's version of 'Mr Postman'. Then the sound of a needle being dragged across a record and then an argument. Suddenly, the door to the attic room changed. It was once again the peeling and unattractive door it had once been. The door flew back and a teenage girl of around the same age of Jess was dragging a small boy along behind her. She roughly pushed the frightened little boy into the room, whilst shouting 'I told you to keep your grubby little fingers away from my records and my record player. Now STAY IN HERE until mum gets home.' She then slammed the door and locked it. The boy sat on the floor and sobbed. Soon the sound of the music started up again, and this time louder than before.

A few seconds later, the boy began to gasp. He furiously checked his pockets. 'My inhaler, I need my inhaler,' he gasped. Then began to bang upon the door. It was to no avail. The music was too loud. The scene then faded away.

Shannon and Jess were in floods of tears. 'So that's what the poor child wanted us to know. He wanted us to know what his cruel sister had done!' Jess said.

Shannon nodded, and then said to the room, 'We know what happened now, my darling. We understand'. She then turned to Jess and said 'He is probably at rest now.'

The rest of the night was uneventful. For several days afterwards everything was quiet. Then around two in the morning again, Jess tapped upon her mother's bedroom door.

When Shannon asked what was wrong, Jess told her that she had seen the little boy again. Shannon said that something struck her as odd. When spirits come back, any ailments that they once had are cured. They are well again. So she wondered why he had the inhaler. That seemed to be at the crux of the mystery.

'Well, it's obvious, Mum. He needed to show us what happened'.

'Yes, he did, but if you remember, he DIDN'T have his inhaler. That's the whole point.'

At that moment they heard a child's voice. It said, 'Tell my sister. Tell her.'

Both of them let out a small whoop of fright. There, behind them, and sitting upright on a bedroom chair was the little boy.

Shannon spoke, and said, 'Tell her what, darling?'

'Tell her it wasn't her fault,' the boy said.

'But it WAS her fault. She was horrid to you,' Jess said.

The little boy was quite calm and resolute. Quietly, but firmly, he said to them, 'My sister knows I always have my inhaler in my pocket - always. I had gone into the kitchen for a new refill for it when I saw her record player. I shouldn't have touched it. She didn't know. She didn't know, and I died. It wasn't her fault'.

A wave of sadness and the futility of it all swept across Shannon and Jess. The boy continued his story. 'She haunts this house too. When Mum found me in here, my sister's life was destroyed. She was my sister and I was her annoying kid brother, but she did love me - she did' he said, whilst nodding defiantly to highlight this fact. 'She couldn't handle what had happened and she took an overdose of pills. When Mum found her it was too late'. 'If you see her, will you tell her that it wasn't her fault? Will you? Please?' the boy said.

Within seconds, the room began to lose its icy coldness. The sound of The Beatles began to drift up the stairs again. Then they heard a voice speak the words, 'I will go to hell. What I did was so, so wrong.' Standing in the room was a young girl in floods of tears.

The boy ran to her and put his arms around her. 'Where have you been. I have wanted to tell you for so long. It wasn't your fault. I love you.' He then said to the girl, 'Look over there. It's Mum. We have all been waiting for you. You are coming with us. There is no hell. There is only hell for those who are not sorry and no not recognise they acted badly. There is no hell any more. You have been there already.' The whole tableau slowly drifted away in front of Shannon and Jess's eyes. The two young spirits were wrapped in a golden light, and were gone.

Both Shannon and Jess were tearful and emotional. 'If ever I tell you again that I hate you, just because I don't get my way. Please remind me of this day' Jess said. Both Shannon and Jess gained a deeper understanding that love is all. Without love, there is nothing. Love can overcome all obstacles in the end.

Sally Daydream

Life springs forth anew and green buds bleed from finger stumps of twigs once ashen grey and dead. The nudity of the bare trees is gone, like blushing maidens, they cover up their limbs and clothe themselves with gay and riotous colour once more. It is a churchyard. The granite and the marble monoliths rise up spectrally. Mute sentinels that mark where loved ones lie, and those forgotten and unmourned.

A place of death yet full of life. The robin pipes its flute-like tune and busies itself in turning over the remaining dead leaves in search of insects and seeds. His size belies his courage. This is his patch and he suffers no intruder. The squirrels care little for anyone but themselves. The robin hates them. They eat birds' eggs. They are second only in being detested to the black cat that stalks the church and grounds like a skulking, murderous felon. The wood pigeons call out almost indignantly. They sit like fat women upon the branches of the yew tree, berating all around them. These are all her friends. These are Sally's closest companions.

Sally prefers the company of creatures to human beings. They do not judge. Neither do they mock or cause her pain. Sally has what some people call a gift. Sally sees it as a curse. The dead tell her things.

At first, Sally would discuss these occurrences with her parents, but her father called her a wicked little girl and thrashed her for telling lies. Her mother concerned herself that her daughter was hearing voices. The doctor, having no answers, sent her away. This is why she had spent all that time. All that time in that bed, in that ward, with those doctors and nurses. They couldn't have taken her to a worse place. To a house filled with restless spirits. Then there was 'that' room. The room where they made her bite down on a piece of rubber, then they put the electrodes on each side of her forehead and her head exploded with the coloured lights.

Sally no longer talked to anyone about the dead, but still. Still they insistently talked to her and asked her to convey messages. Sally ignored them and busied herself in finding small worms in the damp grass to feed to the eager robin, but there was the man that she couldn't ignore. The one who followed her everywhere, and would appear without being bidden. She called him 'The Raggy Man'.

Sally played the game that she called 'The good little girl' game. When asked about the voices, she would smile sweetly and say 'Oh those, the silly voices, they have gone now.' Her father still had very little time for her. He wanted a boy and had been 'Saddled with a stupid girl' as he was fond of saying, to anyone who would listen. Both Sally and her mother lived in mortal fear and dread of him. Then there came a set of circumstances that would throw everything upon its head.

Sally was alone in her bedroom when The Raggy Man appeared. He appeared in his usual frightening and unusual fashion. He would suddenly fly out of a solid wall and hurtle towards Sally until his maggot-riddled face was mere inches from hers. She could smell the stench of his breath. He would always say the same thing 'They want to talk to you'. Sally screamed and yelled 'Go away, I am not talking to you. I am not talking to anyone.'

Sally had no idea that her father was passing on the landing. He burst into the bedroom and yelled at her 'I knew it. I just knew you were lying.' He began to rain down slaps and blows upon her. Sally was screaming when her mother came into the room and tried to make him stop. He did stop, but then turned his attentions upon her. He dragged her to the floor and punched and kicked her, splitting open her nose, so that two scarlet trickles ran from her nose and dripped off the end of her chin. He was drunk - yet again.

He headed towards the stairs, but in his drunken state, he missed his footing and tumbled head over heels to the bottom of the stairs. Her mother found her husband at the foot of the stairs. She could see by the impossible angle that his head lay upon his shoulders that he had broken his neck. He was dead. The police were called, but not before Sally's mum had tidied herself up and changed her clothes. For obvious reasons she didn't want to let the police and the ambulance men into the house with blood all down the front of her dress.

In all honesty, he was well known to the police for his drunken behaviour and violent ways. It came as no surprise that this had happened. The coroner brought forth the verdict of accidental death due to intoxication.

Sally and her mother became much closer after that. Still she played The Good Girl Game, as her mother still thought it had been some kind of mental disorder. The Raggy Man still made his sudden and frightening appearances, but apart from the startled surprise, she still wouldn't talk to him.

It was one day, around ten in the morning when she heard a familiar and frightening voice saying, 'Sally, Sally, please talk to me Sally.' It was her father. He was standing in front of her, his head still at that impossible angle. 'I'm sorry, Sally. I believe you now. Please tell your mummy that I really did love her and that I am sorry'. Sally just ignored him and left the room. He frantically followed her from room to room, shouting hysterically 'I need your mother to forgive me. They want to take me. Take me to the dark place.' Still Sally ignored him.

She skipped down to the churchyard, her father still trailing desperately behind her. 'Good morning Mr Robin. Shall we find some worms?' Sally said. The tiny bird hopped eagerly around her feet. Suddenly The Raggy Man appeared. He hissed through rotten teeth 'Shall I take him away and put him with the others?' Sally looked at her father as he grovelled and begged with her not to let him take him. 'That would be nice. Thank you Mr Raggy Man,' she said. Her father's spirit was no more. Sally knew that the howls of pain and the begging of tortured souls was what fed him. She said to the robin 'That should keep him fed too. Fed for a long, long time.'

Tattoo

'Tattoo?' Amanda was so envious, yet also more than a little intimidated by tattoos. They always reminded her of her father, who wasn't the gentlest or most understanding man in the world. 'Is it Chinese?' she asked.

Jessica said that it was.

'What does it mean?' she asked.

Jessica said that she chose it from a list, and it meant 'Naughty'.

Mandy laughed and said, 'Typical of you'.

Jess and Mandy had known each other since nursery school. They grew up on the same council estate, went to the same schools, and had each other's backs ever since they could walk. They had drunk together, laughed together, and comforted each other when going through any splits with their respective boyfriends. They were as good as sisters.

That had been a week earlier. Much had happened since that day. Jess seemed a completely different person to Mandy. They were always texting each other, but now it seemed that Jess was just perennially irritated by her. Mandy had sent a text with an emoticon saying 'BFF' (Best Friends Forever). Jess didn't reply for an hour or so, before replying with 'Stop sending me this shit. GROW UP'. This reduced her to tears. Something was terribly wrong. It wasn't just Mandy who had noticed either. Their small circle of close friends were all commenting on it too. Jane texted her saying 'WTF is up with Jess. It's like she is permanently PMS'. Jane and Mandy decided that a girls' night out was what was needed. They booked a table at the local Chinese restaurant and gave Jess the ultimatum by text 'Show up or lose us as friends'.

Jess sent back her reply of 'OK, seeing you have asked so

nicely', followed by a manic looking smiley.

The girls met in a pub beside The Golden Palace restaurant. Jane opened the questions with 'Why are you such a moody cow these days?'

Jess bristled, and snapped back with the answer, 'I don't know. I just don't. I just keep having these.....these....thoughts'.

Jane and Mandy glanced at each other in alarm 'What kind of thoughts, love?' Mandy asked.

Jess regained her composure, and answered with 'Dark thoughts. Wanting to lash out and hurt people'. She then broke down into floods of tears. This was far worse than either of them had thought.

'Come on you miserable old slapper, let's go and put some weight on next door' Jane said.

Jess and Mandy both laughed.

The girls arrived at the restaurant. They were no strangers to the place and went there regularly, for everything from birthdays to just girlie nights on the town. Mr Li, the owner, knew them well and always had a laugh with them and spoilt them a little.

'Ahhh, my favourite glamour girls are back,' he said to them, whilst giving them the warmest and widest of smiles. 'Let me take your coats and get you girls a drink' he said.

When Jess took off her coat and he saw the tattoo near her shoulder, his whole expression and demeanour changed. His smile and joviality seemed to cool a little. Mandy was a big 'people reader' and very astute. She spotted it straight away. 'Let me show you ladies to your table,' he said, regaining his smile as he did.

The girls ordered the banquet for three, and soon the exquisite food began to arrive at the table. They had ordered a bottle of white wine to accompany their little feast. The three girls tucked into the food and issued forth little sighs of ecstasy.

Mandy said to them, 'I am just popping to the loo'.

The other two nodded in reply, as both their mouths were stuffed to capacity.

On her way there, she was stopped by Mr Li. 'Can you meet me here tomorrow, before the restaurant opens. I need to speak with you,' he said.

'Erm... sure. What's up?' she asked.

Mr Li told her that it was about Jess.

The girls had a wonderful meal, and Jess seemed to brighten visibly. As they were on the pavement outside, Jane said, 'GROUP HUG' and all three girls hugged each other. As they did, Jess whispered, 'Sorry,' and her bottom lip quivered.

'Oh hush you big, hormonal drama queen,' Jane replied.

All three girls just giggled.

The next day, Mandy went back to the restaurant as promised. It was closed, so she tapped upon the window. Mr Li came and opened the door. He showed her to a table where he had laid out two cups and a pot of tea. 'Don't get excited. It's just builders' tea,' he said, and then laughed.

'What did you want to see me about?' Mandy asked.

Mr Li looked both sad and a little agitated. 'That tattoo that your friend has? Is she behaving differently?'

Mandy felt her stomach turn over and do somersaults. 'How did you know?' she replied.

Mr Li sighed deeply, then said 'I hoped you would say no. Why on earth did she choose that....why??' he asked.

'Well she said that they told her it meant naughty, so she chose it'.

Mr Li thumped his fist down onto the table so hard that the teacups rattled. 'This is what happens. This is what happens when people dabble in other people's cultures'. he said angrily. He then went on to say that it meant no such thing, what the tattoo says is Xie' e, which means evil.

'Bring her back here this evening, even if you have to drag her,' he said.

Mandy said that she would do her level best.

Mandy tried to contact Jess all day, but she wasn't picking up her calls. In her lunch break, she dropped by where Jess worked, but was told that she had rung in sick. That evening, straight after work, Mandy went round to Jess's flat. It was all in darkness. Mandy hammered on the door, but no one answered. She remembered that Jess had given her a spare key in case she ever locked herself out of her flat (which had happened several times before). Mandy opened the door and walked inside. She switched on the lights and shouted, 'Jess, where are you?' It was then that she saw Jess sprawled out on the bed. An empty tablet bottle beside her. The bed was in a mess. She had vomited a few times. Mandy immediately rang for an ambulance.

Fortunately, they had caught Jess in time. Her vomiting had helped to save her, as she had brought back many of the pills. She also had a bandage on her arm. It appeared as if she had tried to remove the tattoo with a sharp instrument. It appeared that she had literally tried to gouge it out.

Jess was obviously tearful when Mandy went to visit her in hospital. She just wept and apologised over and over.

'Oh Jess, please don't apologise. You are my bestie mate. Just promise me you will talk to me in future,' Mandy said. She then asked her about the scarring on her arm, and what possessed her to mutilate herself in such a way. What Jess told her chilled the blood in her veins. 'I didn't do it. The creature did'.

Mandy was at first just dumbfounded, and wondered whether Jess was in some way unbalanced and was hallucinating. 'The creature??' she asked.

Jess told her that she had first seen it two days after she had the tattoo done. 'It wouldn't let me sleep. It would tell me things. It would tell me that you all laugh at me and hate me.'

'WHAT??' Mandy replied.

Jess began to cry and apologise again.

Jess told her that she felt so wretched that she could see no way out, so she took the pills. That was when it tried to chew the tattoo from her arm. She said that it told her that the evil must live on, and the only way was for it to be inside itself.

The scars on Jess's arms healed over time. What remained of the tattoo she had professionally removed. None of the girls ever even entertained the idea of tattoos after that.

Bartram

No one knew how old Bartram was. Everyone called him by his surname, as he hated his Christian name (Cyril), so it suited him down to the ground. Bartram lived in an old, Victorian, red brick detached house. Apparently it had once been a vicarage, but not in anyone's living memory. Bartram seemed to have been there forever. Bartram had a fresh and quite wrinkle-free face and walked with a spring in his step. He was like a man in his prime. The locals knew he must be in his eighties at least by the memory of the local old people.

He had spent time in India and British Malaya. His house was packed with exotic curios which he had brought back. It looked like a museum. There were stuffed animals and all manner of curiosities.

Being a creature of habit, Bartram made his way to a local hotel and restaurant to have his dinner and a few glasses of port, before returning home. For the past few weeks, a pair of local housebreakers had been observing his habits. They waited until he had turned the corner in the road before slipping through the side gate and towards the back of Bartram's property.

'The stupid old sod doesn't even have a burglar alarm,' one of the thieves said, as he prized open a window frame with a small crowbar. Within seconds, the two men were inside.

'This place gives me the creeps. I don't care how soon we are done,' one of the men said.

They had already bagged-up a few nice pieces of Indian silver and a few small pieces of ethnic art. Methodically, they moved from room to room. Pulling out drawers and tipping the contents onto the floor. Any cabinets that were locked they forced open, damaging the beautiful arts and crafts period furniture.

'Look, a gun, and a box of bullets,' one of the men remarked. It was a service revolver from the turn of the century. 'This will fetch good money' he said. He then loaded the gun and tucked it inside his belt loop. 'If the old bugger comes back, he will get more than he bargained for' he said as he laughed.

They had already filled one bag. They put this by the window that they had forced open, and continued with a second bag. Eventually, they made their way up the stairs towards the bedrooms. The first thing that greeted them was a very ornate door. It seemed to be encrusted with precious stones and silver. Neither of them knew what to make of it.

'That can't be real,' one of them remarked.

'Why not?' the other replied.

'Well if that's just the door, imagine what might be on the other side?' the first man said.

The door was unlocked. As they entered the room, they were left completely breathless. There were glass cabinets on both sides of the room that had what seemed to be silver and gold plates, cups and chalices. At the end of the room there was a kind of Indian altar. There was a huge statue of some kind of deity with several arms. They stood in front of the deity and were transfixed. Just at that moment, they heard a hissing noise behind them. They turned to see a cobra around two feet behind them. The snake was erect, with its hood fully puffed out. Slowly, the two men backed away from it. Then something grabbed the men and threw them backwards. This also knocked the gun from the hand of the burglar, who had taken it out of his belt to take a shot at the cobra. It went scattering across the ornately tiled floor. The statue had seemingly come to life and was holding them both fast to its body.

The men struggled in sheer terror. A puddle of urine began to form beside one of their trainers. Such was the man's sheer fright. They were both sobbing uncontrollably.

Slowly, the door opened, and there, silhouetted in the doorway, was the figure of Bartram. In his hand he held a ceremonial, jewel-encrusted dagger. 'We have guests I see,' he said, whilst smiling benignly. Bartram then turned and locked the door. The two petrified men just stared at him in abject terror. One of the men blurted out, between tears. 'Just call the police. We will pay for any damage, please, don't hurt us'. Both men were sobbing like children and had lost control of their bodily functions.

Bartram stood around a foot away from one of the thieves and looked directly into the man's eyes. 'Struggling is useless. He never lets go,' he said, before going on to say, 'I have such a thirst. I think I need a drink'. Quick as a flash, Bartram slashed the neck of one of the thieves wide open, and clamped his mouth over the gushing jugular vein.

The other thief screamed in perfect and abject terror. Bartram was indeed thirsty. He was very thirsty indeed. By the time he had finished, the pale corpse merely flopped forward in the statue's arms. The god then released the man, and his lifeless corpse slithered down upon the floor.

Bartram then turned to face the other thief. He was terrified beyond all compass. He merely held his breath and shook uncontrollably. Bartram placed his hands each side of the man's forehead, and he immediately became peaceful. His mouth fell open in a kind of stupor. Bartram was now inside the man's mind. He was wiping it as clean as would a damp cloth on a blackboard. Saliva began to run out of the man's mouth. He had wiped out every trace of any memory or learning from the man's mind. He could no longer read, write or speak any language.

A few hours later, the man was found stumbling around the streets at two o'clock in the morning. He had been taken to hospital and was still there days later. Bartram disposed of the corpse in the huge boiler in the cellar and made good all the damage.

Two weeks later, Bartram walked through the doors of his favourite hotel and restaurant. The maître d'hôtel greeted him with the words. 'You are looking particularly youthful and refreshed today Mr B. Do you know, I am sure that you have discovered the fountain of life.'

Bartram chuckled and said, 'Why yes, I drank of its rich waters only two weeks ago.' He then winked, and said, 'I'll take the fillet mignon steak please, VERY rare.'

Help Me, Please

There was something about the house that just didn't feel right. It was their first house together, and they had bought a 'do-er-upper', or a house that needed renovating. Some things were beyond them, like rewiring, plumbing, etc. but the rest, Brendan and Jess were more than capable of doing themselves.

'It's just because it's old and run down,' Brendan said, in an attempt to allay her fears, but Jess wasn't at all convinced. Even the plumber said that the place made him feel a little creeped out. Brendan implored him not to mention his feelings to Jess.

The plumber nodded in agreement. 'It will all be done by this afternoon anyway,' he said.

They had both been attracted to the property because it looked absolutely perfect. It was an old farm worker's cottage. It was some hundred yards away from the nearest tarmac road, down a little, twisting farm track. When they first viewed it, it was in summer. Roses and honeysuckle grew around the ramshackle little porch. It looked adorable. They had bought with their hearts rather than their heads, as just about everything needed doing to it. At least now they had a decent bathroom and kitchen, and central heating.

The master bedroom overlooked the porch, and across the track there was a pond. Jess thought it was probably just a couple of feet deep, but when she stood on the bank and looked into it, it was quite a depth. Then she noticed the brick lining. This was obviously purpose-built. It was probably to provide water for the farm. They also owned this little piece of land and the pond. Jess had always wanted to keep ducks and chickens. It would be perfect.

Brendan and Jess were stripping down the walls of the master bedroom when Brendan announced, 'Hello, what's this I wonder?' It was a large piece of plywood that seemed to be nailed over something. It had been skimmed over with plaster to make the walls even.

'Well, it's going to have to come off. God alone knows what it's covering up,'. Brendan said, and was already levering out the nails that held it with his claw hammer.

They were both astounded to find that behind it was an old door. When they opened the door, they saw it was a small cubby hole that was over the stairs. 'Wow, this will be useful,' Brendan said.

Jess was similarly excited, and already had ideas of it being a walk-in wardrobe with shelves and a light. It was she who spotted them first. 'Look, it's a little pair of shoes,' she said excitedly.

Brendan picked them up and said, 'Not shoes, clogs. They look like they belonged to a kid.'

Jess decided to clean them up and polish them. They would be a talking point when friends came round.

Eventually, they made the bedroom serviceable. This meant that they could actually live in the house. Up until then, they had been sleeping in a little caravan outside. They had retained as many of the features as they could. The oak beams looked stunning, and they even sanded down and waxed the old door to the cubby hole. They had bought a reproduction four poster bed. The bedroom looked like something from a magazine. It was gorgeous. That night was to be the first night they slept in there.

They were like two excited children. They were both night-owls, but decided on an early night. When ten o'clock came they made their way to bed. As they entered the bedroom, they saw that the door to the cubby hole was open. Neither of them thought anything of it. Jess closed it again and they both went to bed.

Around 2am, Jess was woken by a creaking noise. She glanced across at the cubby hole and saw that the door was open again. Her rational brain was telling her that it was probably a faulty latch. After all, the door was probably early Victorian. Something made her senses tingle about it, though. She closed her eyes and tried to get back off to sleep. Some minutes later, her nostrils caught the scent of a smell. It was the odour of mud and stagnant water. She opened her eyes, and saw the figure of a small child standing right beside the bed. He was soaking wet and shivering. 'Why didn't you hear me? Why didn't you hear me?' he said.

Jess screamed and shook Brendan violently. 'Wake up, look, look!' she shouted at him, but by then the child had disappeared.

'What's up Jess, are you okay?' Brendan asked.

He switched on the bedside lamp. She wept as she clung to him. She then told him what had happened.

'It was probably just a bad dream, darling. You said he was soaking wet. Look, the floor is perfectly dry,' Brendan said. 'You have been working really hard on the house, and it has all stressed you out a little.'

Jess was now calmer. She was still unconvinced that she hadn't seen a ghost, but her rational brain told her that he was probably right. She convinced herself further when she saw that the cubby hole door was actually closed.

The next day, Brendan had gone off to work. Jess was self-employed and worked from home. She sat at the kitchen table and was typing up a set of reports on her laptop. She had the radio on while she worked. She idly sipped at her cup of tea when she heard some kind of commotion in the background. She switched off the radio and could hear what sounded like a child in distress. She ran outside to see what was happening, but all was quiet again. She scanned the entire area just in case, but found nothing. The mallards were idly floating around on the surface of the pond, and wood pigeons were cooing in the nearby elderberry trees. All seemed like a perfect countryside idyll.

Jess came back inside to continue with her work. 'Christ, it's like living in Borley Rectory,' she mumbled to herself. She had read the books about Borley, and the ghost investigations by Harry Price when she was a little girl. As she approached the kitchen table she caught the smell of the stagnant water odour again. There, beside the chair where she had previously been sitting, were the wet footprints of a child. Jess controlled her feelings remarkably. She even surprised herself. She took out her phone and took several shots of the footprints. She decided to go and sit in the caravan until Brendan returned home.

Jess downloaded the photos onto her laptop and was very relieved that they had come out so well. You could actually see a perfect child's footprint. She had placed a pencil beside it, to give a perspective of the actual size.

Brendan returned home and found Jess in the caravan. 'Why are you in here?' he asked.

Jess then told him what had happened. He seemed extremely sceptical about the whole thing. She could see the look of, 'Oh, not this rubbish again,' on his face. Then Jess showed him the pictures. 'Explain that then,' she said defiantly.

Brendan was completely floored by them. 'Okay, it seems that we have a bit of a problem,' he said.

Jess laughed as if to say, 'That's a bit of an understatement.' She then said, 'I did a bit of poking around online and found this.' It was a newspaper report from 1932 that read, 'Tragic drowning of six-year-old boy in water reservoir.' The report read that Stephen Barry, the son of a farm worker had fallen into the pond and drowned. There was a ball in the nearby pond weed, and his clogs and socks were found on the bank. It had been assumed that he had tried to wade out for his ball, and had slipped and got into difficulties.

'Oh dear God,' Brendan said.

Jess nodded, then said, 'I suppose now is as good a time as any to tell you. I am pregnant.'

Brendan was overjoyed. He hugged and kissed his wife.

Jess brought him back to earth by saying, 'This all needs sorting before I bring a child into the house.'

A couple of days later, they made an appointment to see the pastor of the local church. They told him about the happenings, and even showed him the pictures. He agreed to come round to bless the house. This made them both feel a little easier about the situation. It made no difference. That same night the child returned to the bedside.

Jess had mentally prepared herself for such a contingency. She remembered when she had been reading the books about Borley Rectory and had scared herself. The words of her mum came back to her. 'The dead can't hurt you, darling. They are just unhappy spirits.' Jess was literally terrified, but had steeled herself for the challenge.

Brendan also witnessed the boy, but just stared at him in mute disbelief.

'Were you the little boy who drowned in the pond?' Jess asked the spirit.

He nodded, and said, 'I'm really cold, mummy.'

Jess told him that she wasn't his mummy, but his mummy was probably waiting for him in heaven. 'Did you slip and fall in?' she asked.

'NO!' the boy shouted. He then went on to tell them that the farmer's son had seen him trying to wade out for the ball and had pushed him in. He'd laughed at him, but when he realised that he was drowning, he panicked and ran away.

'Oh sweetie, I am so, so sorry,' Jess said. Then went on to ask how she could help.

The child smiled at her and said, 'You already have. I just needed to tell someone what had happened.' He went on to tell Jess that it had broken his poor mother. She put his clogs into the cubby hole and had her husband nail the door behind a board and plaster over it. 'It was like she wanted to pretend I had never existed,' the child said. He then began to cry.

Then Jess and Brendan heard a woman's voice outside on the stairs landing. 'Mummy is sorry, darling. Mummy is sorry.'

It was Stephen's mother. He ran to her and she hugged him and cried. Over and over she apologised, until the two spirits faded away.

Jess wept for then both.

The last thing she heard was Stephen's voice. He said, 'Thank you for helping me find my mummy. You are going to be such a good mummy yourself.' That was the last they ever saw of Stephen.

Jess and Brendan erected a sturdy fence all the way around the pond.

Year 6017

The archaeology section of the World University (New London Sector) was digging on the former site of a North West city once known as Manchester. The building structures could still be seen, but all records of what once stood on the site had been obliterated in the nuclear holocaust. Certain digital records remained, but were sketchy at best. The calcified and powdered bones of the victims lay buried beneath the rubble on the very day the surprise attack hit them. It had taken four thousand years to bring back the semblance of civilisation. All borders were now open and all countries united for the common good. Religion was examined as an archaic and dangerous doctrine. History showed quite clearly the insidious effect it had on world stability. It seemed almost comical that the whole infrastructure of the world could be based on religious fairy tales, the reliance on dwindling fossil fuels and a metal called gold. It was a strange world to the modern eyes. A world where being different by skin colour could be seen as threatening. 'Did these people fear choice and difference?' the professor said, whilst addressing his chuckling students.

One quiet and thoughtful young person said, 'They did have poetry. They sang and loved. Their primitive minds and hearts could only encompass so much. Their brains had been twisted and distorted by the doctrines taught in their schools and by the bigotry of their guardians. They weren't to blame. They were the true innocents.'

Suddenly the dig became less clinical and more reverent. These were once people just like they were. These people once dreamed and aspired. Their aspirations were flawed, though. Their ability to share had been crippled by the gold that they worshipped. The boundaries between sport and life had become blurred. They could watch their fellow man die of starvation, or freeze to death for lack of basic shelter, yet spend the wherewithal of their 'money' to buy a timepiece that they strapped to their wrists that could have been used to feed and clothe a hundred people for a month. They had become obscene. Their demise was a slow inevitability.

When the holocaust came, the powerful ones hid in their bunkers. They were the unlucky ones. They took the longest to die. The ones in the more remote areas of the world struggled through several nuclear winters, but they were the ones who learned to share and see their fellow man for who he or she was. Colour and previous status no longer mattered. The strong nursed the weak and civilisation was reborn.

In the beginning, the growing of food and the welfare of the people was the only concern. Natural leaders emerged rather than being chosen. People took on tasks because of their natural abilities, be that strength or imagination. Death and illness was rife, and the after effects of radiation threw up many birth abnormalities. Soon though, each generation became immune to the after effects of the dwindling background radiation. Society became another word for nurture. Greed was one of the cardinal crimes. Mental and physical illnesses were seen and treated equally. Neither given less or more importance. No one feared mental illness. It was an ever-present, like the common cold.

Soon violence became less and less common. Society began to realise that violence against any single person was violence against the whole of humanity. People lived all over the globe as they had once done, but a single and common language was spoken by all. There were subtle changes in laws that were dictated by geographical locations and the over-riding natural weather conditions in these areas. New dialects began to emerge and a world council for the celebration of these dialects emerged. Words formed in different areas became assimilated into the global language.

New sports emerged to feed the natural competitiveness of mankind. Now that the nuclear winters were over, and the fight for survival was won, mankind now competed joyfully in their separate geographical regions. House building and design had a world championship. Different prizes were offered up for design and concept, speed of building, resource conservation, etc.

The word wealth was a concept that was only partially revived. It was now called the world happiness index. Now that currency had been replaced by the concepts of love, regard and helpfulness. The need for banks and service industries were a thing of the past. Everything was conceived, made and distributed equally throughout the world. Wills were also a thing of the past as property and possessions no longer really existed.

People were now free of archaic societal frameworks that had previously existed. Birth was seen as a joyous thing, but something that needed regulating. Society grew by mutual consent and the regard of the impact it had upon others and the world in general. Mankind was at last growing up.

Mankind, for all its change, had not become sterile as previously feared. Laughter was ever-present. People held 'Old World' parties, where they elected one of the revellers as President, and he would order everyone around and get them to do menial tasks for him. The revellers would have tears of laughter rolling down their faces as they combed the hair, or washed the face of the president, and fed him like a baby with food, spoonful by spoonful. Then they would depose the president and he would be sent to the corner whilst everyone pointed and booed at him. Then it would be the turn of someone else.

People no longer had jobs as such, as all tasks were done by all people. Specialists emerged and were given time to develop their skills. People like doctors, scientists, philosophers etc, as these were seen as crucial to societal development. Even then, society viewed them as no more or less important than the farming specialist who developed and grew the crops, or the responsible sanitation specialists who recycled absolutely everything. Plastic was no longer synthesized but was grown. It was a kind of biologically engineered fungus. It was also edible when processed.

Now that all stresses and tensions had been removed, people were happy to live closely together. It was realised that animals, birds and fishes were necessary for a natural existence. The five percent rule applied, which meant that only five percent of available land was used for dwelling and production purposes. The rest was used for the natural growing of food in wildlife conditions that benefited both humans and wildlife.

The word family became merely a concept, as everyone's children were seen as a shared asset and every responsible adult was a kind of guardian within their specific district. Children could either be bred and given birth to by the traditional methods, or eggs incubated remotely. Sex had largely become just a recreational activity. Mothers who, for whatever reason (and there were many after the holocaust) couldn't produce children, could jointly raise and look after as many children as they liked. Family basically became a word for mankind, or district.

Laws were there for guidance and the furtherance of a just and peaceful society. People were still people, and squabbles and jealousies naturally existed. These were dealt with by district hearing clinics that were populated and run by people from other districts. All people from all districts took part in such clinics. As property was now all in public ownership, there were very few housing laws and no such thing as mortgages. Houses were built in one size but of different designs so as to be aesthetically pleasing and avoid monotony.

Spirituality became an esoteric activity where people gathered to share joyously the secrets and the mystery of life itself. Prayers became poems and songs of joy. God became merely the force of life itself and the love that existed within it. Inequalities, both physically and mentally were no longer seen as weaknesses. Society had moved beyond labels. Words such as 'disabled' or 'learning difficulties' were merely put aside. A person's usefulness was never brought into question.

It was found that, when all the world became one force, the synergy of it became a tangible force within itself. Stress, disease, mental illness and aggression reduced dramatically. The pursuit of leisure became almost a nonsensical theory, as life itself was constant leisure. Holidays were no longer needed as everywhere was beautiful, merely geographically different.

In every large town or city a building was erected. It was called The House of Lessons. Once a year, each citizen must visit it and re-learn and refresh the memory of what lay inside it. There were two sections. One for children and one for adults. It was a kind of museum. The exhibits were weapons from humanity's past. They showed the weapon itself and images (both film clips and static images) of the results of such weapons on individual people and society as a whole. They showed images of capital punishment and torture. Eventually leading up to the holocaust itself. People were then counselled and helped to come to terms with what they had seen. Each person then had to wear a T Shirt with the words 'Never Again' for a month afterwards.

The words of the new sentient age read as such, 'Love is the reward of the people and the right of everyone. Love cannot be wasted as it is boundless. Love can only die when it is not used, and only truly exist when it is for the good of all'.

The Entity

'You lose who you are. You seem to lose your entire identity!' These were the first words that June spoke to Dan on waking up. She had just been dragged in a state of semi-consciousness from the library of Tidesley Manor House, where she had spent the last four hours on a solo vigil. Her partner, Dan was in the master bedroom on a similar vigil.

'What happened to you. You were absolutely sparked out,' Dan said.

June shook her head and said, 'You probably wouldn't believe me if I told you.' She refused to discuss it any further. The matter was closed. The terrified and haunted expression on her face told Dan not to push her any further on the matter.

That was four years earlier. June could hardly believe that she was back there again. She had told Dan that she just had to go back. It felt as if she had failed. It also felt that there was a part of her in there that had been taken from her. June knew that this time she wouldn't be taken by surprise by the unholy thing. 'This time I am tooled-up,' she growled.

'I'm coming in there with you,' Dan said.

'No... no you aren't. This is me and that thing. I know you mean well, but no.'

Dan knew better than to argue with her. This was why he loved her so much. She could be as stubborn as a mule, but when riled, she was like an Amazon.

Dan had rigged up the library during daylight hours with night-vision cameras, sound recorders, movement sensors, and a remote EMF meter. This time, with any luck, they would see the thing. Dan had set up the control room in the study, where he monitored everything remotely on his laptop. June kissed him and said, 'Wish me luck,' then she ventured into the library clutching a small wooden crucifix and a bottle of holy water. She didn't have long to wait. As she passed through the library door, the word, 'Bitch' was whispered into her ear.

'Maybe I am, but at least I am not a snivelling little shitbag like you are,' she said confidently.

Dan didn't hear the whisper, but he heard her reply to it. 'That's my girl,' he said to himself, whilst smiling. He had never felt more proud of her.

June seated herself on one of the chairs. She placed the crucifix on the table beside her. She heard something sliding around the floor. It hissed almost snake-like in manner. It also carried with it an overpowering stench of faecal matter and rotting flesh. June smiled and said, 'Is this upsetting you?' whilst holding up the crucifix. She heard a growl as an adjacent chair toppled over. It was as if the entity had knocked it over in its eagerness to escape.

'I have that on film,' Dan said excitedly into the earpiece in June's left ear.

'I think we are only just starting,' June said in reply.

There then ensued something of a stand-off. The entity could be heard slowly circling June, but hardly daring to come near her. It could only be assumed that the crucifix did indeed have some hold over the creature.

'You aren't a ghost, are you?' June asked, before adding, 'You have never existed on this side of life. That's why you wanted it - isn't it?'

The entity poured forth a litany of filth, to which June merely laughed.

'Wanted what?' Dan asked through her earpiece.

'Tell you later,' June whispered. She kicked a chair over towards the middle of the library floor. 'Let's see you. Sit down and we will talk,' she said.

Presently, a figure began to take shape upon the chair.

June became very angry. Sitting before her was her departed grandfather. 'You lying piece of shit,' she said. 'I said I want to see *you*, not you trying on the faces of my family. Let me see you - if you dare.'

Dan told her that all he was seeing on the screen was a misty outline of a figure.

'It thinks it's clever,' June told Dan. 'It thinks I believe what it shows me.'

'Just be careful, darling,' Dan replied.

The figure of June's grandfather slowly faded. Sitting in front of her now was a diminutive humanoid figure. It was no taller than around four feet. All its bodily proportions were out of balance. The head was slightly too small for its shoulders. Its ribcage seemed distended outwards. Its legs were small, but its arms were almost the length of its entire body. On the end of each arm were hands, but they had a thumb on each side.

'I'm seeing it. Oh Jesus, I am seeing it,' Dan said, barely disguising the fear in his voice.

The creature spoke. 'Back again, bitch?' it asked. Inside its unholy and distorted ribcage something glowed with a white, pure light.

Quick as a flash, June brought the bottle out of her coat pocket and threw the holy water over the creature. It screamed in pain, and the white, glowing light flew from its body and hit June squarely in her chest. June gasped and was knocked backwards, almost falling off her chair, such was the force.

Dan had witnessed the entire procedure. He sprinted from the study and burst through the library door. He switched on the lights to find June with her head in her hands and weeping.

'Are you okay? What just happened?' he asked.

'It's okay, I have it back now,'. June answered.

'What... What do you have back?' Dan asked.

June let out a long and wearied sigh; then said, 'My soul'.

As they were reviewing the footage, Dan asked June what she meant by getting her soul back.

June told him that she had to keep it to herself until she formulated a plan. 'It was only half of the battle. He wanted me to become the distorted figure, and for his soul to reside inside my body. He wanted mortality,' June said. 'I made a promise to return, in exchange for something,' she said.

'What's that?' Dan asked.

June held her hand against his face and, with tears in her eyes, she whispered, 'Your life. He could have snuffed you out in a second.'

A month later, the media were in a storm. 'Proof of ghosts at last' the newspaper headlines read. They were the hottest thing in decades. They had just made their fifth television appearance in as many days. They were being wined and dined at a top hotel. All paid for by the television company. Life had taken on an exciting and colourful twist. They were earning more money than their entire previous lives, times ten.

At 2.25am, the blue flashing lights of two police cars and an ambulance were seen outside the hotel where they were staying. Dan was found with a table knife thrust through the top of his head and into his brain. There was a mere one inch of the knife's handle still visible. The rest was inside his skull. The entity had given June her soul back, but had also substituted a part of its own. June was found sitting upright in a chair with a maniacal grin upon her face. She laughed and sniggered maliciously. Nothing unusual in that, you may think? The entity had left her mentally unhinged. The only problem with the chair was that it was against the wall, and the legs of the chair were five feet off the ground.

Ted

One day, and without any warning, Sheena found out that not all was as it seems. It started on one bright April morning. She was in the garden, pegging out some washing. There was a light breeze blowing and, combined with the sunshine, it made it a perfect drying day. She was wrestling with a particularly awkward bedsheet, when she heard the words 'What are you doing?' It startled her a little, but the voice was soft and friendly. She turned around and saw no one there. It was then that she saw Ted sitting on the ground. Ted was her life long friend and a teddy bear. She wondered if her granddaughter had been poking around in her bedroom and found him. Ted was very precious to her. 'I must tell Vicky that you are old and not to be played with,' she said to Ted. Then she heard the words, 'Oh, I don't mind.' It seemed to come from her teddy bear.

Sheena stopped dead in her tracks. 'Did you just speak to me?' she said to Ted, before chiding herself with the words, 'Of course you bloody didn't. What am I thinking?' Sheena then examined Ted for any signs that he had been tampered with. She wondered if someone had put some kind of speaker inside him. She started poking at his stomach to see if she could feel anything. Then she heard the words, 'That tickles,' followed by a chuckling sound.

Sheena dropped Ted with the sheer shock of it. She looked at the teddy bear lying on the floor. To her shock and astonishment, she saw it sit up, all on its own. Sheena backed away from Ted. She was now totally in a state of shock. 'OK, now you know this isn't happening for real. Either someone is playing a trick, or...' Sheena said, without finishing the sentence. She was going to say 'You are having another breakdown.'

Sheena had a particularly bad bout of depression in her

youth. Ted was the one constant friend that she could talk to, even rant at, and know that no one would be judging her and analysing her. 'That's it. You are in some way punishing yourself. Ted is your closest confidante, and your mind is telling you to fear him,' she said aloud.

'No, it isn't; it really is me,' Ted said.

Sheena was now absolutely convinced that it was her grandson playing tricks. He was always doing little pranks on her. Then an idea came into her mind. 'OK, if that really is you speaking, you will know the words that I said to you the first night in my hospital bed,'. she said.

Ted tilted his head on one side and seemed to frown. 'How could I forget. You told me that you wanted to kill yourself, and that you were going to try and steal some pills.'

Sheena burst out into tears. She knew that absolutely no one knew that she had spoken those words. She dropped to the grass and sat looking at Ted.

'You are right in one respect, it isn't actually me talking. That would be silly,' Ted said.

Then she recognised the voice. The gentle Scottish lilt. It was her Gran's voice. Her Gran had died when she was six. It was like her entire world had collapsed around her. 'Why... why did Gran have to go to heaven? Doesn't she love us any more?' she remembered saying. It was her first real encounter with death and bereavement. Her mother tried to explain that Gran was old, and old people go to heaven, but Sheena resented it. Up until then she had said her prayers by the bed like a good little girl, but now she hated God. God had taken away her best friend in the whole world.

'I needed to grab your attention. I have been trying to talk to you for some time, but you are stubborn,' her Gran said. 'There is no after-life and it's all mumbo-jumbo. People die and they are at peace, but we have to carry on. Remember saying that only yesterday? her Gran asked.

Sheena nodded. 'Well, I had to take you by surprise. Scare the living daylights out of you,' her Gran said. 'Hence the talking teddy bear.'

Sheena actually laughed. At that very moment she didn't care whether this was all one big psychotic episode. She was talking to dear, sweet Gran.

'There are things that you need to know, and time is of the essence,' her Gran said. 'You need to go around to Michael's house, and you need to go right now.'

Sheena hesitated. Michael was her son, and he had told her in no uncertain terms that he was just fine without her sticking her nose into his business, and who he hung around with was none of her concern. He had virtually thrown her out of the front door with the words, 'Just piss off. I don't want you in my life any more.'

Her Gran spoke again. 'Swallow your stupid pride. He isn't so unlike you, you know. In fact, you are like two peas in a pod. Get your coat and car keys and get round there.'

Sheena could tell by the urgency and the edge to her Gran's voice that something was seriously wrong. She was right. Twenty minutes later, she arrived at Michael's flat. She knocked on the door, but found to her surprise that it wasn't locked. She walked inside shouting his name. Eventually, she found him sprawled across the bed. An empty tablet bottle by his side. He had also been vomiting. She immediately rang for an ambulance.

Fortunately, they arrived just in time to save Michael. Sheena never left his bedside until he regained consciousness. After he did, and the doctor had finished attending to him and checking him over, they were alone. Michael just looked in embarrassment at his mum, before saying, 'Oh, mum. I'm sorry.' He then dissolved into tears. Sheena hugged him, and said,

'Shhh, now. Things will be different. I love you.'

Many weeks later, Michael and Sheena were chatting. 'What on earth made you come around when you did?' Michael asked.

His mum just shrugged.

'You saved my life, and I have never said thank you have I...? Well ,thank you, mum.' Michael then rose from his chair and kissed her cheek.

How could she tell him that a teddy bear had told her! 'I suppose it was just a huge coincidence. I had driven round to have it out with you, and give you a piece of my mind,' Sheena said.

Michael smiled and said, 'Glad you did, mum. I love you.' Then he said, 'I had a really strange dream last night. This will make you laugh. I dreamt you were pegging out some washing on the washing line when your old teddy bear dropped by for a chat.'

Ring a Ring O' Roses

'Why do you want to see a ghost?' This was one of the questions that was asked by Jennifer's counsellor. Jennifer's mind had rapidly learned to guard her replies. She didn't want to release too much too soon, especially as everything was still a blur in her mind.

'Because in a way I would find it comforting. Scary, yes - but comforting,' she replied.

'How can seeing a dead person be comforting? Can you explain?' the counsellor continued.

Jennifer began to feel a little irritated and hemmed in. 'Isn't it obvious?' she snarled.

'Not to me,' the counsellor replied.

'Because it means there is something after we die. We go on,' Jennifer replied.

'Ah, I see,' the counsellor said.

Jennifer inwardly sneered at this supercilious reply. Oh, you see do you? Well whoopie-fucking-doo, she thought to herself. Her face conveyed none of these thoughts. She merely smiled benignly and nodded.

Jennifer had been found wandering around the grounds of a disused mental hospital mumbling incoherently to herself. She had been in a group of people who had been conducting a paranormal investigation of the old building. Jennifer remembered nothing after hearing one of the group scream, and the feeling of falling through space.

'What were you doing wandering around the hospital grounds?' the counsellor asked.

'Was I?' Jennifer answered. No one had actually told her this. The first thing she remembered was coming to consciousness in her hospital bed.

'Yes, you were wandering around the grounds and singing part of a nursery rhyme over and over. The words, Atishoo, Atishoo, We all fall down.'

Jennifer's interest had now been piqued. All this was actually new to her. 'I had no idea I had done that,' she replied. The counsellor made notes in her notepad.

Inwardly, Jennifer's mind scrambled to try and make sense of the latest revelations, and to piece everything together. She remembered very little of the night.

'Why do you think you were singing that particular part of the rhyme?' the counsellor asked.

'You're the shrink. Why do YOU think I was singing it?' Jennifer replied.

The counsellor remained calm and answered, 'What I think is of little importance. We are trying to piece everything together and ascertain what caused you to be in such a state.'

Jennifer felt somewhat abashed at her petulant outbreak. 'Yes, I know, I apologise... sorry,' she answered.

'It's fine' the counsellor replied, whilst sporting her best, comforting smile. Immediately, Jennifer bristled inwardly again.

'I think we will leave it there for today. I feel we are making progress,' the counsellor said.

Jennifer lay back in her hospital bed and was soon asleep again. It had only happened the previous night, and the effects of the drugs she had been given to calm her down were still fairly prevalent. Jennifer slept whilst she could. Inwardly, she was dreading nightfall, and had no idea why. It was just a strong sense of foreboding.

When Jennifer awoke it was dark. Immediately her senses were on high alert. The dimmed lights of the ward bathed everything in an eerie and other-worldly light. Then Jennifer heard the words, 'Ah, hello Sleeping Beauty,' from right beside her. She jumped with fright, before seeing the smiling face of a nurse, sitting in a chair beside her.

'I'm sorry, I didn't mean to startle you,' the nurse said.

'No, no, it's fine' Jennifer replied.

'You look like you could do with a nice cup of tea,' the nurse said.

'Oh, I could absolutely DIE for one,' Jennifer replied.

The nurse chuckled, before saying, 'Coming right up. One lump or two?'

'No sugar thanks,' Jennifer replied, and the nurse scurried away.

Soon the nurse returned with a cup of tea and a round of buttered toast on a plate. 'You haven't eaten all day. I thought you had better have something,' she said.

Both the tea and toast tasted absolutely divine. 'I needed that, thank you,' Jennifer said to the nurse.

'Well, if you are enjoying your food, that's a good sign,' the nurse replied.

Soon Jennifer was asleep again. The last thing she remembered was the nurse taking up her seat again at her bedside.

Soon she awoke to the sunshine streaming in through the window and the bustle of the ward. Within minutes a bowl of cornflakes and a cup of tea was placed in front of her. Again, these tasted like nectar. Then, out of the corner of her eye, she saw the advancing counsellor. 'Oh God, not more grilling,' she mumbled to herself.

A few moments later, the counsellor was sitting by her bedside. Her opening gambit was, 'Well, the nurse tells me that you are eating well and seem to be quite cheerful this morning?'

Jennifer nodded in reply.

'Well that's good news. Maybe you can go home today,' the counsellor said.

This perked Jennifer up remarkably. She hardly had enough face with which to smile. 'They will come and take you across later today,' the counsellor said.

'Across? Across where? Across town? What?' Jennifer asked.

'The other side of course. The newly deceased often feel dazed and confused on dying,' the counsellor replied. 'Now do you remember?' she continued. 'Do you remember that rotten floor giving way and that drop onto the concrete beneath?'

Jennifer began to panic. She opened her mouth to scream but no sound came forth. 'They are here for you now. Your friends are waiting on the other side. They all passed away too. They are already across.'

These were the last words she heard from her counsellor. Soon she felt as if the world was melting away. It felt like floating on the softest water of exactly the same temperature as her body so that she couldn't actually feel it. The light beckoned and all fear ceased. The feeling she experienced can only be described as the weight of all her worldly cares falling away. She almost chuckled at the thrill of it.

The nurse turned to the counsellor and said, 'She handled it well for one so young. At least her spirit won't be joining all the other poor, grounded, tortured souls in that dreadful building.'

Don't Let Go

The swallows had returned, and his heart soared acrobatically along with them. How he loved those little birds. They always reminded him of his childhood, and long, hot summers that seemed to go on forever. As he dug over one of the flowerbeds the edge of his spade hit something. Thinking it was a pebble, he went to clear it. On closer inspection, he found it to be a lead soldier. A small cloud drifted across his horizon. It was probably one of his own as a child. Those lonely and frightened days drifted back into his mind. The days when his father was somewhere abroad, and no one knew where. All his mum would say is that 'Daddy has to go away'. It was many years later that Hamish found out that his father worked for MI5. The feeling of melancholy was quickly dispelled by the robin bobbing around at his feet. 'Sorry your highness, I am falling down on my duties. Let me dig you up a juicy worm for your breakfast'. Hamish said. He slipped the lead soldier into his waistcoat pocket and continued with his tasks.

The day passed pleasurably. Hamish loved his 'little patch of heaven'. This was how he referred to his garden. It was part formal and part wildlife haven. No chemicals were ever used, and he didn't really mind the blurring of the lines between his garden and the rolling fields beyond. The big old apple tree was a magnet in springtime for the Bullfinches. They would peck away at the sweet, young buds. He knew that this would mean a few less apples, but what a feast for the soul to see those gorgeous, scarlet chested birds busying themselves amongst the branches. 'I am a very lucky man,' he said, whilst smiling broadly.

'Yes you are, you have me for a wife. Lucky sod.' It was his wife, Barbara, who spoke, whilst bringing him a cup of tea.

Hamish laughed and said, 'Never a truer word spoken, darling.' The two of them sat companionably beside a little, rustic table in the garden and drank their tea.

'Look what I dug up in the rose bed,' Hamish said. Then he put the lead soldier on the table.

'Oh, how sweet. One of yours?' Barbara asked. Hamish nodded. Barbara noticed the flicker of a dark thought flash across his brow. She knew he was thinking about his father. She reached across and touched his hand.

His face instantly returned the gesture with a warm smile. 'A long time ago in a land far, far away,' he said, and Barbara nodded.

Hamish's father hadn't had the easiest time, and didn't come away from his service days unscathed. Hamish had grown up with the whole gambit of feelings. A loving and gentle father one minute, then a brooding and unapproachable one the next. He had the knack of reading his father's moods down to a very fine art. One thought always surfaced, though. The same thought in moments when he allowed it all to bubble up and plague him. A school sports day when he was eleven. He had been out in front in the 400 yards and being watched by his proud father. Suddenly he tripped and went flying onto the cinder track, taking the skin off his knees and the tip of his chin. He would never forget the look of disappointment on his father's face, or his later words of, 'Don't blubber. You are a big boy now.' That was when he began to hate his father.

That evening, Hamish brushed away the oxidation from the little lead soldier and put it on top of the old, wooden-cased radio. It almost felt like a talisman. A key to a forgotten time, and to memories still unsorted, and long overdue for the need of doing so. 'We should have talked more. No, I should have listened more. Sorry, Dad,' Hamish said. He knew little about what his father had been through at the time. All he saw were the effects upon his own life, and not the symptoms that lay behind them. Hamish was leaving to go to university, and his father had started to give him a little advice and wish him good luck. Hamish had cut him dead with the words, 'A bit late to start playing the loving father now, isn't it?'

He looked at his son and nodded, whilst saying, 'I suppose I asked for that.'

Those were the last words he'd ever spoken to his father. His dad died of a heart attack two weeks later.

Hamish had learned to bury these feelings, and brush them away with the words, 'Everyone has regrets.' These were words he dearly wished to take back. To re-live that moment and react in the fashion of the man he had become: the man that recognised the pain and suffering behind the actions and forgive such frailties of character. He switched on the radio to try and lift his mood a little. The song that came out of the speakers couldn't have been more apt. It was 'Little man, you've had a busy day' by Henry Hall and his orchestra. Hamish actually laughed out loud. The irony of it wasn't lost on him. He poured himself a glass of single malt whisky and settled into his armchair to read a book. Then a smell drifted into his nostrils. A smell he recognised immediately. It threw him back to his childhood in an instant. It was the smell of his father's pipe tobacco.

Hamish dismissed this as an over-active imagination and mere wishful thinking. Then the lead soldier on top of the radio caught his eye. Instead of the battered old toy it had once been, it now looked like new. The red tunic and black bearskin hat were as fresh as the day it was made. Hamish picked up the soldier, opened the back door and hurled it over the fields. 'I do not want to know. Leave me alone,' he said. Then he switched off the radio and went to bed.

Hamish didn't rest well. Too much had happened, and once again, he had forced it all under and tried to drown the thoughts like the demon that they had become. Finally, he fell asleep. He awoke to a nice, fresh, spring morning. The smell of bacon assailed his nostrils. Barbara greeted him with the words 'Good morning Mr Sleepy Head.'

Hamish stuck out his tongue at her as a reply, which made her chuckle. Then he noticed the old, battered lead soldier was back on top of the radio. He almost spat his tea all over the tablecloth.

'Something gone down the wrong way?' Barbara asked.

'Yes, must have,' Hamish replied. He began to wonder what in holy hell was going on. He ate his breakfast, then made his way to his shed. This was where he did most of his thinking.

Once inside his shed he busied himself repotting a few seedlings. Something that always made him feel more cheerful. The little sparks of new life that would soon brighten his flower beds. He idly glanced through the shed window and almost dropped the pot he was holding. There, in the garden, digging with his hands in the soil, was a boy. 'What the bloody hell...' he started to say, before the realism hit him. 'Oh good god above, it's me!' he said, hardly believing his own words. Then he saw him. A man kneeling beside him. It was his father. He watched in total fascination. A myriad of thoughts tumbled through his mind. 'Am I going mad? Am I dead and I am seeing my past?' Everything around him still felt very real and very current. His flesh still felt solid to his touch. Then a vague and tiny fragment of a memory began to surface. One that had been suppressed - buried and forgotten.

The full weight of the memory resurfaced. It was the day after his grandfather's funeral. It was thought unwise to subject one so young to a funeral, so he had been left in the care of his aunt. He had been most upset that he hadn't been allowed to say a proper farewell, so he had taken one of his toy soldiers and held his own funeral. His father had knelt to ask what he was doing, and when he realised, one of the most tender moments between a father and his son occurred. 'Shall we say a prayer, Hamish. A prayer for your grandad?' His father said.

Hamish said nothing. He just clung to his father whilst he recited The Lord's Prayer over the toy soldier's grave. When he looked into his father's face he saw his tears. It was the first and last time he ever saw tears in his fathers eyes, until the day when he said those unkind words on his departure to university. 'Oh my god. Why didn't I remember? Why didn't I remember that this happened?' he said to himself. Then he shouted the words 'I didn't mean what I said, dad. I was wrong. Please believe me, I was so very wrong.'

His father raised his head to look at him. He smiled and said, 'I know, son, I know, and there is nothing to forgive.'

Hamish then felt an agonising pain in his chest and all went black. He felt a peacefulness and acceptance. 'So this is it, ah well, I've had a good innings, Seventy-two isn't bad,' he said to himself. He saw the light and totally accepted his fate.

Then a strong hand gripped his shoulder and he heard the words, 'No son, it isn't your time yet.' It was his father, but his father as a young and athletic man.

'It's okay, dad, I don't mind,' Hamish said.

His father gave him a big, beaming smile and said, 'I thought you said you would listen to your old man in future?' He then said, 'Take my hand and don't let go.'

The next thing that Hamish experienced was waking up in a hospital bed. His wife, Barbara was holding his hand. The concern and worry heavily etched upon her brow. 'I thought we had lost you, my darling,' she said to him.

'It wasn't my time so it seemed,' Hamish replied.

'It's a good job he came and told me about you,' Barbara said.

Hamish looked puzzled. 'A little boy knocked on my door and said, 'The old man in the shed isn't very well," Barbara said. 'He looked really familiar. I think he must live locally,' she said.

'Ah yes, him. I know him well,' Hamish said. Hamish did indeed know him. How could he not, when it was himself? Although, until his reunion with his father and his apology, he had forgotten the loving father that he had really had. A man with problems, and a man fighting his own demons. A man that did all he could.

'I will give that little boy that lead soldier as a thank you,' Hamish said.

One Careful Owner

'Jazzy, do me a favour. Sit in my driver's seat and look into my rear view mirror and tell me what you see, please.' Helen had been experiencing a bizarre and quite disturbing set of occurrences with her recently acquired second hand car. Her friend, Jane, (or Jazzy as everyone called her), sat in the driver's seat and said, 'What do you mean? I just see the back window and the road behind it'.

'So you don't see any people... on the back seat?' Helen replied. Jazzy asked her if it was some kind of joke. Being honest, her exact words were, 'Are you taking the piss?'

Helen assured her that no urine of any kind was being extracted, and that she was deadly serious.

Jazzy asked the usual questions. Do you see people where they shouldn't be quite often? Have you been working too hard? Do you think you should see a doctor?

Helen began to become quite irritated with her stark and quite obvious disbelief in her situation. 'I'm being serious for god's sake. You know me. I'm not the weirdo, ghosty shithead kind' Helen answered.

Jazzy then came up with an idea. 'Let's go for a drive tonight. You drive and tell me if they appear in the mirror. I will use the little mirror on the sunshade to see behind. If you see them, tell me and I will tell you if I see them too,' Jazzy suggested. The plan was made and Jazzy said that she would come round to her house at eight o'clock that evening.

Right on schedule, Jazzy knocked at Helen's door. When she opened it, Jazzy said, 'Okay, are we ready for our evening with the dead?'

Helen just gave her a sickly, sarcastic smile, as if to say, 'Kiss my arse'. Both girls got inside the car and off they drove.

Jazzy asked if there was any particular place where she saw the apparitions. Up until then, it hadn't even crossed Helen's mind, but when she thought about it, it was always on the new bypass on her way home from work. 'Let's go there then' Jazzy suggested.

As they drove along the bypass, Jazzy kept on glancing idly into the small vanity mirror on the sun shade. Suddenly, she let out an ear piercing scream. It surprised Helen so much that she almost swerved into the ditch. 'STOP THE CAR. THERE ARE TWO OLD PEOPLE ON THE BACK SEAT!' she screamed in terror.

Helen pulled onto the side of the road. Both girls leapt from the car and stared into the back. It was completely empty. 'It looks like you might have been working too hard too, Jazzy. You are seeing them now' Helen sarcastically remarked. 'Well, now you have seen them too, we had better head back home' she added.

Jazzy refused point blank. 'There is no way I am getting back in that car - no way' she said.

Helen offered the alternative of waiting out in the middle of nowhere for a cab to arrive, or walking eight miles or so home. 'Look, just get in. They have never harmed me. Sit in the back seat if you like' Helen said.

Jazzy asked if that was a joke. Helen answered that it quite obviously was. Both girls got into the car and drove home.

The next evening, Jazzy called round at Helen's house. She was still quite traumatised from the previous evening's happenings. 'They were just two old folks, just sitting there. They were neither frowning or smiling. They were sitting there looking bored,' she said.

Helen nodded in agreement and said, 'That is how they always appear. I've contacted the previous owner and asked if I can speak to her. She has invited me round there tomorrow.'

The next evening, Helen timidly knocked upon the door of the car's previous owner. Her name was Janet. Janet's first words were, 'Don't tell me. You see two old people sitting in the back of the car.' Helen nodded, then burst into tears.

'Sit down and I will put the kettle on,' she said. When she came back with the teas, she said to Helen, 'I suppose it was unfair of me to trade it in without saying something, but I just wanted rid of the damn thing'. She then went on to tell her that she'd thought it might just be her that saw them. 'I suppose we should get to the bottom of this once and for all,' Janet said.

Helen agreed.

The two of them looked back through the other previous owners. One was a man by the name of Allan. They contacted him and asked if they could speak to him about the car. He said, 'Sure, what would you like to know?'

They asked if they might pop round to see him as it was all a little bit weird. He sounded somewhat confused, but said, 'Erm, okay. I am in tonight if you would like to come round.'

That night, they both went round to Allan's house and he welcomed them into his living room. 'This all sounded very mysterious over the phone. What do you want to know?' he said.

Helen smiled, then said, 'Promise me that you won't think we are a pair of nutcases.'

Allan said that it all depended on what they were about to tell him. The two took turns in relaying their separate stories.

Allan listened to what they had to say. 'This old couple. Is the old chap bald with a grey moustache, and does she have silver, curly hair?' Allan asked.

Both were astonished, and said almost in unison, 'Yes.'

Allan then went on to tell them a story. A car had once been owned by an elderly couple. They were called Joe and Madge. One winter's night they had been travelling home. A blizzard ensued and Joe lost control of the car. They ploughed into a ditch and the car was wedged. They decided to huddle together on the back seat and wait until daylight to try and get help. They died of hypothermia.

Helen and Janet were horrified. 'That was OUR car?' they asked.

Allan said, 'No, it wasn't.' He went on to tell them that although the car was repairable, their family didn't want it. His car needed a new engine as his had seized, so he bought it cheaply from them and swapped engines. That was the car that Helen now owned.

Allan told them that he had no luck with the car at all, and something just felt strange about it, so he part-exchanged it for a newer model. Then Allan went on to say, 'In a way, they made history. They were the very first fatality on the new bypass.'

Godfrey and the Elemental

'There is a residue. A malaise that sticks to you. Sometimes things even follow you home. There occurs a need to be cleansed. To bathe in a brighter light and wash away all negative spirits. There is a clear and distinct tipping point, when it is they who have control, and all negative energies join forces to form an unholy synergy created from the souls of the dead. An elemental can be born. A soul that has never existed, but feeds upon you. Oh it feeds upon you completely. Any embattled old ghost hunter knows this, and the ones that don't? Well, they find out the hard way.' Thus spoke Godfrey.

Godfrey was a man of advancing years who had been on the paranormal scene way before it became fashionable on television. He had been to countless haunted properties and helped scores of frightened and grateful people come to terms with what was happening in their homes. It was now his turn. It was he who needed to come to terms with the scars that had been left behind. Ghosts and spirits can leave scars that take many years to heal. They work on the psyche and imprint negativity. They switch off all happy thoughts. Deal with the dead on an almost daily basis, and you find nought but death.

Georgina (or George, as everyone called her), listened patiently. Not a flicker of any emotion appeared upon her face. As a psychologist, she had been trained to be empathetic rather than sympathetic. Sympathy was one of the negative emotions to be avoided. Sympathy meant immersing herself in another's misery. It compounded the problem. Something that she and Godfrey both knew, but at different ends of the belief spectrum. George wasn't a believer. Not in the least!

After Godfrey had spoken, George made him aware that she wasn't a believer, but kept an open mind in such matters, and hoped this wouldn't be an insurmountable problem.

Godfrey smiled benevolently, and said, 'Of course, I understand completely. No, it isn't a problem.'

George smiled back at him, and said, 'That's good... now tell me more about this elemental.'

Godfrey told her that there was little more to tell. He had dealt with them before, and each time, they left scars. There they ended the session. George wrote up her notes and slipped them into a file. She would bring them out in a week's time when his next appointment was. She thought no more about it and engaged her brain with thoughts of her next client. Her name was Alicia.

Alicia had been through an acrimonious divorce after an abusive and violent marriage. They were a few weeks into their sessions. As Alicia sat down in the armchair opposite George, she was very restless and anxious. George picked up on it immediately. 'Tell me how you are feeling right now, Alicia,' she asked.

Alicia seemed very ill at ease, and said, 'You look... different. There is something dark that seems to be surrounding you. It is like you are sitting in a shadow.'

George wondered what had triggered this somewhat paranoid outbreak, and answered her. 'Well, it's just little old me... George. I'm no different'.

Alicia herself wondered if she was having some kind of episode. 'I'm trying to keep calm, but there is definitely a shadow surrounding you, and it is frightening me. Am I having some kind of mental breakdown?'

George tried to calm her and said, 'No, it is probably just the stress you are under, and once an idea gets into someone's mind, it can be difficult to shake.' It was then that she noticed the look of terror on Alicia's face.

'I can see a dark figure standing behind you... oh my god.

This can't be happening.' Alicia ran from the room in abject terror.

George called after her, but to no avail. 'I can see it's going to be one of those days,' George mumbled under her breath.

As George opened her front door, she was greeted by her cat. He usually purred loudly, and would sinuously wrap himself around her ankles, asking to be fed and tickled. This time, he arched his back. His fur was standing on end, and he hissed at her before running off into the kitchen. 'Moses, it's mummy. What on earth is the matter?' she said to the absent cat. Moses was sitting on the kitchen table. His tail flicked from side to side. She held out a hand to stroke him, and he yowled at her and lashed out. Three shiny, red lines appeared on the back of her hand.

'You little shit. Find your own dinner then!' she yelled after the cat as he retreated through the cat flap.

George had felt strangely under the weather all day. She thanked the heavens that it was Friday. Friday meant one thing. She and Chrissie, her best mate, would order a takeaway to be delivered. She already had the white wine on chill in the fridge. Chrissie would usually bring some kind of lurid DVD with her, and the two girls would watch together and enjoy each other's company.

Around eight thirty in the evening, George heard a knock at her front door. It was Chrissie. As she opened the door, Chrissie's face at first had its usual beaming smile, but then George saw it change to a look of concern. Once inside, Chrissie said 'You look washed out. You look like shit'.

George chuckled, and replied, 'I love you too, darling'.

Then Chrissie remarked, 'God, it's freezing in here. Have you switched off the central heating?'

George glanced at the thermostat in the hall and all seemed right. 'You must be coming down with something. Don't give it to me, you diseased old slapper,' George replied.

Both girls giggled and awaited the delivery of their takeaway. It was Indian that night.

As they devoured their curry and sipped at their wine, Chrissie said, 'Look, I know you don't believe in the paranormal. Will you indulge me and answer one question... please?'

George agreed that she would.

'Have you been dabbling in the dark arts, or been playing on a ouija board?' she asked.

George was astounded at the question. 'No... no, I haven't,' she answered. Something then began to surface in her mind, and she began to string all the day's events together. She told her about Godfrey, Alicia and then the cat.

'KNEW IT,' Chrissie said.

'Knew what??' George asked.

'It's followed you home. The dark thing. You are soaked in it'.

George's impeccably ordered and rational mind began to show doubts. It can't be real, she thought. Chrissie then asked her if she felt unnaturally tired, a bit depressed, even tearful. What happened next took both girls by absolute surprise. George burst out into floods of tears. She was sobbing so much that she could hardly speak. She just nodded. Chrissie would usually have given her a massive hug, but this time there was no way she was going to touch her. Not whilst she had that darkness surrounding her. She told her this, and followed it with 'But don't worry sweetie, I will fight this with you.' George was in no fit state to argue.

'This Godfrey bloke. Do you have his phone number?' Chrissie asked.

George handed her the diary and pointed to it. She picked up the phone and dialled the number. After a couple of rings, she heard a voice. It said, 'Hello, this is Godfrey speaking. Can I help you?' Chrissie told Godfrey what had happened. There was a silence at the other end of the phone as he collected his thoughts. Finally, he said, 'I prayed that this wouldn't happen. I need to confront this entity. May I come round?'

Chrissie asked George and she nodded her approval. 'He's coming right now,' she told her.

An hour or so later, Godfrey knocked upon George's door. As soon as he saw the poor, wretched girl he let out a deep and mournful sigh. 'Oh, please forgive me. I didn't think that this would attach itself to you,'. he said, before turning to Chrissie and asking her the question, 'Do you truly love your friend? This is important, for you must truly love her.'

Chrissie told him that she was her dearest friend and they had been through so much together that they were practically sisters.

'Good, she is going to need you during all this,' Godfrey replied.

Godfrey sat opposite George on a chair he had brought in from the kitchen. 'Raise your head and look at me please,' he asked.

She did as requested. As she looked into his eyes she felt real and imminent danger and looked away.

'You must be strong, my dear. You must be brave and continue to look at me,' Godfrey said.

It took all the strength that she had, but she did as he requested.

'You have no issue with this girl. You are my elemental. I am the one you seek. What hold have you over this innocent?' he asked.

A sound came from George's lips that had both he and Chrissie shocked and mortified. 'He protects her but he should be mine. He died an unhappy and lonely man,' the elemental replied, in a deep and gruff voice of pure evil.

'Which man protects her? I demand you tell me his name' Godfrey said.

What happened next made both Chrissie and George break down in floods of tears. A new and familiar voice then spoke through George, and said, 'I am Michael. I am her father'.

The elemental then took over her again and hissed in defiance.

'Don't let him hurt my father. He can do whatever he likes with me. Don't let him hurt him,' George implored.

'It is lying to you. It is using your weaknesses. That wasn't your father,' Godfrey said.

Again, the elemental hissed at him. Godfrey then took out a copy of the bible and a crucifix from his coat pocket. He also had a small bottle of holy water.

George began to feel truly terrified. The entity was using her own 'fight or flight' responses to protect itself. George began to beg him not to carry on, but Godfrey disregarded her. He instructed Chrissie to sit beside her and hold her tight to her. He began to chant in Latin. 'Sáncte Míchael Archángele, defénde nos in proélio, cóntra nequítiam et insídias diáboli ésto præsídium.'

George begged and implored him to stop, but Godfrey carried on with the The Prayer of St Michael. The fight for George's very sanity and soul began. The battle ebbed and flowed, and Godfrey feared that this may be one battle that he may lose.

It was at this moment a golden glow emerged around George. A tear ran down Godfrey's cheek. 'NOW, your father is here,' he said. 'Your father and someone called Gamps.'

George dissolved into floods of tears. The two dearest people who ever lived had come to her aid. Her father and her dear, sweet grandfather.

Godfrey slumped in his chair and threw back his head. 'He is gone from you' he said. Both Chrissie and George could see Godfrey was now shrouded in the darkness. 'If you will pardon me, I must leave now,' Godfrey said. He rose from his chair and bid them both goodbye.

Days later, George received the news that Godfrey had taken his own life. The telephone fell from her hand and she dissolved into floods of tears. She realised that he had literally given his life for her. George then heard a comforting and familiar voice. That of her father. He said, 'He is safe now. He is with us. None can hurt him now.'

His funeral was a very simple affair and, oddly, a non-religious one. He had no surviving family, but literally hundreds turned up at his funeral.

On The Street Where You Lived

'Oh, this is weird. Take a look at this. This is frightening,'. Josh said to his partner Daisy. He was compiling a series of clips that showed people falling in the street as one of those amusing online slapstick videos. 'I have slowed this right down. Look at what happens at 15 seconds,' he said.

Daisy took a look as he ran it frame by frame. 'THERE, did you see it?' he said.

Daisy let out a gasp, and said, 'Run it again.' Sure enough, it was exactly what she had seen. 'A hand came out of nowhere and grabbed that man's ankle,' she said.

Josh had put out the call online for anyone who had clips of this kind. This had been sent via email to him. 'It must have been edited,' he said. 'Very cleverly done, but there can be no other explanation.'

Daisy agreed. They thought little more about it. Then came another email from the sender. It said, 'It isn't edited. It happened.' Then the sender sent the details of the location, with a request to meet him there.

Daisy and Josh discussed whether to go or not. Josh was just too intrigued by it all. He loved anything paranormal. Daisy came up with a good idea. She said, 'Just in case this guy is a nut job, which he probably is, we need backup.' They were going to contact their friends, Craig and Winston, and they would all drive down in one car. Both of them were big lads, and would be very useful in case anything kicked off.

As arranged, they made the forty-five minute journey to a quiet village on the outskirts of the city. Josh and Daisy got out of the car, leaving their 'minders' keeping look-out in the car. There they met a very quiet, frail and studious young man by the name of Alex. Josh bowled straight in with the opening statement of 'OK, what's the story, and is it fake?'

Alex sighed quietly and said, 'I only wish it was.' He then told them that there was a coffee shop around the corner. 'Bring your two friends as well. I'll buy the coffees.' Soon they were all seated in the café. They had the place to themselves.

Alex began to tell them about a story that had begun to circulate locally. It started first amongst the homeless people who happened to pass through the village, but it had soon spread. Stories began to circulate about people feeling a hand grip their ankle as they walked along, causing many to trip and fall. They started calling the phenomenon 'Pavement Pete'. At first it was taken as just one of those silly urban legends, until one victim happened to be a WPC. So now the story gathered a little credence now that a police officer was saying it was real. Alex told them that he had sat on the wall opposite the affected pavement for days, armed with a small action camera on a tripod. To his disbelief, he saw a man fall headlong, and then look back in terror, only to leap to his feet and run away.

Alex then told them that the original footage was still on the camera if he wished to examine it himself. Obviously, Josh leapt at the chance. Already he could smell the fame that he had always dreamt of. This would hit the media big time. Josh told Alex to bring his camera around to his editing studio and they would examine the film together.

Two days later, as arranged, Alex arrived at his editing studio. Josh had hardly slept with the excitement. Alex handed over the camera and Josh plugged the USB into his PC.

'That's the one there,' Alex said, as he pointed at a file on the monitor.

Josh downloaded a copy of the file. He played the file and found that the clip was slightly longer. In the full length clip he heard the man say, 'It grabbed me. It grabbed my ankle.' He also heard Alex swear with the shock of what he had just filmed. Alex then spoke, and said, 'Maybe I should have told you this first. He might visit you.'

Daisy had been listening in the background, and said, 'MAYBE?... there's no maybe about it'.

Josh asked him to explain what he meant. Alex looked a little sheepish, then said, 'I think I know who Pavement Pete is.'

Both Josh and Daisy now hung on his every word. 'Well, go on, who?' Daisy said impatiently.

Alex told them that a homeless man used to sit in the same spot and beg. He was a good humoured sort and did no one any harm. He would play his harmonica and beg for change from passers-by. At first, the police used to move him on, but he just came straight back again. They knew he wouldn't mind a night in the cells in the very least, and in the absence of any complaints, they just turned a blind eye to him. One morning, he was found dead on the pavement. It looked like he had been violently attacked. 'Did they get anyone for it?' Daisy asked. Alex shook his head, and said 'But all the locals have a good idea. A bunch of local thugs, but nothing could be proven'.

Alex asked Josh what he intended to do with the footage. 'I rather thought that we could approach the newspapers with it?' Josh replied.

Alex looked suddenly frightened, and said 'You weren't listening were you?' He told Josh that he could happily have the rights to the film clip, and that he could even keep the camera. His parting words were 'I hope you have better luck than I have had these past weeks.'

Josh asked him for his address and Alex gave it to them, but with the parting words, 'This belongs to you now. Don't try and bring it back. Oh, and further on in the camera files, there's some footage I took at home. Only fair that you should know.'

Daisy was now officially creeped out by the whole thing. 'Just bin it - get rid of it,' she said.

Josh told her that he had absolutely no intention of doing that.

She continued by saying, 'I just have a very bad feeling about this, and you know how intuitive I am.'

They agreed that they would see what happened in the next couple of days. They didn't have long to wait.

That night, as Josh and Daisy were getting undressed to get into bed, Daisy suddenly screamed and fell from view. Josh ran round the other side of the bed, but she was nowhere to be found. He looked underneath the bed, in the wardrobe, everywhere. Oddly enough, he wasn't panicking. It was like watching from outside his body. His mind had closed down with the shock of it. A mere five seconds or so after this, he heard his name screamed out. It sounded like it was coming from downstairs. He ran like a man with the strength of five. He took the stairs three at a time, almost falling as he did. He found Daisy crouched up in a ball on the floor, dressed just in her knickers and bra. She was hysterical when he touched her and started beating him away. He held her tightly and said, 'It's me, sweetie. It's your Joshie'. Slowly she settled down and started to weep uncontrollably.

She told him that she felt a hand grab her ankle. The next thing she was going through the bedroom floor as if it was a mirage. She had drifted down onto the floor like a feather. She had been paralysed with the shock and fear of it, until she came to her senses and screamed out his name. 'He warned you. It's that film. It is Josh. You KNOW it is' she said, then collapsed into floods of tears.

'COME OUT YOU BASTARD AND FACE ME!' Josh shouted. He was more angry than he could ever remember being in his life. That night, Josh rang Alex and hysterically told him what had happened. He just hung up. They got absolutely no sleep that night.

The next day was something of a blur. In desperation they looked online and found a local medium. She arrived that evening, but it soon became apparent that she was out of her depth - if indeed she was a medium at all. As she was about to leave, a knock came at their door. It was Alex.

'This is my fault, and it is up to me to fix this mess. You see, I gave him a way back,' Alex said.

Josh and Daisy said nothing, but continued to listen.

'By capturing him on camera it gave him a link. A physical link. It is like I hooked him.'

Josh then asked what it was that they needed to do.

'Did you watch the other film clips on the camera?' Alex asked.

They both said that they hadn't. 'He wants the addresses of the lads who attacked him,' Alex said. 'I didn't want to give them to him because one of them is my cousin, but now I realise that I must.'

Alex placed a sheet of paper onto Josh and Daisy's coffee table; then said, 'This is what you need. These are the addresses'.

At that, the piece of paper lifted into the air, hovered there for a second, then burst into flames. The pieces of ash drifted down like feathers.

Alex stood up to leave. As he was leaving, he said, 'Destroy the camera and erase any copies of the video.' Josh assured him that he would.

Two days later, the newspaper reported a spate of mysterious deaths. Four young men had been found dead in their beds. The cause of death was unknown, but there was a look of terror upon their faces. Josh destroyed the camera and deleted the copy of the video from his computer... at least, that's what he told Daisy.

The Smiler

'Do you think he's a bit soft in the head? - He's been sitting on that little wall all morning just smiling.' Barbara ran the wool shop on the high street and was discussing with her assistant, Janice, about the arrival of the 'Smiler', as they had christened him. He wore something resembling a green set of overalls, a pair of work boots and a black baseball cap. 'He's still sitting there, still smiling, and now it's pouring down,' she said.

A while later, she slipped on her jacket and went outside to talk to the man. Janice witnessed the spectacle from the safety of the shop. She saw Barbara speaking to him, but he just tilted his head slightly on one side as if listening, but made absolutely no reply - neither did he stop smiling.

When Barbara returned, she was even more puzzled than before. 'It's so odd. He just sits there smiling. He never seems to blink. He just looks straight into your eyes. That's another thing. NEVER have I seen such blue eyes.'

It puzzled the pair of them. 'Do you think that he might not speak English, and that's why he says nothing?' Janice asked.

Barbara pondered for a moment before saying, 'Now when I tell you this, you will think I am going a bit daft.'

Janice was totally intrigued. 'Do tell. I can't wait!' she replied.

Barbara went on to say that when she asked him questions, somehow she intuitively knew and heard the answers. 'It's the oddest thing. He seems to be able to speak straight inside your head,' she said.

Janice laughed, then said, 'You are correct. I DO think you are going daft! You think he can talk inside your head - seriously?'

Barbara's feathers were a little ruffled at this statement and said, 'Well YOU go out and talk to him and tell me what you think.'

Janice picked up the gauntlet that Barbara had mentally thrown her way and did just that.

Five minutes later, Janice came back into the shop. She looked visibly shaken.

'Are you okay, love?' Barbara asked.

Her bottom lip trembled a little before she said, 'I'm bloody scared'. Janice went on to tell her that as soon as she stood in front of him, she heard a voice inside her head say quite clearly and distinctively, 'Your friend is correct. I CAN speak inside your mind. I can read it too.' Janice then went on to say that he had told her what her son said in bed that previous night. He'd told her that her son was called Alex and that he was very bright and intuitive. He'd then told her, 'Tell Alex, he is quite correct. The kind spaceman DOES talk to him.'

The two women were in quite a tizzy about the whole thing. 'Do you think we should call the police?' Janice asked.

Barbara was never one for using bad language, but her immediate response was, 'Are you going fucking mad? ... and tell them what exactly? ... this strange man that sits outside our shop can talk inside our heads? They will lock US TWO up, not him!' As they were speaking, they both heard the same words inside their heads. 'There is no reason to fear me. Quite the opposite in fact'. They turned to see that 'The Smiler' was now standing inside their shop. Above the door there was a little bell that announced anyone entering the shop. The bell had remained silent.

'I can talk in the conventional way, if you are more comfortable with it?' the man said. His accent was a perfect, nondescript, BBC English.

'Who are you and what do you want?' Barbara defiantly asked.

The man smiled and said, 'The vowels and consonants of my language are difficult to master. You may call me Adam'.

Janice then joined in the conversation by saying, 'Okay, Adam. So what do you want?'

Adam smiled and said, 'Needs and wants are words we no longer have in our vocabulary, but sadly, they are prevalent and powerful words to your race.'

'YOUR race?' Janice asked.

'Yes,' Adam replied.

Adam then said, 'Ask your friend to describe my face.'

Not being in a position to argue, Janice readily agreed. She asked the question and Barbara replied.

'He has the bluest of blue eyes, sandy coloured hair and is clean shaven. He has a Nordic look about him.

Janice looked at her as if she had said he had horns sprouting from his head and was wearing a clown's outfit. 'Are you taking the piss?' she asked.

Barbara was too non-plussed to reply.

Janice went on to describe him as having a grey, close-cropped beard, brown eyes and was middle eastern in looks.

Adam chuckled, then said, 'Interesting, isn't it?'

'Let me try and explain,' Adam said. He then went on to tell them that some children they call 'The Blessed Ones'. They have the purest of minds, a strong sense of right and wrong, a deep and caring concern for the earth and mankind as a whole but, more importantly, they are beacons. 'We can talk to them,' he said. He then went on to tell Janice that her son, Alex, was one such child.

Janice became suddenly infuriated and massively over-protective. 'You just leave my son alone, you bastard!' she said.

Adam's face never changed. He smiled his usual patient smile and said, 'Had I left him alone when he was ten months old, well, would we be talking about him?'

Janice suddenly realised. She turned to Barbara and said, 'The miracle, oh dear god, the miracle. Do you remember?'

Barbara's blood ran cold. Indeed she did remember. Alex had acute myeloid leukaemia. The doctors gave him zero to five percent chance of surviving it. The two women had sobbed uncontrollably on each other's shoulders; then the doctors rang up and were completely baffled. He had made a complete and total recovery within twenty-four hours.

It was all too much for Janice. 'That was you. You did that?' she asked, before dissolving into tears.

Adam went on to tell them that Alex was one of thousands of children all over the world. Thousands of 'Blessed Ones'. He told them that they were there to become leaders. People would naturally and unquestioningly follow them. 'The earth is dying, and you are still taking from it. Still polluting it, still poisoning it,' he said. 'The Blessed Ones will lead your race away from the brink. They will take down the borders, they will declare all wars obsolete; they will share and use the earth's resources wisely and none shall starve whilst an obscene few profit and grow rich.'

Adam smiled, then said, 'Now, here is the real me.' Standing before them was a countenance so dazzling. He shone as bright as a neon light. His wings extended to their full magnificence. 'I believe your primitive culture calls us angels,' he said. 'Your son knows me better as The Kind Spaceman.'

Adam had laid bare their souls; he had conveyed to them a vision of what would be. 'The transformation starts now. It begins with you two, and do you know why?'

The two ladies shook their heads in astonishment.

Adam smiled, then said, 'Only Blessed Ones can see and hear me. You two were amongst the first.'

The Reading

'I'm picking up the energy of a young man. Someone who passed way too soon. He is saying that he was warned that he would kill himself one day with that damned motorbike.' The medium spoke to the assembled crowd. It passed through Kristina's mind that he could be referring to her son, but still she didn't move or make her presence known. 'It's somewhere in this area here' said the medium, pointing towards Kristina's general vicinity in the audience. Still Kristina didn't acknowledge him. She was a confirmed non-believer, and had gone along with her friends for 'a bit of a giggle', as she worded it. Then the medium pointed directly at Kristina and said, 'It's for you. He says he wants to speak to you.' Kristina was furious. She rose from her seat and made her way from the auditorium to the gasps of the assembled crowd. As she passed the people on her way out, she heard mumbled remarks such as, 'Why did she bloody come here if she didn't want a reading?'. Many were going there hoping for exactly that.

It was towards the end of the show, so Kris decided to wait in the foyer for her friends. When they emerged, they didn't look too pleased. Her best friend Tanya said, 'Even though you were bloody ignorant, he passed the message on anyway. It was your Mark. He wanted to tell you that you were right about the motorbike, but the accident really wasn't his fault.'

Kris was almost incandescent with anger. 'This is what these people do. They prey on the grief stricken and the vulnerable,' she said.

Tanya threw her hands up and said, 'I said I would tell you, and I have. Kiss my arse, Kris.. Stop shouting at me. If you knew you were going to be this bloody touchy, why did you come?'

Kris burst into tears, and Tanya comforted her. 'It's been

seven years now, and I still grieve. I still think that one day he will come striding in through the door and ask if there was anything to eat.'

Tayna hugged her friend, and said, 'I know love. I know.'

Two weeks had passed since the episode with the medium. Something troubled Kris about the message her friend had relayed to her. It was the bit about the accident not being his fault. The coroner's report had clearly stated that there was no presence of alcohol or drugs in his bloodstream. The marks on the road indicated that his motorcycle had gone on to its side and skidded off the road before wrapping itself around the edge of a dry stone wall, killing him instantly. The verdict was that it was an accidental death due to unknown causes. Probably just a freak accident, or loss of control. His funeral had been attended by dozens and dozens of his friends and the motorcycle fraternity. Mark was a well-liked and very popular young man.

Tanya and Kris were having a glass of wine whilst having an Italian meal. It was something of a bridge-building exercise after their spat at the clairvoyant evening.

'Look, I'm sorry I went about things the way I did. I just over-reacted,' Kris said.

Tanya told her that it was fine and already forgotten. 'I wonder what he meant about it not being Mark's fault though?' she said.

Kris replied that she had actually been having the same thoughts.

'We got to speak to him afterwards. He signed our programme. He said that he was sorry if he had upset you'.

Kris went very quiet. She was wrestling with her own thoughts and beliefs. 'But what if it WAS Mark?' she thought to herself.

Tanya could almost read her thoughts. 'I asked him for a

business card, and he said he would be glad to speak to you again,' she said.

Kris said, 'Oh well, no doubt he will want paying, but what price peace of mind?'

Tanya told her that he had said that he would happily speak to her and had never mentioned any charges at all.

Tanya contacted the medium on behalf of Kris. He lived about an hour's drive away. A week later they were pulling up outside a very unassuming semi-detached house. Tanya had driven there as she didn't fancy the idea of Kris driving whilst her mind was distracted.

'Is this it then?' Kris asked.

'What did you expect. Count Dracula's castle?' Tanya replied.

The two women laughed then got out of the car. The door was opened by James the medium himself. 'Come on in. Call me Jim. Would you both like a cup of tea?' he asked.

The two ladies said that they would indeed. He told them to follow him through to the kitchen.

A while later, they were all seated around Jim's kitchen table with a mug of hot tea each, and a plate of biscuits in the middle. 'I know you don't believe in all this stuff, and I am not here to make you a convert. If you want me to tell you what he said to me, then I will.' Jim said.

Kris apologised for her previous behaviour, before going on to say, 'I have always had an open mind. I won't lie and say I believe what you do is real, but I am here and willing to listen.'

Jim smiled and said, 'Well, that's all that I can ask for.'

'He had a girlfriend, didn't he? I see a petite blonde girl. Very giggly type.'

Tanya and Kris both looked at one another, and both said, simultaneously, 'He means Kelly.'

'I wouldn't call her his girlfriend. A friend who is a girl more like,' Kris said.

Jim smiled and said, 'Well, that isn't what he is telling me.'

Kris looked both bemused and amazed. 'Where does she fit into this?' she asked.

Jim told her that they had been seeing each other for a few weeks. Mark had fallen for her. head over heels. On the night of the accident, Kelly had told him that she no longer wanted to see him. When he pressed her to tell him why, she told him that she was seeing one of his friends. He insisted that she told him who, and she said, 'It's Todd'.

Tanya and Kris looked at each other in disbelief. Both of them knew that Todd was his best friend.

Jim told them that he only had one thought on his mind. To have it out with Todd and tell him exactly what he thought of him. He was going to 'punch his lights out,' he told them. Mark had set off at speed to go round to Todd's house. He was riding way too fast and hit a small pot-hole in the road whilst approaching a bend at speed. It was enough to throw the bike off balance. 'He is telling me he was gone instantly and felt very little pain,' Jim told her.

'But I thought you said that it wasn't an accident? The way you have just described it, that is exactly what it was,' Tanya said.

'He is saying that he is sorry, but he had to get to talk to you somehow, and this was his only way. To make you believe something else had happened. It didn't. It was just an accident.'

Kris didn't know whether to laugh or cry. 'The little sod,' she said. 'So why did he need to talk to me so badly. I already knew that?'

Jim relayed the message why he needed to talk to her so badly. 'He wants to tell you that he is great now and still living his life on the other side. He says he watches over you and sends you little messages.'

Kris was confused, and said, 'What messages?'

Jim laughed, then said, 'You keep seeing butterflies against the kitchen window. They often appear when you are thinking of him. He wants you to know that yes, it is him.'

Kris broke down into floods of tears. Even Tanya didn't know about the butterflies.

'He also says that you need to tell Todd that they are still 'best friends forever' and to stop blaming himself.' Jim went on to tell them that he said that the roads in heaven were long and straight and went on for miles. He told them to say this to Todd. 'Tell him that when he is an old man and passes away, we will meet on this side. I have a Harley-Davidson ready and waiting for him, and the two of us will take that bike trip we always planned. We will ride forever.'

Kris still sees butterflies at her kitchen window, and greets them with, 'Hello Mark.'

The Begrudged

It was an old country inn that was being converted into a dwelling. Renovations were coming along nicely. With many old buildings, organic materials were often incorporated into the fabric of the building. The plaster on the walls contained human hair as a binding material. As they chipped away, the occasional tuft of hair would be revealed within the plaster.

'It gives me the creeps. This is the hair of some person who has probably been dead for over two hundred years,' Jack said. He and his wife Jean were doing many of the renovations themselves.

As often happens when an old property is having any building work done, it also disturbs the spirits. Jack was extremely sceptical about the whole matter, but Jean was a different kettle of fish entirely. Every creak and knock in the old house scared the living daylights out of her.

'God almighty Jean, will you stop freaking out,' Jack said after one of her perfunctory whoops. 'It's like living with her off Most Haunted'.

'I can't help getting scared if you bought us a haunted house, now can I?' she said in her defence.

'Who says it's haunted?' Jack asked.

'Oh, just piss off,' Jean said, and carried on watching TV.

These mini spats were quite common. A sort of way of relieving stress. Occasionally they had 'a right up and downer' as Jack referred to one of their massive rows. This usually involved quite a lot of bad language, and the dragging out and dusting down of several of Jack's past misdemeanours. Jean forgot nothing. She had the lot. Times, dates and places, and the plot and sub-plot of everyone involved. Jack's response was always the same. 'Here we go again. Perry effing Mason. You missed your way in life you did. You should have been a criminal lawyer,' Underneath it all they loved each other, though.

One of the features of the house was a beautiful granite doorstep. A sinuous curve had been worn into the centre of it by centuries of feet. It had tilted over time and needed lifting out and re-setting. Jack manhandled the hefty step out from its position by the use of a long lever bar. As the stone toppled out of its position, Jack saw that there was something beneath it. 'Hey Jean, come and take a look at this,' he said. Beneath the step was a tiny, leather shoe. It looked like it had belonged to a toddler. Judging by its design, it looked the same age as the property. 'I bet they put this in when it was being built,' Jack remarked.

Jack put the shoe on the mantlepiece in the main room. He thought that it would make a great talking piece. Jean wasn't very happy about it. She told Jack that it gave her 'bad vibes'. Jack just walked away from her, whilst mumbling something about 'Mystic Meg'. Jean was about to say something, but ended up just shrugging, and saying to herself, 'It just isn't worth the bloody effort.' The shoe stayed where it was.

That evening, they retired to their bed around twelve fifteen. They were both asleep within minutes. It had been an exhausting day. They were both abruptly awoken from their sleep at around two in the morning. It sounded like there were several children playing in the small courtyard in front of their property. 'Ring a ring o' roses, a pocketful of posies'. The sound of the old nursery rhyme and the giggles of the children drifted in from the window. Jack was out of bed in a flash, followed closely by Jean. Both looked through the window and were amazed at the scene below them. A group of eight or so children were playing as if it was midday. Jack opened the window to shout down to tell them to clear off and they just faded away.

Jean was hysterical. 'NOW will you believe me. I told you, I told you,' she said.

Jack was totally nonplussed. He had seen what he had seen, which had been corroborated by his wife, but how was it possible? 'But... ghosts don't exist,' he said.

'Tell that to those effing kids then,' Jean angrily retorted.

Both of them went down to the kitchen to make a cup of tea. Sleep was out of the question for the night after that. As they sat around the kitchen table trying to calm their nerves, Jack said, 'I'm sure that there's a rational explanation for all this.'

That was the last straw for Jean. 'Will you stop talking stupid. WILL YOU?' she shouted at him. 'You just saw eight or nine kids just dissolve into thin air as if they were smoke and you are blathering on about a rational explanation. SERIOUSLY??'

Jack had to concede that there wasn't an explanation. 'What do we do now?' he asked meekly.

'I have absolutely no idea,' Jean replied.

The next day, Jack contacted a local paranormal investigation team. Neither he nor Jean were churchgoers, so a vicar or priest were out of the picture. The next night the team arrived, and soon their house was wired with cameras and microphones from top to bottom. A team of people in their twenties descended on them and wandered around wafting bits of equipment around and taking readings.

'Well, the background EMF readings look normal,' one team member told Jack.

'So they should be too. We have just had it rewired'.

Jean scowled at Jack, but Jack just shrugged and smiled.

Jack was still secretly in 'rational explanation' territory. No matter how unlikely, there had to be a sane reason. Anything else would shatter his convictions and leave his mind open to utter chaos.

Amongst the team was a young lady by the name of Shona. She professed to be the team 'sensitive'. She saw the little leather shoe on the fireplace and immediately walked towards it. As soon as she touched it she gasped and said, 'Oh no, please... no'. 'What's the story behind this shoe?' she asked Jean.

Jean told her that they had found it under the doorstep.

Shona looked at them both in disbelief, and said, 'And you moved it?'

'Did we do wrong or something?' Jack asked.

'Did all the activity start as soon as the shoe was moved?' Shona asked.

Both agreed that it had.

Shona turned to the group and said, 'We have a problem. They have invited them inside.'

She went on to tell them that they may have looked like mere children, but these weren't. 'I call them The Begrudged,' she told them. 'They are the spirits of children that either died in birth and feel robbed of their future, or those that died in cruel or unnatural ways.'

Jean began to quietly sob. She herself had miscarried a child. The thought that his spirit could be wandering with these waifs was heartbreaking.

Shona assured her that these were the unwanted and unloved ones. The ones that went unmourned. She assured her that hers would be in a beautiful place of love and light. It was at this moment, one of the team that had been monitoring the cameras said, 'Oh my god, look at this.'

Everyone gathered around the monitor. To their horror, all 'The Begrudged' were gathered around the fireplace and the shoe. They seemed to be passing something between themselves and each eating hungrily upon it. It appeared to be the arm of a baby. No one even suggested the idea that it was until Shona mentioned, 'They are feasting upon the innocents,' Their teeth appeared razor sharp, and soon the arm was literally just bone and cartilege. 'Someone needs to go in there now. Someone needs to take that shoe outside again, and it has to be whoever took it from its place. They are the only one who can put it back.'

Jack felt his stomach lurch with fear. Over and over he kept repeating inside his head 'This isn't happening. This is impossible.' He leapt to his feet and strode with purpose towards the main room and the waiting ensemble.

'Jack... be careful darling,' Jean called after him.

As he pushed open the door a chuckle ensued from the gathered crowd. The one thing that Jack had on his side was the fact that if any of them touched the shoe, they would perish. Unfortunately, Jack was unaware of this vital piece of knowledge. He decided to try and reason with them. 'I want you all to leave my house right now,' he said.

They just giggled; then one of their ensemble shot forward as fast as lightning. Jack felt a searing pain in his thigh. He saw a hole in his trousers and a gaping wound behind this. One of them had bitten him. Jack was enraged. He lunged forward and grabbed a large, ornate fire poker. He whacked one of them beside the head, sending him flying across the room. In the same split second he grabbed the shoe and waved it at them. To his astonishment he saw them back away as if he had been holding a gun. By pure chance, he had discovered the shoe's power. Jack was like a man possessed with the fear of self-preservation. He waded into them whilst wielding the shoe like a knife. They scattered back through the door. They were howling and whimpering like wolf cubs.

As good fortune would have it, he hadn't replaced the stone step. It was still propped up alongside the door. He placed the shoe back into position and dropped the stone step back into its place. 'Level or not. Sod it. It stays put,' Jack said. He slammed the door behind them and shouted, 'Stay out!'

Literally seconds afterwards the lights were on. The team had a first aid box and were administering to Jack's wound.

Shona was muttering incantations around the door and pouring what Jack assumed was holy water.

'As long as you leave that shoe in place, they should give you no trouble,' Shona assured them. The team packed away all their equipment, and by four in the morning they were saying their goodbyes. The house felt suddenly lighter. It even felt a few degrees warmer. They both went to bed and slept.

The house came on a treat and there were just a few jobs left to do. It had been a week since the paranormal episode. It is fair to say that Jack had seriously reconsidered his 'there are no such things as ghosts' stance. They were in bed and watching their bedroom TV. They were sharing a bottle of white wine and watching a 'chick flick'. Suddenly, Jean let out a scream. She threw back the bed clothes and saw a bloodied and raw wound. Then they both heard a giggle and the sound of a set of feet pattering away. From the next room they heard, 'Ring a ring o' roses, a pocketful of posies.'

Little Alfie's Playmate

Little Alfie was only four and, as do a lot of kids of his age, he had an imaginary playmate. He told his mum that his friend was called Rupert. She wondered where on earth he had thought up such a name. She wondered if perhaps another child at the nursery had that name, or maybe he had seen a Rupert the Bear story book somewhere. Either way, Rupert was here to stay - at least for the time being anyway!

Rupert became one of those annoying anomalies. A place at the dinner table always had to be set for him, but Alfie said that all that Rupert wanted was a glass of water, so every mealtime, a glass of water and an empty plate was set in front of a seemingly empty chair. One day, Sheila, his mum, saw that the water level in Rupert's glass had gone down to almost empty. She smiled to herself and naturally assumed that Alfie had drunk it when her back was turned. 'Would you like a top up of your water, Rupert darling?' Sheila asked. Then she saw the most remarkable thing happen. The last inch or so of water in the glass gradually dropped away. Sheila shook her head in disbelief. I think I need a break, I'm seeing things now, she thought to herself.

'Rupert says that he has had enough water, Mummy,' Alfie said.

Sheila began to worry a little about this unwanted house guest. She would check in on Alfie when he was playing. One day she had given him some felt-tip pens and a few sheets of paper. When she came back to see what he had drawn, it frightened her almost senseless. He had drawn a kind of gallows, and hanging from it he had drawn a woman in a black dress. 'What are you drawing Alfie darling?' she asked.

Alfie replied that it was Rupert who had drawn it. 'They are hanging a witch, mummy,' he said, almost gleefully. He had also drawn a figure that wore a crucifix on a chain. She assumed this to be some kind of man of the cloth.

Alfie's Dad was in the army and was away on a tour of duty, so Sheila had to sort the particular little problem on her own. She asked the ladies at the nursery about Alfie. They looked rather uncomfortable about the whole conversation.

'We have had to let Alfie play on his own. He seems to like it better,' one of them said. The other one interjected, and said, 'Tell her the rest of it', and then nodded in encouragement.

The first lady then went on to relay a few disturbing stories. 'He frightens the other kids. Some mums have told us that their kids have been traumatised by him,' she said. 'He tells them about all kinds of torture. He seems especially fond of talking about red hot branding irons,' she went on to say.

Sheila was staggered. 'Why the f...' she began to say, before stopping herself swearing. 'Why the hell didn't you tell me this before?' she asked angrily.

Then the second lady said, 'This may sound silly, but he scares us too.'

Sheila looked quizzically at her. She continued by saying 'This... friend of his. This Rupert...'

'What about him?' Sheila enquired.

'Well, he can move stuff. We have both seen it. There... I've said it,' she said.

The two nursery nurses said, almost in unison, 'Perhaps it would be best if you found somewhere else after today.'

Sheila said, 'Bugger that, we are going right now.' She lifted little Alfie into her arms and stamped off out of the building. She strapped Alfie into his car seat and she sat in the driver's seat. She was fuming. 'Scary... my child?' she thought to herself, before actually saying the words, 'How dare they say that!' She phoned in to work from her mobile and said that something had cropped up and she wouldn't be in that day, but she would work from home.

It was the following morning. She was giving Alfie his breakfast, when he suddenly announced,. 'Daddy's friend has just stood on something. It went BANG, mummy.' Then he giggled.

Sheila knew immediately what he meant. An icy chill ran through her veins. 'Did Rupert tell you that, darling?' she asked (as nonchalantly sounding as she could possibly muster up).

'Aye, I did mistress,' she heard. The voice came from somewhere behind Alfie.

Sheila let out an involuntary whoop of fear.

Alfie giggled. 'You scared mummy, Rupert' he said.

'She then heard a low, malevolent sounding chuckle.

They lived inside the army base and, as do all military establishments, they had a chaplain. She didn't even wait until Alfie had properly finished his breakfast before scooping him up into her arms and heading off to the chaplain's office. She timidly knocked on the door and was invited inside by a pleasant looking man in his forties.

'What can I do for you?' the chaplain asked.

Sheila told him the story. The chaplain's eyes widened a little, then he said, 'We have just had reports that there has been an injury. Someone has stepped on an explosive device. They keep me informed as they like me to come along when they break the news,' he said.

Sheila broke down in tears.

Suddenly, Alfie's face took on a serious, almost blank and dead-pan expression. He walked up to the chaplain and said, 'Be strong and courageous, do not be afraid or tremble at them, for the lord your God is the one who goes with thee. He will not fail or forsake thee.' Then he added 'that's Deuteronomy, chapter thirty one.' Both the chaplain and Sheila were stupefied at this occurrence. 'Did you teach him that??' the chaplain asked.

'Of course I bloody didn't. Are you mad?' she screamed at him. She then apologised profusely and dissolved into tears.

The chaplain admitted that he was way out of his depth. 'I think we need to bring in a child psychologist,' he said, before adding, 'Leave it with me, please.'

Sheila nodded and then left the room and headed off home.

Sheila's mind was in turmoil. A couple of days ago. life had been quite mundane and ordinary. Now she felt like she was living inside an episode of The Twilight Zone. A knock came at the door. She opened the door and one of her friends stood before her. She seemed very agitated and was clutching her toddler tightly in her arms.

'Gina, whatever is the matter?' Sheila asked.

'Oh God, it was awful,' Gina answered.

Sheila invited her inside. Gina then told Sheila that she had been at the nursery half an hour earlier. She went to the same one that Sheila took Alfie to. She went on to tell her that as she was dropping off her son, she happened to be talking to one of the nursery assistants when they heard a loud crack come from the playroom. The children then started to scream. When they went inside, they found that a large crack had appeared in the floor, and an awful stench was issuing forth from it. 'Everyone thought a drain had ruptured, or something similar,' Gina told her. But then went on to say 'Then thousands of cockroaches started to pour out of the crack in the floor.' She went on to tell Sheila that the kids had them all over them, and they had to rush everyone outside and brush all the bugs off the children. Sheila felt it in her bones that Rupert had something to do with this.

A couple of days later, the chaplain contacted Sheila to say that the child psychologist would be calling round later in the afternoon to assess Alfie. She arrived at the chaplain's office at two in the afternoon. The psychologist was a pleasant looking woman who was in her early fifties. She asked if she could be left alone to have a little chat with Alfie. Sheila and the chaplain went into the prayer room next door with a cup of coffee each. Within ten minutes she emerged from the room looking flustered and agitated. She had a small crucifix on a chain around her neck. She was rubbing this between her fingers. She looked really shaken and more than a little nervous. 'That child needs something that I can't give him. He needs deliverance. He needs a priest,' she said, and promptly walked out of the office. They heard her tyres squeal on the tarmac outside. Such was her desire to escape the place.

'Now what do we do?' Sheila asked desperately.

The chaplain just looked down at his shoes and said, 'It looks like we need a rather novel approach. Leave this with me.'

A couple of days passed and Sheila heard a knock at her door. She opened it to find the chaplain standing there, and with him a kindly looking oldish man, somewhere in his sixties.

'This is Peter. May we come in?' the chaplain said.

Sheila welcomed them both inside. Alfie was sitting at the table eating his breakfast. He saw the old man and he smiled. The man smiled back. He then turned to Sheila and the chaplain and said, 'I see the child has a protector.'

'A protector?' Sheila said. She was barely able to contain her rising anger and hysteria.

'Alfie has a spirit friend. He is a small and raggedy little child. He means no harm,' Peter said.

'Surely this can't be good for the child?' the chaplain asked.

Peter answered by saying, 'Shall we all have a cup of tea and a chat?'

'We better bloody well had,' Sheila said pointedly.

Peter began to tell them not only about Alfie, but also about

Rupert. 'Have you ever heard of guardian angels?' Peter asked.

They both nodded. 'Well, he is Alfie's' Peter said.

Both of them looked singularly unconvinced.

'Well, to me he seems evil' Sheila said.

Peter tilted his head to one side and smiled. 'He is far from evil' he said. 'In fact, you almost lost him whilst you were carrying him, didn't you?'

This shook Sheila to the core 'But how did you...?' she began to say.

'How did I know?' Peter answered. 'It was Rupert who told me, and Rupert who looked after Alfie in your womb'.

He went on to tell Sheila that Alfie should have been a twin, and the other egg just ceased to develop. 'Alfie knew about his twin and sort of gave up hope' he said. 'It was Rupert who was also one of twins. Also one born alone in the womb. He kept little Alfie company. You owe Alfie's life to him.' He then went on to tell her that Rupert was far far from being evil. He told her that he loves and protects Alfie.

Sheila began to cry and the chaplain put his arm around her shoulder to give her support. 'In fact, in his own primitive way, he has been warning Alfie about evil people,' Peter said. 'So that explains the drawings?' Sheila asked.

Peter nodded in agreement.

What Peter said next both amazed and humbled Sheila. He went on to tell her that Rupert's own father had died in the English Civil War, and that little Rupert knew all about war. He and his mother were left without support when his father was killed. They both starved to death. 'That's why he is so thin, and why he never eats,' he said. 'What's more, you owe him a huge debt of gratitude for saving another loved one,' Peter said. 'It was your husband who was about to step on that device, but Rupert diverted his attention so that he stopped'.

Alfie came across and stood by his mummy. He put his hand

inside hers and smiled up at her and said, 'Rupert says he will go if you want him to.'

Sheila's eyes brimmed with tears, then she said, 'You tell Rupert he is a brave little boy. He is always welcome in our house, but tell him that his mummy also needs him.'

Sheila then felt a kiss on her cheek. 'Rupert says he is going home now, mummy. Can he come again?' Sheila smiled and said 'Of course he can.'

That was fifteen years previously. Alfie is now a tall and handsome young man. His father returned home from every one of his tours of duty. To this very day, Sheila still lays an extra plate at the table, with an empty plate and a glass of water.

End Game

It was no bigger than a tennis ball; it was a perfect sphere and was hovering exactly one yard above the surface of the top of the nuclear reactor. Its presence definitely hadn't gone unnoticed! It was silver, but also vaguely iridescent. The surface of it moved and morphed in rainbow patterns, like the reflection of oil upon water. The army and a whole team of scientists were surrounding it and measuring any possible radiation or electromagnetic force that may be coming from it. Both came back negative. They suspended a steel net beneath it and hooked it up to a central bar. An army helicopter then began to winch the offending object upwards, but it wouldn't budge. The pilot of the helicopter radioed down to the commander on the ground that it just wouldn't budge. 'It's like it is fastened to the ground,' he said.

It was at this moment that the ball moved rapidly, one hundred yards to the left. This flung the helicopter sideways and towards the ground. Fortunately, the anchor bolts holding the net sheared away and the pilot managed to regain control of the helicopter. Once free of the net, the ball flew back at the same speed to take up its exact position above the reactor once more. It was precisely where it had been before to within a thousandth of an inch.

'I almost said that it doesn't want to play ball, but that would be an unfortunate choice of words,' Lieutenant Colonel Bell said. This was followed by nervous laughter from the assembled crew of soldiers and scientists.

'Shall I take a shot at it, sir?' one of the troops asked.

Bell said that he thought this might be an extremely bad idea. 'What if the little bastard shoots back?' he asked the eager soldier.

The soldier didn't answer. There was little else that they could do but keep a guard on the anomaly. Six soldiers were left behind to guard the object and monitor the situation.

The soldiers that were detailed guard duty were nervous to say the very least. They knew that this wasn't 'one of theirs'. This was no secret weapon being tested, but what was it? Some wondered whether this was something from either the US or the Russians. Something being tested in secret under field conditions - but why? What kind of weapon would just sit there? It gave off no waves of any kind. They had checked for everything from subsonic waves through to microwaves. It had no measurable form of propulsion. It gave off no heat signals. It was just there. Like some insolent ball of nothing. The one word on everyone's mind that no one spoke was 'Extraterrestrial'.

It would be approximately three in the morning when one of the soldiers said 'What the fuck is that?' Coming from beneath the ball was a slender beam of light. It was no thicker than a human hair and glowed green in colour. The beam then began to move rapidly, and all within the same width as the ball. It almost appeared to be a solid beam of light the same diameter as the ball itself.

One of the troops radioed Lieutenant Colonel Bell. 'Something's happening sir. It is emitting a beam of light'.

Bell was there and on site within four minutes. He and the soldiers watched in trepidation as beneath the first ball, a second ball was forming. Within minutes it was complete. It flew from its position to take up a position some ten yards away to the right.

'Its had a baby. I wonder if it's a boy or a girl?' Bell mumbled to himself, before saying 'Well isn't that just perfect. Now we have two of them'.

This pattern repeated itself four times more until there were six spheres. Each of them sat perfectly equidistant between each other. Each making one corner of a perfect hexagon. Again they were within a thousandth of an inch of the same distance. There they sat. Six perfect, menacing spheres. Between each sphere was the same beam of light, no more than the breadth of a hair, interconnecting them into a perfect hexagonal shape. Things then began to happen. More spheres were produced, and the whole process was speeding up. More hexagons connected to yet more hexagons. It took almost a full day until the entire surface of the planet had been covered.

Understandably, the entire planet was gripped with panic. All forms of communication had been cut. All power had been switched off. The whole planet was plunged back into the dark ages. Miners were trapped below ground with no idea what was happening, and due to the pumps being turned off they were both running out of air and the tunnels were slowly filling with water. Nuclear reactors began to go into critical condition as all controls had ceased. Soon they went into meltdown, polluting everything for thousands of miles. Within two years, all life forms on the planet were extinct, except a few exceptional microbes and bacteria. The earth was dead.

The spheres dispersed leaving behind them an extinct planet. The director of life force research wrote up his notes:

Planetary experiment 2176/1/BB/7 - Earth.

The hybridisation between our species and the primitive earth forms at first seemed promising. They developed speech, democracy, music, poetry and literature, but such was the power of the rogue genes that they became dominant. Violence was the dominating force and the whole experiment had become dangerous to the stability of the universe. They had developed propulsion units enabling them to extend beyond their own planet. This was a contamination that the Life Force

Governance could not risk. It is with regret that the experiment has been terminated. The planet has been scheduled for disposal.

Black Dust and a Packet of No 6

Craig was a battler. Born in the smoky northern town that had been steeped in the cotton and the coal for generations. Those two Goliaths had once dominated the town. The last pit had closed many years ago, and cotton weaving was but a memory. In his mind he could still hear those clogs on the streets. The pit men off to work. The idle chatter and their 'snap' tins and water cans carried with them. Craig was now self employed as an odd job man. He was a qualified electrician from his time at the pit, and could turn his hand to most tasks. Times were difficult, and work wasn't exactly plentiful. Sometimes the wolf felt remarkably close to the door!

Craig had been doing some work for a local firm, and was owed money by them, only for them to go bust. This meant he had to borrow money from the bank and hope he could recoup his losses, and maybe get some back from the defunct firm's insolvency money. It was then, of all times, his van was stolen, along with all his tools. He only discovered it missing when he got up in the morning. He had a sick feeling in the pit of his stomach. He rang the police and the insurance firm immediately. His wife berated him for leaving his tools inside the van. He did it every night. The van was always locked and parked under the street lamp outside their house. His van was decked out with shelving and all his tools. It would be a major task to unship it all every night, but he made up his mind that it was something that he would have to do next time - if indeed there *was* a next time.

Craig told his wife, June, that he was going for a walk to clear his head. His dog, Prince pricked up his ears in expectation. 'Come on then, lad,' Craig said.

Prince didn't need asking twice. He was out through the door like a flash. They strode across the same fields that he had walked as a kid. Down towards the colliery spoil heaps, and towards 'The Flash'. A lake that had been formed by mining subsidence, and was now a wildlife haven. Many was the big perch he'd caught in there as a kid with a big lobworm for bait. He sat on the bankside and looked out over the lake. A tear began to trickle down his cheek. Craig gritted his teeth and said, 'You big soft sod' to himself - but then the thought of his dad came to his mind and he burst into tears.

His dog, Prince, nuzzled beneath his arm and lay his head upon Craig's knee. 'Aye, I know lad, thi dad is turning soft,' he said, then ruffled the dog's fur.

All kinds of thoughts were drifting through his mind. The final demands that he had kept back from his wife that came so regularly from his suppliers. The fact that his van was only insured for third party, fire and theft, and he wasn't sure whether that covered his tools as well.

'I'm a strong, hard workin' man. How did this bloody happen?' he shouted to the winds. He thought of his wife and son who depended on him and how he felt he had let them down. He was more than seriously contemplating the best way to kill himself. 'I wish I could talk to you, dad. You always knew what to do,' Craig said. Then bowed his head and wept.

He was woken from his despair by the sound of the pit hooter. Craig raised his head to see the pit in full swing across the other side of the flash. The headgear was turning, bringing up a cage full of men for the change of shift. The smoke rose lazily from the tall chimney of the mill. Within a few seconds, the whole scene returned back to the present day. Craig was totally non-plussed by the whole affair. Even his dog seemed to have a worried look on his face when he looked at his master. 'Don't speak a word of this,' Craig said to Prince, before saying to himself 'I'm now thinking the effing dog can talk as well.' He burst out laughing. Half through the comedy of the situation, and half through hysteria.

As he walked back towards home he noticed a cigarette packet on the floor. It was a 'No 6' packet. The same brand that his dad used to smoke. I didn't know they still made those, he thought to himself. He hadn't noticed another small time slip had occurred.

When Craig arrived home, his wife was watching TV. The dog hopped up on the couch beside her. Craig sat on the sofa too, with Prince between the two of them. 'Is there owt good on?' Craig asked.

'Corrie is on in ten minutes,' June replied.

'I said good, not crap,' Craig replied.

His wife merely smiled smugly as she settled down and awaited her beloved Coronation Street.

A moment later there was a knock at the door. Craig opened it and two police officers were standing outside. One of the officers said, 'We have some good news for you, sir. We have recovered your van and all of your tools.'

'Oh thank God. Is the van okay?' he asked eagerly.

'Well, they damaged the back doors a little getting in, and they have broken the steering lock, but that apart, it seems fine,' the officer replied. 'It's the weirdest thing. The two lads who stole it drove it to the police station and told us that it was they who had stolen the van. They just gave themselves up. Apparently some blokes had put the fear of god up them,' the officer said. 'They kept going on about two men. One called Billy Pigeon and one called Geoff Paint.'

Craig almost tumbled backwards, before saying, 'Are you sure those were the names?'

Both officers looked at one another, before they both said 'Yes, those were the names they gave. Why do you ask. Do you know them?'

Craig was about to say that he did indeed know them, but stopped himself. Billy Pigeon was his dad's nickname because he kept racing pigeons, and Geoff Paint was his brother, Craig's uncle, who was a painter and decorator. Both were dead some years.

'No, just sounded like comical names,' Craig told the officers. He then went to the station to collect his van.

That night, Craig slept, but was troubled by dreams. He was back at school. He was sitting outside the headmaster's office when he saw his dad walking along the corridor. Craig's legs were shaking with the fear of it. His dad looked upset. The headmaster told his dad that due to Craig's constant cheek to the teachers and his general disruptive behaviour, he was seriously considering expelling him. Craig expected to feel the full wrath of his father's anger, and probably a couple of clips around the back of his head. What happened was far, far worse.

His dad looked him straight in the eye and said, 'I'm ashamed of you. Me and your mam work hard to give you decent clothes and some spending money, and you let us down like this. You are no son of mine.'

Craig idolized this gentle giant. His dad was Superman and Batman all rolled together, and now his dad had disowned him. He would happily have had his dad shout at him. Even to have his pit belt across his backside, but for those words to have been said. He felt bereft. 'I'm sorry, dad. I'll behave. You see. You won't hear any more bad things. I promise, dad,' Craig said, as he walked home beside his sullen and silent father.

In the next dream, Craig was a teenager and playing for the county schoolboys' team at rugby. It was the finals. Craig had seen a hefty, big lad come sprinting down the wing. It seemed odds-on that he would score. He heard his dad's booming voice shout, 'Tackle him lad!' The big forward was head and shoulders above Craig, but like the true battler that he was, he took his legs from beneath him and brought him toppling to the ground. He glanced up at his dad and received a proud smile and a wink. Craig's team went on to win, and the newspaper report said that 'It was down to the skill of the forwards and the spirited defence put up by Craig'.

In the next dream he was sitting in his living room. His dad was sitting opposite him in the armchair. This dream felt strange. It felt very vivid. His dad had his old tweed jacket on and his ever-present flat cap. His dad said, 'Now then lad, has tha learned nowt from me?'

Craig was confused, and replied, 'What do you mean, Dad?'

Craig's dad said, 'I mean about you being a quitter. I heard what you were thinkin'. You wanted to do yourself in.'

Craig felt the butterflies in the pit of his stomach. Is this real? he thought to himself.

His dad shook his head and said, 'Daft bugger. You would leave your lad without his dad, just because things are gettin' a bit hard? Have you forgotten what it was like when we were on strike? Well, have you? This is nowt.' His dad then took out his packet of No 6 cigarettes and lit one.

'Sorry dad,' Craig said. It felt like being back outside the headmaster's office all over again.

Craig woke the next morning with an entirely different mindset. He had a good talking to off his dad, even if it was just a dream. As his wife made his sandwiches she remarked 'Have you started smoking again?' Craig said, 'No, I haven't. Why do you ask?'

'I found a packet of No 6 cigarettes down the side of the armchair. I hope that little bugger hasn't started smoking. I will tackle him about it when he gets in from his paper round,' June answered.

A second later, Craig heard the words, 'Think on now, lad. I'll be watching,' spoken directly into his ear. It was his dad's voice.

'Did you say something, love?' June asked.

Craig just kissed her and said, 'Yes, I said I love you my little darling.'

June laughed and said, 'Yeah, right. I bet you did. Give us a kiss.'

Craig kissed his June, and picked her up like a rag doll and gave her a huge hug. 'See you later, lovey. I have a good feeling about today,' Craig said.

As he jumped into his van he happened to glance at the passenger's seat. There, upon the seat was a beautiful, pristine, iridescent pigeon feather.

A Friend in Need

It was a clear, crisp January morning. The ground was firm underfoot and the breeze was minimal. The frost on the spiders' webs in the trees and grasses made the whole scene one of breathtaking magic. It felt like walking past the jewellery cabinet of an empress, and seeing her tiaras and necklaces shining in pristine splendour. The ambient background noises of the jackdaw's quarrelsome and busy chuckling, and the indignant flurry of feathers and vocal admonishment from a startled partridge added the soundtrack to a perfect day of walking on his beloved Lake District hills and moorland. Occasionally the haunting cry of the Curlew could be heard, echoing down the valley. This was the kind of day that Tom lived for. To him, the cold air was like the finest vintage wine to be drunk in deeply and savoured.

Tom was known as 'Shock' by his friends. This was due to his unruly mop of bright red, curly hair on his head, and beard to match. One of his friends once remarked 'It looks like someone's given you an electric shock and your head has lit up like a bulb'. For the rest of that particular walking trip, his mates called him Shock, and the nickname stuck!

Shock never went out without equipment. It always annoyed him when he heard about hapless tourists being rescued off the hills and being found wearing a football shirt, jeans and a pair of flip-flops. Apart from his waterproof thermal clothing, he always carried a backpack that contained a flask, a first aid kit, a small tarpaulin that could be used for emergency shelter, a whistle, a compass and a map. Along with this he had things like chocolate and mint cake for energy, a Swiss army knife, bits of cord to tie down the emergency tarpaulin and a few tent pegs. His mobile phone was also fully charged and in his top pocket.

He had been out a little more than an hour as he rested against a dry stone wall to pour out a cup of tea from his flask. The cup began to tumble from the top of the dry stone wall where he had placed it. Not wanting to lose the precious warming fluid, he lunged forward to try and catch it. As he did, he slipped. His boot was semi-wedged between a few fallen stones. As he went over he heard the soft crack come from the vicinity of his ankle. He knew immediately by the severe pain that this wasn't just a sprain.

Shock slowly and painfully shuffled his body around until his back rested against the wall. All the time he had been out walking he hadn't seen another soul. He knew that the prospect of a passing walker finding him was remote. He took his mobile phone from his pocket, but to his dismay he found that he couldn't get a signal. To make things worse, it would be dark in a couple of hours, and the black clouds began to roll down the valley towards him. He took out his whistle in the hopes that another walker would recognise and hear the familiar call for help known by all experienced walkers, and come to his rescue.

He blew on his whistle for twenty minutes or so before he felt the breeze rising a little. With it, it carried the first few flecks of snow. With great difficulty, he managed to secure the tarpaulin underneath some of the stones on the dry stone wall and peg out the bottom of it making an impromptu little lean-to shelter. The snow was now almost a white-out and the darkness was falling rapidly. For the first time in his life, Shock wondered if his beloved mistress-of-the moorland would take him to her bosom and carry him off on his final journey. He wondered if he would become another statistic, and maybe his passing would be remembered by a bunch of flowers tucked into the dry stone wall that had been his final resting place. He was scared - and with good reason.

He could already feel the cold creeping into his bones.

Having lost his cup over the other side of the wall, he drank directly from the flask. He could only sip at it as the scalding liquid burnt his lips. He nibbled at a bit of chocolate and, as he did, his lip trembled a little. The words of his Dad sprang to his mind. 'Always tell someone where you are going, and what time you expect to be back'. Did I tell Jean where I was going? he thought to himself. In all honesty, he couldn't remember if he had told his wife anything about his journey at all. A small wave of fear and misery swept over him.

Shortly after this, something quite remarkable happened. He heard a shuffling outside, and a dog's snout pushed itself under the flap of his shelter. Oh thank Christ, he thought to himself. He stuck his head out from the shelter, and as he did, the snow stung his eyes. Visibility was virtually zero. He blew and blew on his whistle, but to no avail. He began to wonder whether another poor, hapless walker was out there and had become parted from his dog.

The dog settled down beside him and the two sheltering waifs and strays found comfort from each other's warmth and companionship. The dog was a sort of Border Collie cross. His face was black on one side and white on the other. Circling his eye on the white side was a patch of black. To add to the dog's uniqueness, one eye was the usual dark brown, but the other was almost grey. 'I'll call you Patch' Shock said. As if in reply, the dog stretched upwards and licked his face. They settled down for the night.

When morning came and Shock woke from his fitful sleep, Patch was still by his side. The dog welcomed him by leaning his head on his chest. Shock stroked the dog's head. He was so very, very cold. He began to shake almost uncontrollably. Then he heard a noise. It was the sound of an engine. He peered from beneath the tarpaulin and was dazzled by the sun glinting off the surface of the snow. Coming towards him was an old tractor. He recognised it as an old David Brown VAK1 from the 1940s. It was being driven by a portly, red faced farmer wearing a mackintosh coat, a scarf and a flat cap. It was pulling a small trailer with bales of hay in it. The dog recognised him immediately and leapt on his trailer as if he had been doing it all his life.

'Now then young fella, it looks like you are in the wars,' the farmer shouted down to him, before adding, 'I thought I saw thi from the bottom of the valley. Mountain rescue is on its way. Five minutes and no more,' he said. Then he gave him a cheery wave and drove on past. The dog looked back at him and wagged his tail, as if to say, 'Nice meeting you'.

Five minutes later, the Landrover appeared on the horizon. He saw the welcoming words on the door stating that it was the Mountain Rescue. A medic strapped up Shock's ankle and splinted it. He was then gently lifted onto a stretcher and placed in the back of the vehicle. Then they slowly made their way back down the valley.

One of the rescuers, a man in his fifties said to Shock. 'It's odd you should pick that exact spot against that wall.' When Shock asked him why, he told him that the son of a local farmer had broken his leg and had propped himself up against that very spot. 'We call it Bertie's corner, seeing as that's where Bert was found partially buried under the snow.' He then went on to tell him that his Dad had found him the day afterwards. He had driven up there in the tractor to feed the sheep. His Dad thought that his son had just gone on home after seeing the sheep were okay. 'His dog never left his side. That dog stayed with him all the time,' the rescuer said.

'This might sound daft, but can you remember what the dog looked like?' Shock asked.

'I can as it happens,' he answered. 'It was a comical looking thing. Black on one side of its face and white on the other, and a black patch over its eye. It was called Patch.'

Raymond

'Let's get something straight. You are telling me that you want us, the housing department, to find you another property to live in because you say this one is haunted?' the housing officer asked.

Caroline nodded defiantly and said, 'Yes, that is precisely what I am asking, and I invite you to spend a night there, and see for yourself.'

The housing officer seemed intrigued by the whole thing. He had more than a passing interest in these things himself, but was a sceptic. 'It would be strictly off the record, and on my own time, but okay,' he said.

'Good!' Caroline replied, and so the plan was set in motion.

The story started some six months previously. Caroline wasn't the kind of person to be easily spooked by 'things that go bump in the night'. As an ex police officer, she had seen her fair share of spooky old properties and deserted streets. She had more fear of living people who hid in the shadows. The ones that could do her harm. The dead were the dead, as far as she was concerned.

Caroline had lived in her council flat for about two years, ever since her husband died. She had moved there because the children were now grown up, and their previous council house was just too big for one person. It started off with silly little things. She would take a dish out of the kitchen cupboard and close the door straight away again afterwards, only to turn around a few seconds later to find it wide open again. The cupboards had spring loaded hinges, so that once closed, they stayed closed, unless someone opened them wide again. They couldn't just slowly swing open on their own. She put this down, at first, to her own absent mindedness, but it began to happen more and more often. One day, she even took a notepad and pen, opened the cupboard door to take out a cup, closed the door again, then wrote on the pad 'You definitely closed the cupboard door.' Alongside this, she wrote the time. Once again, when she turned around, the doors were wide open. These occurrences were a little unnerving to Caroline, but mostly, they were merely one of life's annoying little happenings. She began to wonder if the hinges were merely faulty in some way. A few days later, things became immeasurably worse.

She was in the kitchen making herself a cup of coffee when she heard someone whisper in her ear, 'I'm watching you... bitch.' She spun around in fear, brandishing the coffee spoon as if it was a dagger. There was no one there at all. She knew the door was locked, and that no one could have left the room that quickly. Her mind was in complete turmoil. She wondered if this is what schizophrenia felt like, and if she was becoming mentally unstable. It was then that she saw a teacup fly off the draining board and smash against the wall just behind her. It narrowly avoided hitting her face as it did. She whooped with fright and ran from the flat. She knocked on the door of the next door flat. They were complete strangers, but she was in a state of panic. Two minutes later she was inside their flat and explaining to the young Jamaican couple what had just happened. Far from ridiculing her, they said that they too had experienced odd happenings.

Things didn't improve a great deal, and no matter how high she turned up the central heating, the flat felt cold - especially the kitchen. She had also started to experience a presence in the bedroom. One morning, she had risen and walked into the bathroom to take a shower. When she returned to her bedroom, the entire contents of her underwear drawer were strewn across the bed and floor, with the exception of a matching pair of scarlet red, bra and panties. These were laid out perfectly and precisely in the centre of the bed. This angered Caroline beyond belief. 'Just fuck off you nasty little creep. You don't tell me what to wear,' she screamed.

She heard a tearing sound come from the wardrobe. When she opened the door, one of her dresses was swinging on its hanger. When she examined it more closely, it looked as if the claws of some animal had torn four parallel cuts down the whole length of the dress. Caroline flopped down onto the bed and wept. She was at the end of her tether. That was when she decided to make an appointment to speak to the housing department. It was two weeks into the future before she could get to see someone.

She would quite often wake in the morning and find scratches and bruises on her body. Especially her breasts and legs. She would wake up as if fighting for her life. Some monstrosity was always trying to rape her. She would feel rough hands holding her arms and the feeling of someone trying to enter her. She virtually abandoned her flat and slept in her car. Anything was better than being attacked in her sleep.

After her appointment, true to his word, the housing officer knocked on Caroline's door at eight thirty that same evening. In his hand he carried an aluminium flight case. 'Mind if I come in?' he said.

Caroline wordlessly beckoned him inside and showed him into the flat. 'Would you like a brew. The kettle has just boiled?' she said, and he answered, 'Yes please, tea with milk and no sugar thanks.'

She asked him what was in the case. He smiled coyly and said, 'I fancy myself as a bit of a ghost hunter. It's some of my stuff.'

Caroline wondered what other surprises he had up his sleeve. 'You know my name, it's Caroline. Can I ask yours or do I have to call you Mr Broughton?' she asked.

He smiled and said, 'It's Francis - or Frank, whichever you prefer'.

'Do you know what EVPs are?' Frank asked.

Caroline did know, as she had been a devotee of *Most Haunted*, but she chose to answer flippantly by saying, 'No idea. Is it contagious?'

Frank suspected that she was poking fun at him, but proceeded to patiently explain that he would leave a recording device running and start to ask questions. 'Sometimes, when you play the tapes back, you can hear faint voices answering the questions,' he said. He then placed the digital recorder in the middle of the kitchen table and began to ask questions. When they played the tapes back, they weren't at all prepared for what they heard.

Frank's opening question was, 'Do you want to talk to us? You can talk into this machine and leave an answer.'

When they played the tape back, they heard something that sounded vaguely like electronic feedback. It sounded like a long and protracted wail. Then the words, 'Die, bitch.' This wasn't at all faint. The voice sounded evil and rasping.

The next question asked was, 'What do you want here? What do you want with Caroline?'

The voice answered with cruel laughter, and the words, 'She's getting none. She wants it, the bitch does. I'll give it to her.'

Caroline sat in total, wide-eyed disbelief as she listened to the replies.

The last question was, 'Is Raymond here?' There followed a moment of silence before the answer. 'I WILL HAVE YOU. YOU WILL DIE!'

Caroline looked directly at Frank and said. 'OK, tell me just what the hell is going on? Who is this nasty little piece of shit, Raymond?'

Frank looked down in embarrassment, and proceeded to tell

her the story. It transpired that the previous occupants were an old lady and her son Raymond. Raymond had always been a little strange, and had been in minor scrapes with the law. He was a known 'Peeping Tom' in the local area, and had stolen items of women's underwear from washing lines in the locality. Unfortunately, no one was aware of quite how disturbed Raymond really was. One day, he had a severe psychotic episode. He had a furious argument with his mother, after which he took out a kitchen knife from the drawer and stabbed her in her right eye. He then cut open her throat, and also disembowelled her, laying out her entrails across the kitchen work surfaces like gruesome decorations. He had also stripped her naked and put her clothes beside her in a neatly folded little pile. When the police arrived, he was sitting on the sofa eating a microwave meal and watching TV as if nothing had happened. When he saw the police officers, he bundled past them and threw himself to his death from the balcony. The flat being five storeys up, his death must have been instantaneous.

Caroline sat in complete dismay and bewilderment, before saying, 'And this... this... THING, is still living here?...Well... IS HE?'

'So it would seem,' Frank answered.

Caroline was furious. 'A great little flat in a lovely neighbourhood. I thought I was SO LUCKY finding this place - but I wasn't lucky at all WAS I?' She said.

Frank just apologised on behalf of the council. 'So, what do we do now?' Caroline asked tearfully.

Before Frank could answer, they heard a voice from the other side of the kitchen door. 'He's my boy. I'll sort him out,' it said.

They then stood transfixed as they saw the shimmering silhouette of an old lady standing at the open kitchen door. 'RAYMOND, just look at the mess you have caused. Apologise AT ONCE!' the old lady said in a very authoritarian voice. They then heard crying coming from somewhere in the kitchen, and a voice said 'I'm sorry mummy. I'm so, so sorry mummy. Don't hit me. I'm sorry. Don't send me back to that hospital. I don't like it there.'

The two shapes seemed to merge into one, as if they were hugging. 'He will be no more trouble, I am taking him home,' the old lady said. It then seemed as if a small tunnel of light appeared, and they were swallowed up by it.

Immediately the flat felt warmer and brighter. It felt as if someone had let the sunshine back in. Raymond's mother was good to her word, and Raymond never appeared again. She had taken him off to whatever fate befell him on the other side. Caroline stayed for a while afterwards, but never felt at home there.

'How can I relax knowing a sweet old lady was murdered in my kitchen?' she told the housing people. Helped by Frank, they found her a new flat on the other side of town. It wasn't quite as nice an area, but Caroline didn't mind one bit. It felt as if a massive weight had been lifted from her.

It was about the third day in her new flat. Caroline reached up to the cupboard to bring down a cup to make a cup of tea. When she heard the sound of someone scrape a chair along the kitchen floor and sit down. She froze in terror, and said to herself, 'Oh Christ no, please tell me he hasn't followed me'.

'No he hasn't, love. He's gone for good,' a voice said.

She hardly dared believe it. It was her husband's voice. She turned around to see him sitting at her kitchen table.

'He was just too strong, love. He was evil, and drew strength from his mother. I held him off from the first day you moved in there, but eventually they overpowered me. Can you ever forgive me?' he said. Caroline burst into tears and said. 'Oh darling. Oh, sweet, sweet man, of course I do.' He then blew her a kiss and gradually faded from her sight. Caroline knew that whatever might befall her in life, she knew that her husband would be watching over her as she slept.

The Well

'Well, his advert says that he can find everything from water to buried treasure through the use of dowsing rods.'

Tim looked at his wife in total exasperation. 'Jennifer, are you seriously suggesting that we find the old well by hiring the services of a crackpot with a couple of twigs?'

Jenny always hated it when Tim took the supposed moral high ground and talked down to her. 'He doesn't use twigs, he has metal divining rods. Look at his website,' she replied.

'I don't want to bloody look, but if it pleases you I will. Oh yes, they look very scientific indeed. A couple of old wire coat-hangers bent into an 'L' shape,' Tim replied.

Jenny told him that he was a sarcastic old git, and it would do no harm to at least give him a go.

'Anything for a quiet life' Tim replied.

Two days later, George, the dowser arrived at their farm cottage. He was a ruddy faced, grey haired man of around five feet four in height. He had the kind of serene and unlined face that could make him anything from early sixties to late eighties. Jenny greeted him enthusiastically, 'It's so nice to meet you. Would you like a cup of tea?' she asked. George said that he would love one, and so they retired to the kitchen.

Once inside the kitchen, George said, 'Do you mind if I try dowsing in here?'

Jenny was both puzzled and intrigued and said, 'Feel free.'

George walked up and down across the kitchen. In certain spots the dowsing rods reacted. He chuckled and said, 'Thought so.' He turned to Jenny and apologized. 'Sorry, just checking something out. Call it a feeling. I was right,' he said.

'Right about what?' Jenny asked.

'Your house is built on a ley line,' George replied.

George went on to explain the significance of ley lines. 'I personally believe that they are an ancient source of spiritual power. That power can be used for both good and bad. Sensitive people can find themselves suffering certain side effects by living on top of a ley line'.

'Like what?' Jenny asked.

'Oh, a feeling of exhaustion in certain rooms, a heaviness, headaches, feeling like they are not alone, that kind of thing,' he answered.

Jenny's mouth fell open in shock and amazement. 'That's how I always feel in the pantry. It is just the other side of that door,' she said, whilst pointing to the far end of the kitchen.

'Yes, that would be right on top of the ley line, and with the walls being made of local granite, it would act as an amplifier with the room being so small.'

Jenny began to feel a little creeped out.

'Do you ever feel that someone is in there with you. A child?' George asked.

Jenny told him that she often felt a presence in there with her, but had just put it down to imagination.

'It's a child. A young girl about four years old. She died in there,' George said.

Jenny said nothing at first, but then she blurted out, 'Are you trying to frighten me? If so, you are succeeding!'

George chuckled and shook his head.

Unbeknown to Jenny and to George, Tim had been listening outside the door. He burst into the room and said, 'I think we have heard enough of your bullshit. I want you to leave right now. Is this how you get your kicks, by frightening old ladies?'

'I'm younger than you, you cheeky bastard,' Jenny shouted at Tim in retaliation. Before going on to say, 'Just because YOU don't believe in anything deeper than football and scotch whisky, doesn't mean that it doesn't exist.'

George shuffled uncomfortably in his chair, then rose to his feet and said 'I'm sorry. I didn't mean to cause any trouble. I'll be on my way.' He then left the kitchen and walked back to his car. Jenny was absolutely blazing mad.

'You really, really piss me off, Tim. He was right in describing absolutely every feeling I have in there. There are things I don't tell you because you are such a sarcastic prick, but he was right about the little girl too, because I have seen her'.

Tim stood open-mouthed in amazement, then (unwisely) said, 'Why didn't you tell me this?'

'BECAUSE YOU WOULD HAVE SAID WHAT YOU JUST SAID TO THAT NICE OLD MAN," she shouted at him. Such was her absolute temper, she picked up one of the mugs from the table and flung it at the wall, then collapsed with her head upon her arms on the table and wept.

Tim crept around Jenny feeling like a naughty schoolboy. Every time he smiled at her, it was met with a face of thunder. He knew that expression very, very well. They had been married for thirty-seven years. He had learned not to push his luck when she was like that.

Some time later, Jenny had settled down into feeling mildly irritated, but communicative. 'You are a bit of a hypocrite you know,' she said to Tim.

'In what way?' he asked.

Jenny then went on to remind him about his childhood, and the man he always saw in his wardrobe. 'So, because you saw him, he was real, but anything anyone else sees is bullshit?'

Tim shuffled and squirmed in his chair. 'OK, I'm listening. What do we do next?' he asked. 'Well what YOU do is phone up George, apologize, give him one of your bottles of single malt as an apology, and ask him to come back'

Tim opened his mouth as if to argue, but merely said, 'Okay love'.

Fortunately for Tim, George declined his kind offer of a bottle of Highland Park, and told him that he drank nothing stronger than tea. Tim still felt a little wounded and a tad embarrassed by the previous day's events, but he was the perfect host. George's opening words were, 'The well is the other side of the pantry wall, about six feet past it. There's a slight depression in the ground. It's probably capped off with a stone.'

They all went outside, and Tim took a spade and removed the grass. Lo and behold they found a stone slab. 'It's under there, but be careful, it's an old well,' George said.

'How did you know?' Tim asked.

George smiled and said, 'Common sense really. They had it where it was handy, plus I saw the depression. Above all that though, I felt its presence.'

Tim felt Jenny's hand squeeze his a little tighter, and he knew better than to ask any more questions.

'What do we owe you?' Tim asked.

'I'll tell you after we have finished,' George replied.

'But... you found the well,' Tim replied.

George looked at him patiently and said, 'There's still a frightened child who is lost and stuck on this side. We have to attend to her.'

'Will that be extra?' Tim asked.

Jenny promptly kicked him in the shins with no attempt to disguise it. 'Owwww... only asking,' Tim said.

George chuckled and said, 'No, I don't charge for helping spirits across to the other side.' He made arrangements to return the next evening after dark. 'They come through better in the darkness,' he said.

The next evening arrived, and with it, so did George. He had instructed Jenny to place a lit candle on the kitchen table and switch off all the lights.

Tim was dying to ask if he was going to go all weird like the mediums on the old black and white films and say, 'Is there anybody there?'

George disappointed him by merely sitting there with his eyes closed. Eventually, he spoke. 'She is frightened, and is apologizing over and over again. She is asking if she is still loved and wanted. Before she died, she was told that she was a bad little girl'.

Jenny burst into tears and said, 'Tell her of course she is still loved.'

George said, 'It isn't you she is frightened of, and is asking. It's him,' he said, whilst nodding towards Tim.

'ME??' Tim blurted out in total shock and surprise.

George went on to explain that she thought he was her daddy. On the morning that she died, her daddy was about to leave to go and work in the fields when he saw his little girl playing with a china figurine. 'Be careful with that,' he yelled at her. Such was her shock, she dropped it and it smashed on the floor. 'You stupid little girl. Now look what you have done. I don't love you any more. Get out of my sight!'. her father had yelled. George went on to tell them that her name was Florence. She had run into the living room and wept into a pillow on the sofa. The figurine had belonged to her father's mother, her grandma. He left to go off into the fields to work.

Florence had a little jam jar where she kept any pennies that were given to her. It was kept on a shelf in the pantry. Florence was going to give the money to her daddy to buy another figurine. She loved and adored her daddy very much. This was her small way of addressing the balance. She stood upon a stool, but the jam jar was just out of reach. She stood on her tip-toes and the stool toppled away from beneath her. As she fell, she hit her head against a marble slab that was used to keep the butter cool. She was killed instantly. Her father never forgave himself, he took to drink and died a few years later.

Tim was becoming emotional himself, just imagining how he would have dealt with it.

George snapped him out of it by saying, 'She wants to know if she can come and sit on your knee?'

Tim dissolved into tears. 'Of course she can' he said. Tim felt the presence and the gentle weight of something snuggling up to his chest whilst sitting upon his knee. Then he found himself speaking, but his voice wasn't his own. He said, 'Daddy does love you. Daddy is so so sorry'. Florence's father was speaking through Tim.

Then Jenny and George saw Tim's appearance change. He was a man in his thirties wearing blue overalls and a flat cap, and on his knee, cuddled up to him was a pretty little girl in a gingham dress. He was hugging her and sobbing.

Slowly, the image faded away. Tim was drained and emotional. 'Something happened, tell me, what the hell happened?' he asked.

George said, 'You set her free. She has moved across to the other side. You became her daddy for a moment.'

Tim slumped back in his chair and said, 'I need a whisky.' Then he heard a little girl's voice say. 'Don't drink. It hurts you.'

It was Florence. She was standing in the kitchen doorway with her father holding her hand. They both faded away and were seen no more.

George wanted no money from Tim and Jenny, and Jenny still occasionally felt the presence of little Florence, but she was no longer frightened. She was a happy little girl now that she knew her daddy loved her.

Oh, and Tim? He drank just a little less scotch.

Know Who Your Friends Are

It was a simple act of kindness, like opening a door for someone. It just happened to be that I gave someone my seat on a train. I didn't mind standing, and she looked so weary. I'm guessing she was in her early fifties, but I am notoriously bad at guessing women's ages. I think I have learned through experience that it carries too many pitfalls. She smiled and said, 'Thank you kindly, sir.' She spoke perfect English, but with an accent that I couldn't quite pin down. It sounded vaguely Eastern Bloc. She had a sort of gypsy look about her, but she was dressed in modern and western fashion. Had she not spoken, I would have had her down as being a local.

A couple of stops later, the person who had been sitting next to her alighted, leaving the seat vacant. She moved across towards the window, allowing me to sit beside her. 'May I say something?' she said.

'By all means,' I replied.

Her face took on a strange expression, somewhere between sadness and concern. 'You are going somewhere tonight, and I believe that what awaits you may do you harm. There is a darkness in that place.'

My expression must have been an absolute picture. It was as if someone had pulled off an impromptu conjurer's trick. 'But... how... I mean?' I stuttered out.

'How did I know?' she asked. I merely nodded in reply. 'You have the darkness still upon you. You have met spirits before. I see their dirty fingermarks upon you. Tonight may be a step too far,' she replied. She took out a small notepad from her handbag and scribbled down a name and a mobile phone number, then handed it to me. 'Keep this - I would prefer you didn't go to this place, but you are a man. Men are so stupid. If you need my help, call me,' she said. Then rose from her seat and left the train at the next stop. She had basically called me a man, and therefore stupid, but I took it almost as a kindness. There was a certain confident air about her.

I looked at the scrap of paper. It bore the name, 'Irina' and what I assumed to be her mobile number. I tucked this into my wallet. For some strange reason it felt almost like a precious gift. It felt like an amulet. I felt somehow lighter in mood. At the same time I felt mildly uneasy. It was a sort of excitement. I felt like a child about to go off on holiday.

That evening I had agreed to investigate a building in the countryside. It was at the bottom of an old concrete road that had seen better days. Parts of it had degraded, and there were weeds sprouting through the cracks. At the end of the lane I found a very plain looking rectangular building that was built of red brick, which had then been pebble-dashed. Bits of this had fallen off, leaving patches of bare brick showing. Other than that, the building was intact. It had been part of some kind of military installation. It was one of those places that the locals knew not to ask too many questions about. The remains of a tall, chain link fence and the concrete posts still surrounded it, though sections of it were now missing. The security gate was pushed back, and was leaning at a slight angle. It hadn't been moved for many years. Brambles were growing through the wire framework.

It was owned by a farmer who had the idea of converting it into a mechanical workshop, but he had become terrified of even setting foot back in the place. He had reported hearing screams followed by a loud voice shouting 'GET OUT'. He didn't need to be asked twice. He ran through the door and slammed it shut behind himself. He then locked it. He gave me the keys to the place a few days previously when I went to visit him, and told me very plainly indeed that he didn't intend accompanying me. So, here I was, about to turn the key in the lock, when my mobile phone rang.

I looked at my phone and the name 'Irina' was displayed there. I almost dropped the phone in shock. There were several reasons for this. The main two being that I hadn't added her number to my phone, and so it couldn't have displayed her name, the second being that I hadn't given her my phone number in return. Very timidly I answered the call and whispered 'Hello'.

'You are a stupid man. Do not open that door until I get there,' she said.

I started to say, 'But how do you know that I am...?' and the line went dead.

I took several steps away from the door and walked back to the gate. I paced up and down in confusion, desperately trying to make sense of what had just happened. Was she some kind of government spy? I wondered. Was I under some kind of surveillance? What the hell was going on? I didn't have long to wait to find out. Within ten minutes, Irina arrived. I heard her footsteps behind me on the lane.

I was about to ask her how she got here, but before I could, she said, 'The taxi driver didn't want to come up this road.' She scared me a little. It's like she could read minds, but I had a strong feeling that she was here to protect me.

'May we sit in your car? There are things I must tell you before we enter that building,' she asked.

If she had said to run naked round the perimeter fence I would have. Something about this woman and the situation I found myself in made me feel powerless. 'Yes, of course,' I answered, then pressed my key fob to open the doors.

Once inside the car she looked me straight in the eyes and said, 'Behind that door is evil. A kind of sickening, skulking creature. Once a man, but was then and is now, a monster.'

I gestured to speak up, but she placed a finger upon my lips to stop me. 'Please don't interrupt me again,' she said.

I felt like a schoolboy who had just had a ticking off.

She smiled at me and said, 'Sorry, I am not good at small talk.'

She told me that behind that door, unspeakable acts had been performed. This was once a satellite of an army intelligence base. This is where they brought prisoners for investigation and torture.

'Torture? Surely not,' I said.

She laughed and said, 'Why... because the British don't do things like that? We live in a kill or be killed world.'

I shifted uneasily in my seat, before saying 'I'm not too happy about all this. Am I acting in any way illegally?'

She looked at me with incredulity upon her face, before saying, 'Does this look like an army base now? Would they give YOU the keys to a government building? Do I have to say the words and tell you that we are talking about a malevolent spirit?'

I shook my head. I felt that I was now a bit-part player in some third rate horror drama.

'Besides, he has already seen you. There's no going back now.'

My stomach lurched at these words.

Irana took a couple of deep breaths, then said, 'It's me he wants. I assassinated him. We have unfinished business.'

Involuntarily, I blurted out, 'What the fuck??'

She smiled and said 'Don't worry, I have retired'.

I have never felt so thoroughly intimidated and emasculated by a woman as I felt at that moment.

'I'm on your side anyway,' she said. Then slapped my thigh and kissed my cheek. Suddenly I felt like a pretend James Bond.

'Let's get one thing straight,' she said, before continuing to say, 'I was a British agent and working on behalf of the British to... erm... let's say, neutralise certain traitors and double agents.'

Again, my stomach lurched. 'Please don't tell me any more,' I said.

'You need to know. This is crucial. When we get inside those doors, you will struggle to tell friend from foe.'

I suddenly felt like bursting into tears.

She saw this, and said, 'Reach inside. You have a well of bravery inside you. That's why you were chosen.'

'Chosen?... By who?' I said. 'The farmer rang me and said he has ghosts.'

Her face took on a steely expression; then she said, 'Certain actions define certain ends.'

By now, you could have tapped one of my veins and bottled neat adrenaline from it. All my senses were heightened. If even a bird had chirped, I would probably have sprinted down the lane screaming.

'Once inside, let me do the talking,' she said.

I nodded, whilst thinking, 'Don't worry about that. I have no intention of saying a word.'

'Hand me the keys and keep behind me,' she said. I heard the lock click open. Immediately it reminded me of the click of a rifle bolt. She pushed the door open and strode inside. 'Shall we have a little dance, Johnnie boy?' she said.

This was greeted by a chair flying across the room, narrowly missing us. Suddenly, I felt a sickening pain in my neck as if steely fingers were pressing into it. I whimpered and dropped to my knees. 'Leave him, it is me you called for' she said.

The pressure disappeared instantaneously. I shuffled into a corner with my back to the wall.

Irana moved like a street fighter around the room. As she did, the figure of an athletically framed soldier appeared. They traded blows, and she gave every bit as good as she received. He drew a revolver from a holster and, in a split second, she kicked the gun from his hands and it came sliding across the floor towards me. I grabbed it and shakily held it in front of myself.

'You can't shoot ghosts, stupid,' Irana said.

I lowered the gun, but kept hold of it just in case. He whirled around after missing her with a swing of his arm, and I saw her plunge a knife into his side somewhere around the kidney area. He dropped with a groan of pain and disappeared.

She then started speaking in what sounded like Russian, and the room took on a sudden icy chill. Two military policemen entered the room. They appeared to be unarmed. 'Give me the gun, sir. She is a Russian spy,' one of them said.

I was about to hand it over when I heard her words inside my head, 'When we get inside those doors, you will struggle to tell friend from foe.' I pointed the gun towards the soldiers, and said, 'Two big, strapping lads like you against one weak little woman? My, my, what is the army coming to?'

At that, he made a step towards me, and I shouted, 'I am really that scared that I no longer give a fuck just who I shoot. FUCK OFF!' He backed away.

'Meet the other two, his colleagues, the REAL Russian spies,' Irana said.

They laughed, and said, 'You are the only traitor in this room. Traitor to our country'.

I could see that they were about to make their move. 'Catch!' I shouted, and threw the gun towards her. She plucked it out of thin air and, in one perfectly practised move, she put a hole just above the right eye of one of the men with one shot. The other one made a move for the door. Three more shots rang out, and he too fell to the ground.

By this stage I was a whimpering wreck who was trying to shelter behind a wooden chair.

The room grew warmer and the atmosphere lifted. I looked at where the bodies had once been and they were gone. 'It's okay, James Bond, you can come out now,' Irana said.

I was still panting from the sheer terror of what I had just witnessed. 'Where have they gone?' I asked.

'They were ghosts; where do you think they have gone? Back to the grave, stupid man,' she replied.

'You told me that you can't shoot a ghost, but you did,' I said.

She laughed and said, 'But a ghost can shoot another ghost. I am dead too.' She looked at me again, and said, 'You haven't figured it out yet have you? Just why you were chosen?

I shook my head in total bewilderment. 'You had the keys in your possession after you collected them from the farmer. They were found on your body after your fatal car crash,' she said.

Release

When you have been with someone for so long, you begin to recognise the tiny, insignificant things about them. A particular clearing of the throat, the tunes they hum, and most subtle of all, their footsteps. It's just a series of staccato clicks, but you recognise it. You know it almost like their voice. It was two thirty-six in the morning and he was woken by the sound of footsteps outside. 'She is late' he thought to himself. It took his mind a few seconds to catch up. Then reality hit him, he knew it couldn't be her, as she had died in a car crash four years previously. Justin desperately missed his Delia, or Dee-Dee as he called her.

Abruptly, the footsteps stopped. He sighed and put it all down to being between sleep and wakefulness, combined with a heavy dose of wishful thinking. Then he glanced at the time on his alarm clock. It was exactly the time that the fatal car accident had happened.

Eventually, he drifted off to sleep again, but his dreams were horrendous. Everything was playing over and over in his mind. The tears in the eyes of the young policeman who broke the news to him. Her parents' reaction. They were absolutely devastated. She was their only daughter. Once again he was sobbing. The grief of losing her was all-consuming. Secretly, he wished that it had been him, or that he could have been with her and died too. Life had lost all its appeal. He just existed until he could go to bed and switch off the pain with sleep.

He rose wearily from his bed and padded downstairs in his slippers. The first duty was to put the kettle on. He couldn't even think of starting the day without his cup of life support - his beloved coffee. He was about to go for a shower when he caught the delicate aroma of perfume. He knew that aroma as if it was handwriting. It was Chanel, Coco Mademoiselle. It was Dee-Dee's perfume of choice. As quickly as it arrived, it departed. The ache returned to his chest and his stomach turned over again.

He had no idea why he did it, as he didn't believe in ghosts 'or any of that palaver' as he described it, but he said, 'Dee-Dee, if you are trying to tell me something, give me a sign.'

Almost immediately he became aware of a tapping sound. He was almost too scared to turn around and look, but when he did, he saw a goldfinch perched on the kitchen windowsill outside. It was tapping on the window and cocking its head to one side and looking at him. A few seconds later it flew off in a blaze of red and gold.

The strange part was that the window that the bird was tapping at overlooked the side passage. The bird feeders were in the garden, outside the main window. Then he remembered. When she came home from work, she knew he would be preparing dinner, so she would knock on the small window and say, 'Put the kettle on while I put the car in the garage.' Now he was beginning to think he may have been wrong in calling it all rubbish.

He got dressed and headed off to work, and painted on his 'I'm just fine, thanks' face. He didn't want them asking how he was, and he most certainly didn't want their pity. In the same office there was a woman by the name of Franciszka, or Fran as everyone called her. She was English, but born of Polish parents. She and Justin were work colleagues and acquaintances. She told him that she was clairvoyant and clairaudient, but he just poked fun at her and called her Mystic Meg, so she had stopped mentioning it.

This particular morning she seemed as if she had to say something. 'Look, tell me to piss off, or call me names, but there's something hanging onto you. Have you had any weird happenings?'

Justin stared open-mouthed for a few seconds before saying, 'Odd you should say that'.

She replied with, 'No, it isn't, but never mind. Meet me in The Red Cat at seven tonight and don't be late, oh and you are buying.'

True to his word, Justin found a table in a quiet corner and awaited the arrival of Fran. She finally made her appearance at seven fifteen. 'What's with all this don't be late shit, then you go and turn up late yourself?' Justin asked testily.

Fran just grinned and said, 'It's a woman's prerogative. Stop whining and buy me a vodka and tonic.'

Justin returned with Fran's drink and put it down in front of her.

'Thanks love,' she said, and then launched into him. 'So, I take it she had finally managed to communicate with you?'

Immediately, Justin was on the defensive. 'It's probably all coincidence and wishful thinking,' he replied.

'Oh bollocks, you know it isn't. It's hanging all over you, the energy. You are soaked in it. Tell me what happened,' Fran replied. So Justin told her everything.

'You do know she visits you every day, at work? Fran said.

Justin looked totally bewildered.

'She stands behind you and is shouting at you. I know you feel something, because when she touches your shoulder you shrug as if something touched it'.

Justin slid back his chair, almost knocking the drinks over, and ran into the toilets. He sat in a cubicle and wept buckets. After a little while, he composed himself and went back to the table to make his excuses. 'Sorry, when ya gotta go, ya gotta go,' he said.

Fran's face never changed expression as she said, 'You don't have to be embarrassed by crying in front of me.' She then reached across and touched his hand.

He took her hand in his and gently brushed her fingers with his thumb.

'Drink up and we will go back to my place for coffee,' Fran said, and followed it up with 'And yes, I DO mean coffee.'

Justin laughed.

They arrived at Fran's place and she made them coffee. She put them on the coffee table and patted the sofa alongside her and beckoned Justin over. He sat down beside her and she put her arm around his shoulder, and said, 'You need a hug'.

Justin made a sort of small whimper, and tears sprang to his eyes again.

She held him close to her and said, 'Tears are healing. Let it all go.'.

He felt safe and warm. He felt cared for. It was almost like when mum would kiss it all better. Unbeknown to himself, he had missed physical contact desperately.

After a while he regained control and began to apologise profusely.

'Now stop that. Don't you dare,' Fran said. 'Do you know what kind of men don't cry?' she said. Then she answered her own question by saying, 'Unfeeling, uncaring arseholes. That's what. You are a lovely, warm bloke and you have had a terrible loss. I would think far, far less of you if you hadn't cried.'

'May I kiss you?' Justin asked. Then began to stumble out the words, 'I'm sorry. I don't know what made me say that. Please forgive...' but she stopped him in mid sentence by leaning across and kissing him so softly that he momentarily lost his breath. She smiled at him and said, 'A lot has happened to you and you are reaching out. Don't worry, I will be here to catch you. We will have a few kisses, then I will pack you off home like a good boy.' Before he left she said, 'Don't feel guilty. She is fine about it. She wants you to live your life.' Fran knew that he would feel like he was betraying her whatever she said.

That night, Justin sat upright in bed and said, 'Okay, Dee-Dee. I'm listening'. A few moments later he heard music. It was coming from outside. A car parked up to drop someone off, and the tune, 'Have I told you Lately' was playing on the car radio. It was their song. They even danced to it at their wedding. He then heard the people saying their goodbyes. He heard a woman's voice saying to her friend. 'I'm so glad you have decided to move on. Bye love'. Justin smiled to himself and a warmth crept over him. Soon he was asleep.

The next day, Justin's emotions were in turmoil. He couldn't get Fran out of his mind, but also felt pangs of guilt. It almost felt as if he was having an affair. Just then he heard a knock at the back door. He almost jumped out of his skin. It was Dee-Dee's mother. She looked somewhat flustered and emotional. 'I hoped I would catch you before you went to work,' she said. He invited her in and made her a cup of tea.

She looked across at Justin and said, 'I had such a vivid dream last night, I just had to come and tell you. You will probably think me a silly old woman. I know you don't believe in ghosts.'

Justin replied with, 'I dunno so much these days. Try me'.

She told him that her daughter came to her in a dream.

She told him that he and Dee-Dee were dancing on their wedding day. She then kissed Justin and told him to wait on the dance floor whilst she came across to speak to her.

'What did she say to you?' Justin asked.

'She just wanted me to tell you that by loving someone else it doesn't make your love for her any less. Then she said to tell you that you were a wonderful kisser. It would be a shame for someone else not to have the benefit.'

Justin let out a cross between tears and laughter.

'Do you know what?' she continued. 'I agree with her. You

deserve to be happy again, darling' At that, her mother said her goodbyes and left.

As he entered the office, Fran smiled at him and said, 'Wow, the colours that are around you are dazzling. All the darkness has gone.'

Justin never spoke a word. He just walked over to her and kissed her. The whole office (mostly women) broke into a chorus of 'Awwwww' and then cheered and clapped. They were married a year later. They chose another song for their first dance as that song would always be Dee-Dee's.

Count Your Blessings

'How do you do that? How do you make things work just by picking them up?' she asked. Of course, this was a seemingly ridiculous question, except for one thing. It happened to be true. Ian had a sort of talent, or an ability. Call it what you will. Most people would say that he wasn't 'the sharpest knife in the drawer'. He wasn't well educated or astute. In fact, he could barely read and write, but Ian had this way about him. He fixed things.

Sheila had brought her laptop in for Ian to check over. 'What's up with it then?' he asked. 'It just won't boot up' Sheila replied. Ian took the laptop from her and just held it in his hands. He turned it over and looked over every square inch of it. The whole examination took about five minutes. Sheila began to wonder if he even knew what it was! 'Well, aren't you going to open it up and switch it on?' she said irritably. Ian just gave her one of his patient and bemused smiles and said 'Yes, okay. I will'.

Ian carefully opened the laptop and pressed the power button, and the laptop sprang into life. He looked through all the files and programmes, then said, 'It's fixed.'

Sheila was agog. She just stared at him as if he was Dynamo the magician and he had just pulled off an astounding piece of street magic. 'What the fuck!' she said, before going on to say, 'I had it down to the computer shop and they examined it. They told me that they reckoned that the hard drive was trashed, but a friend told me about you'.

'Oh, that's nice. Who was it?' Ian asked.

'It was June from the corner shop,' she replied. 'Anyway, never mind about that. What did you do to fix it?' she asked, barely able to disguise the joy and incredulity in her voice.

'Oh, sometimes they just need a bit of a rest - don't we all?' he answered. Then he gave her the same disarming, gentle smile.

'What do I owe you?' she asked.

'Five pounds. Everything is five pounds. All jobs are five pounds,' Ian replied.

'You've saved me a fortune. Here's twenty,' Sheila replied.

'No, that's very kind, but all jobs are five pounds. That's the magic number,' he replied, and handed back the twenty pound note. Sheila paid him the five pounds and then left.

When Sheila got home she switched on her laptop and it booted up with such rapidity that it startled her. It was like someone had massively enhanced the speed of the machine. Everything worked magnificently. She checked through all her important files and documents to make sure nothing was missing or corrupted, but everything was fine. She then checked to see if there were any updates, and she saw that the machine had taken an update named 'Ichthys'. In fact, her machine was now running Windows 10 - Ichthys edition. She Googled this and found that it didn't exist. Sheila was both astounded and completely bamboozled. Her machine was running as fast, if not faster, than any machine she had been on, and was running a fictitious version of Windows.

Sheila took her laptop back to Ian.

'Oh, hello again. Has it stopped working?' he asked.

Sheila was almost stuck for words, but then just blurted out, 'I know you fixed the machine, but you did nothing. How, just how did you fix it?'

'Are you not happy with it?' Ian asked. 'If so, I will give you your money back'.

Sheila laughed almost hysterically. 'I am delighted with it, but did you somehow install an update without me knowing?' she asked.

'The machine did that. It blessed itself.' Ian replied.

'What the holy fuck are you talking about?' she said to him. Ian winced a little and said, 'Please, please don't blaspheme'.

Ian asked Sheila if she would like a cup of tea.

Sheila said that she felt in the mood for something stronger, but tea would do for now. Ian then went on to tell her a remarkable story. He told her that he was out walking the dog one evening when he saw an angel.

Sheila said nothing, and kept her face straight, whilst at the same time thinking, 'Here we go. This one is away with the fairies'.

Then Ian astounded her by, 'No, I told you, it was an angel, not a fairy.'

Fortunately, Sheila had already put her cup down on his counter, or she would assuredly have spilled it all down herself. She stared blankly at him. Her mouth hung open loosely in sheer amazement.

He gently touched her jaw with one finger, then said. 'That loose crown. It's okay now.'

She felt the tooth with her tongue, and indeed, it was now rock solid, where before it had been slightly wobbly. She actually had a dentist appointment that very afternoon to get it fixed. Sheila fled the little shop in sheer panic. On her way out, she heard Ian say, 'That was free. You didn't ask me to fix it so it is free. No five pounds.'

Once outside, Sheila only ran about ten yards or so before stopping, and saying to herself, 'Okay, everything has a rational explanation. You just haven't found out what it is yet. No need to panic.' She hadn't convinced herself one little bit. Sheila then walked home.

The next day, she happened to be in the corner shop. June served her as she always did.

Sheila asked her, 'You know that bloke Ian, the chap you told me about who fixes everything?'

June merely looked at her in a confused manner, before replying, 'Ian? Ian who? I don't remember me telling you that.'

Sheila then went on to tell her that she had taken her broken laptop down to the little shop beside the post office on the High Road just as she told her to do. 'Do you mean Ian Harris, at the old sewing machine shop?' June said. 'If you do, he's been closed for donkey's years. He had a bit of a nervous breakdown. Kept telling everyone he spoke to angels. He committed suicide. He left a note saying that God wanted him to be an angel. The shop wasn't doing well. All that was left in the till was five pounds.'

Forgive Me

'We are here to observe - nothing more. Their pain and suffering is just that. It is theirs. There is a secret on this side of the veil that we must keep. To let them know that we are real would upset the equilibrium.' The words spoken by the Great Spirit were in themselves sacred, but not of any god. The novice listened and also grieved his own passing. 'If we cannot intervene, then why must we watch?' the novice said. 'It is part of our healing process. Our penance, if you will. I have been observing for centuries, and still my soul is not fully forgiven'. The novice looked alarmed, then said 'God has not forgiven you?' The Great Spirit laughed, and said 'God IS forgiveness. He is that very power. Had he not made us flawed, then we would not seek it'. 'Seek what?' the novice asked. The Great Spirit sighed and laid his hand upon his broken soul, and said 'The ability to forgive ourselves. This is the true hell my little one.'

In life, the novice had been the most ordinary of men. He saw the posters in the village hall. He saw the finger pointing at him saying, 'Your Country Needs YOU'. Although he was working class, and the poorest of the poor, he still loved his country. His country that gave him so little in return. The recruiting sergeant barked these words at him, 'They bayonet women and children. Are you a man? Are you going to stand by and do NOTHING?' He signed on the dotted line, and a few weeks later he was in Flanders. He had never really found religion. Not the church kind anyway. His religion was hearing the lark rise and ascend to the heavens, or seeing the tiny droplets of dew on the whiskers of a rabbit as the sun crept over the horizon. This was Robert's church. Robert was the simplest of men, but like many of his kind, his chest was barely big enough to encompass the heart, the courage and the love he was capable of. When the slaughter came, he was one of the innocents. On his first bayonet charge across 'No Man's Land' he was scythed down like the ripe corn by the obscene and unfeeling lead of a machine gun. The one who fired the bullets never even saw him. He had his eyes closed to the butchery. Not his real eyes. The one's inside his mind. The mind that screamed over and over, 'Kill or be killed. Kill or be killed. Kill or be killed'.

It wasn't an easy death. It took him two hours. The last thought that prevailed in his mind was a combination of thoughts about home and the fervent hope that The Lancashire Fusiliers won the day. The ultimate obscenity was that none returned. The famous 'Pals Regiment' were no more. Twelve streets with drawn curtains and uncertain, desperate futures.

'Great spirit, am I an evil man?' The novice asked. 'To answer that question, I would have to know more than a mere spirit is capable of.' the Great spirit replied.

'I know I have killed men. It says in the good book thou shalt not kill, am I an evil man?'

The great spirit smiled, then said, 'You have taken the first step upon your journey.' He went on to tell him that death is a part of being human, and therefore, in many ways, humans can cause the death of others without even understanding that they do. 'Your brother, Thomas, he is on this side, you have met him?' the Great Spirit asked. The novice smiled, and said, 'We are reunited'. 'The rich people and the doctors. Could they have helped him? Could their medicines have healed him?' the novice nodded. 'Then did they not kill HIM by not helping?' The novice realised that these were the stumbling baby steps that he must take to find his final peace.

The Great spirit and the novice trudged heavily across the carpet of years that spread before them. There was no horizon, merely the warm glow of the pure light of understanding and humanity in the distance. It glowed like a camp fire on a distant shore. 'They burn candles in their churches, yet extinguish the lights inside their very hearts. They pray not for peace, but for the butchery of people they have never met. They follow the book you spoke of. The good book. The one with the wise words. Do they even know what the words mean?' the Great Spirit asked.

The novice said his first wise words, 'They manipulate the words for their own greed and folly, don't they?'

The Great Spirit smiled and said, 'Your words and your footsteps are the truth that will release you. No book of stories can do this.'

Thus the novice and the Great Spirit arrived at their journey's end. 'One last question oh great sage' the novice entreated.

'I am listening, but I am no great sage. I am a simple soul,' the Great Spirit answered.

'We have journeyed oh so very far, and your hand has caught me more than once as I stumbled. Am I permitted to know your name?' the novice asked.

'But you already know it. Do you not know your own name? Every man must walk with his own spirit and be reunited with it to be whole again. I am you and all your ancestors. We are as one again,' the Great Spirit answered. The weightlessness of love, understanding, forgiveness and warmth enveloped them and they became part of the pure ecstasy. Rooted in the past, the present and the future. They are in a land where there is no amen.

The Returned

'It is so cold. It is bitterly cold, and very dark here. Where am I? I'm frightened. Where am I... please? I can hear your voice but I can't see you.'

Always these words, or ones very similar were heard when the digital voice recorder was left switched on inside the guest room. This had started off after a series of paranormal events. They always thought the spare room was the centre of activity, so a friend came up with the idea of leaving a digital voice recorder in there. They ended up with far more than they bargained for, or could imagine in their wildest nightmares.

The houses had once been fisherman's cottages. They were small, humble dwellings close to the harbour. The fishing industry had long since left the area, and now it was a quaint tourist destination. Mark and Jackie had bought the house with their retirement handouts and had retired to their idyllic cottage by the sea. At first everything was wonderful. The sun shone brightly and they spent their days frequenting the wonderful restaurants and sea-front bars. The place was bright, vibrant and bustling with people who came to experience the beauties of the coastline and its interesting history of smugglers and ship-wreckers.

Now it was late January. The sea looked constantly angry and oppressive. It hissed at their bedroom windowpane at night-time. All the happy throngs of people had gone and most restaurants and bars had either closed for the winter or existed on a skeleton staff. The whole atmosphere had changed to one almost of menace. The quaint buildings and ruins now looked like something from a Victorian melodrama. It became overbearing and depressive. They also found that the log burning stove heated the living room adequately, but fell short of keeping all the radiators warm in other rooms.

They felt it the most at Christmas. They felt totally cut off and isolated from everyone they knew and loved. The village being a tourist village and out-of-season, there were no colourful lights or a tree in the village square. They both secretly wished to be back in their lovely little semi-detached in the Midlands, and their former social life. Of course, neither one told the other how they felt. They had made their bed, and funds dictated that they must now lie in it.

The night-times were the worst. The bedroom was icy cold and they could hear the sea. Always the sea. The constant, constant, horrendous black and menacing sea. They began to hate it. In a moment of clarity and honesty, Jackie asked Mark how he was feeling. He told her 'I hate the sea and the cold. It feels like being on a convict ship'. Jackie turned away and quietly wept. So, this was our dream was it? This dreadful place, she thought to herself. Mark was also thinking something remarkably similar.

The noises at first were subtle. They were almost subliminal. The odd thud and bump. It could so easily have been the cottage next door, but it was a holiday home and unoccupied. More alarming was the sound of someone sobbing bitterly. It sounded like a young boy or girl. Mark dismissed this by saying that sound can travel. It was probably in the next cottage along after the unoccupied one. They had children. Jackie placated herself with this until Mark himself was jolted into acceptance.

He was in bed. A stench assailed his nostrils. So pungent was it that it woke him up. When he opened his eyes, he was confronted by the image of a child around the age of twelve. She was dressed in rags and tattered cloth. Her hair was matted with dried blood, and a section of her cheek was missing, through which Mark could see her teeth. He was frozen with terror and tried to scream, but no noise would come forth. This vision then reached over with her talon-like fingers and raked open his cheek. He could then scream, and she vanished before his eyes.

Jackie awoke in panic herself and fumbled for the switch on the bedside lamp. When the light came on, she could see the blood on his cheek. She too screamed in fear. 'Mark, what has happened?' she shouted in panic.

All he could stumble out were the words, 'Child' and 'She scratched me.'

She dragged Mark out of bed and into the bathroom. She switched on the lights and reached for a flannel. Remarkably, once the blood had been removed, his face was completely free of wounds. There were, however, three pale red marks on his cheek. Mark was still weeping. He was also mortally embarrassed, as in his sheer terror, he had also wet himself. This, above all, was the worst part of it all for him. He was a proud man. Jackie pretended not to notice. She suggested that they should both get dressed and go downstairs.

'We have to move,' Mark said. 'I hate it... there... I've said it.'

Jackie offered no resistance, apart from saying, 'If we try and sell now, in the middle of winter, we will lose a fortune.'

Mark had to agree. Were they to sell, they had to sell for enough to buy a similar property to what they had back home. Ahhhhh home. That word seemed like salvation. They both longed for the familiar accents and the familiar ways. They rekindled the wood burning stove and settled down on the couch together. They fell asleep in each other's arms.

The next morning, Jackie walked down to the newsagents to buy a paper and a few overpriced necessities. There she was confronted by Julie, the owner of the shop. A rotund lady of advancing years and an abrupt and callous manner about her. 'My God, you look bloody awful,' she said to Jackie. She told her briefly about the incident. Julie, of course, knew all about it.

'Oh, that will be Mad Becky,' she announced gleefully, before going on to ask, 'Didn't they tell you about the murders and cannibalism thing?' She asked with a sort of feigned innocence.

Jackie just looked completely shocked. She paid for her items and left. She could hear Julie chuckling as she closed the door behind her.

When she arrived home, she was in tears. She told Mark what Julie had said. 'She's a nasty, malicious old bag. Take no notice of her. She probably made it all up,' Mark said. He detested the woman from the moment he clapped eyes on her. 'We will go into the big town and ask the librarian at the local history section. If any bugger has been eaten, it surely would have made the papers,'. Mark said. This made Jackie chuckle. They did just that.

Eventually, they were introduced to a nice old lady by the name of Rosie. She was the local historian. Jackie related the story that Julie had told her.

Rosie sighed, and said 'That bloody woman again. She must have a screw loose somewhere.' Apparently, she had told the story to the two previous occupants of other cottages on that row.

She told them that she was indeed correct that there was a Mad Becky. She was a local girl who was mentally subnormal. Her father was a drunkard and a thief. One day, a baby went missing from one of the houses. Mad Becky had been seen close to there at the time. Someone said that they had seen her eating something that looked like raw meat. This was all that the superstitious villagers needed. They marched upon her house and dragged her into the streets. There the angry mob questioned her. As she couldn't speak properly and had a severe learning disability, she just talked gibberish. She was kicked and punched to death outside her own door.

The sad irony of the story was that the baby's aunt had taken her down to the dockside to look at the boats. She had done this many times. Why this time they panicked had been lost in the mists of time. One of the fishermen took her body out to sea. She was placed inside an old potato sack and a boulder was lashed to the bag. She was then thrown into the sea beyond the harbour walls.

Rosie told them that this happened in the 1600s and was probably just a folk tale told in pubs to entertain tourists, but Jackie could tell that behind these words, Rosie believed it as well. They made their way home after collecting a few provisions. Mark had forbade Jackie from setting foot inside Julie's shop. Not that he had any power to do this in any way, but Jackie happily turned a blind eye to it. She realised that he was still trying to repair his injured pride and manliness after he had wet himself.

The next morning, Mark heard the clatter of the letterbox and thought it was the postman. When he reached the door his blood ran cold. Someone had pushed a small plastic doll through his letterbox, but someone had cut away the side of the doll's head with a knife. 'Inbred bastards. Sick fuckers,' he hissed under his breath. He felt relieved that Jackie hadn't gone to the door. He opened the stove door and threw it onto the fire. He knew in his mind that there was only one mind sick enough to do this - Julie.

Things became so bad in their bedroom with the noises and the cries, they took to sleeping in front of the log burner downstairs on a makeshift bed. They felt that the epicentre of activity was the spare bedroom. A friend had loaned them a digital voice recorder. He told them to leave it running in the room and to play it back in the morning. This they did.

The first thing that they heard, faintly in the background of the recording was the voice of a woman pleading with someone. 'Don't hit her. She knows no better. Please, George.' This was followed by the plaintiff sobs and cries of a young girl and the sound of her being slapped and punched. A little later, they heard those words. 'It is so cold. It is bitterly cold, and very dark here. Where am I? I'm frightened. Where am I... please? I can hear your voice but I can't see you.' The background noise sounded like the bubbling and swooshing of water. They both felt quite sick to their stomachs. Were these the words of the spirit of Becky as she lay on the sea bed. Was her spirit feeling the chill, deathly deeps of her watery grave? As they listened to the recording, drips of water began to drop from the ceiling. Three or four heavy drops. They seemed to fall from thin air. There were no droplets clinging to the ceiling. Mark dipped his little finger into the liquid and placed it on the tip of his tongue then spat it out. 'It tastes like sea water,' he said.

Both of them were gripped by a feeling of hopelessness and fear. 'We are out of our depth,' Mark said.

Jackie burst into tears. It was then that they heard a knock at the door. Mark opened it and it was Julie. He was incandescent with rage. 'What the fuck do you want? You have a nerve showing up here after what you did,' he said.

Julie looked at him with an air of superiority and arrogance and said, 'I have no idea what you mean.' The semblance of a smile was upon her lips.

'Is that so? I have seen those little plastic dolls on sale in your shop,' Mark said.

'Well, that doesn't mean that I did it, does it?' she said.

Mark had her. 'Did what? What did you do?

For once she seemed flustered and said 'Well... erm... well... you said I had done something.'. She regained her composure and said, 'I wish to speak to your wife.'

Mark was about to tell her what to do and slam the door in her face when he heard Jackie's voice. 'What do you want with me?' she said.

'Well, aren't you going to invite me inside?' Julie said.

Jackie said, 'Please come in'.

At this, Julie seemed to let out a sigh. It was as if she couldn't have stepped over the threshold without being invited. 'She is here. I can taste her,' Julie said.

Mark said that he was taking no further part in any of this. Jackie looked at him almost pleadingly.

'Taste her?' Jackie asked.

'Yes, I can smell and taste her,' Julie replied. As she smiled, Jackie could swear that her two canine teeth had grown ever so slightly, but then chided herself for her stupidity.

'I can help you. I can make her go away,' Julie said. 'I will return this evening.'

Jackie showed her to the door. Mark had seen and heard enough. He quietly slipped away and made a call on his mobile.

That evening, as night fell, Mark and Jackie heard a tap at their windowpane. Mark pulled the curtain to one side and was greeted by the face of Julie. Her face looked even more malevolent and evil by the light from their reading lamp. Jackie walked towards the door and was about to open it, when she heard the voice of a stranger. He said, 'Do NOT invite her in.'

Jackie whooped with fear and surprise. 'Who are you?' she asked.

Mark interjected and told her that he was here to help.

The man spoke again and told Jackie that Julie was not all that she seemed. 'Listen to what he is telling you,' Mark said. Then the man addressed Julie. He opened the door and Julie hissed and shrank away from him. He threw salt upon the doorstep and to her it seemed almost like acid. A string of oaths and curses fell from her lips. 'It is time you went back. Time you slept again. I will be here every time. Here to put you back. Begone,' he said.

At this, Julie seemed to just fade back into the night.

The next day, the body of Julie was found washed up upon the shore. A verdict of accidental drowning was put forward by the coroner. In absence of any next of kin, she was given a funeral supplied by the little money that she had in her savings. She was cremated.

Mark invited the man back to their cottage. He then told Mark and Jackie the full story. What he told them they could scarcely believe. He told them that Julie was a Hellion. She was a malevolent child spirit, neither living nor dead. A spirit who could adopt a persona. Imitate the living. Julie was, in fact, Mad Becky herself, or the evil part of her that was grabbed and held onto as she died. Her soul was invaded at point of death. Her mortal soul had been torn into two pieces. The innocent part went to the heaven of the innocents. Her evil undead part would enter the soul of an unwanted and unloved child. This was Julie. She had ironically been born into descendants of the progeny of her drunken father. Thus, the power was doubled. By inviting her into the cottage, she could reunite the living and dead parts in an unholy ritual.

'I will always be here to put her back,' the man said. 'If not me, one of my descendants. My apprentice is already learning my trade.' At this, he smiled, and bid the couple a fond farewell.

On the far side of the village a baby had been born to an unmarried mother and a drug addicted father. The nurses remarked on how little she cried. 'It is almost as if she feels nothing. Nothing at all,' one nurse remarked.

Beer Barrels and Brigands

The old brewery had been in the same family since its inception in 1817. Greg was the latest incumbent to inherit the reins and run the brewery. He had worked in every department ever since leaving school. No one knew the brewery as well as he did. All his father's staff wondered if he would take a new broom to the place and employ younger, more go-getting staff, but he didn't. He knew their true value.

He had grown up knowing every person in the place and had been taught the ropes by most of them. They were as good as family. A couple of them had even passed retirement but asked to stay on. As he was fond of saying, 'There are two things you can't buy. Loyalty and love.' When he sat in his father's chair for the first time, and all the welcomes had been given, he put his head in his hands and wept. It had only been the previous month that his father had passed away.

He had a young son himself who would be leaving school soon. He may go on to college or university, or he may come straight into the business as he himself had. Whichever route he chose, he would give him the opportunity.

The first job of the day was to go through the books with the accountant. This gave him rather a nasty shock. They were just about limping on. The sensible thing to do would be to make a couple of redundancies. He knew very well that there were a few that could have their jobs amalgamated with someone else's. The computer system had streamlined things massively. This he staunchly refused to do. They were a team, and the team never left anyone behind.

There was an oil painting on his office wall. It was of his great, great grandfather, Tobias. The founder of the brewery. It was like a holy effigy. Any family news, be it joyous or tragic, a family member would stand opposite the picture and tell Tobias. He himself had done this when he announced the birth of his son, and also when he announced the sad demise of his father. Maybe it was a trick of the light, or his mind playing tricks with him, but he could swear that Tobias looked sad. His eyes appeared to be full of tears.

The year would mark the two hundredth anniversary of the brewery, so to mark the occasion, they were going to devise and brew a bicentennial range of beers. They had kept every beer recipe since the beginning. They were all kept in what was lovingly known as the crypt. It was a locked room in the cellar. They were going to call their best bitter 'Tobias' after the founder. Greg made his way down into the crypt and opened the door. He smiled to himself as the old door creaked reassuringly, as all spooky old cellar doors should. He took down a leather bound tome marked 1817 and opened it. Sure enough, there were the original recipes.

He brought the book up into the daylight of his office desk and dusted down the cover. The book had a damp and musty smell about it, but it was in remarkable condition. All the recipes were written in copperplate. He found one of their original recipes and saw that it hadn't changed that much. The first variety was made with only one variety of hops, which luckily were still available. Just by looking at the ingredients, his eye told him that this would be a lighter and more refreshing beer. More like an IPA than a traditional bitter. He spoke with his head brewer and it was decided that they would brew a sample batch for tasting.

Greg was fascinated with the old crypt and its documents. He wanted these to be kept safe. Maybe he would even open up a small brewery museum and have these on display. He began to look through the old documents and came across an oak strongbox. It was locked and the key wasn't in the lock. In the office there was an old key safe. There were several old keys hung up in it, and some of them, no one had any idea what locks they were the keys for. He selected a handful of these keys and went back to the box. He inserted the third key into the keyhole and turned it, and he heard a pleasing click as it unlocked. He opened the lid and it was like Christmas day. They were the personal belongings of Tobias himself.

He and one of the employees carried the box back up the cellar stairs and into his office. He could see that the employee was just as fascinated by the contents as he was, but Greg thanked him for his efforts and sent him back to his job. This was family history, and for his eyes only. He found all kinds of fascinating things: a silver snuff box, a family seal and several other items of the period. Then he saw a scroll that was tied up in a black velvet ribbon. When he opened it and began to read it, he could hardly believe his eyes. It was written on parchment by a calligrapher of some skill. The ink was a sort of reddish brown in colour. He wondered whether it actually had been written in blood. It was a covenant between Tobias and the devil in the form of a wager.

A bet had been drawn up between Tobias and a gentleman by the name of Jacob. So sure of the superiority of his beer, Jacob had bet his soul against that of Tobias. A panel of judges from the masonic lodge would be drafted by secret ballot. Each man would try a pint from the tap of each brewer. The loser would forfeit his soul to the devil. The winner would receive a golden medallion. Greg was quite dumbfounded by the whole affair.

Later that evening, he happened to meet up with the vicar of the parish church. He told the vicar of the document. He was invited back to the vicarage so that the vicar could look at the document more clearly. The vicar read it and, like Greg, he too was quite staggered. 'I wonder which man won?' he said.

Greg told him the same thing had run through his own mind. 'Would such a document be legally binding?' Greg asked.

The vicar said that it had been signed by three witnesses, so in essence it would be, but then went on to say 'That doesn't mean that the devil actually collected though.'

The vicar suggested that he would look through the old parish records from the time. Records from the parish council were quite methodical and full. All misdemeanours were recorded fully and painstakingly. Greg thanked him and bid him a farewell.

On his journey home, Greg had to drive past the brewery offices. As he did, he noticed a flickering light in his office window. At first he wondered if it was an intruder's torch, but the alarm hadn't gone off and he had no reports from the night-watchman. He rang through to security from his mobile and asked Jack, the watchman to meet him at the side door. The two then went towards his office. They could hear two men talking rather loudly and passionately. They burst through the door.

The scene that greeted them was completely other-worldly. The room looked completely different. The old cast iron fireplace had been opened up and a fire was burning in the grate. A candelabra containing three candles burned upon his desk. There, sitting at his desk, was a man in Regency costume. Standing before him was a wretched looking man. The man seemed to be asking a favour from him. To his shock, he saw that the man behind the desk was none other than Tobias. The watchman ran away in terror, but Greg was quite transfixed by the whole thing. He realised that in disturbing the document he had disturbed their spirits.

The two spirits seemed completely oblivious to his presence. 'Oh come man, it was a drunken wager. It was a braggard's tongue due to your fine ale sir. Release me and be done.'

Tobias eyed his rival and said, 'I will give it my consideration.

Meet me here in a week hence and I will deliver unto you my answer.' At this the tableau faded away and the room was back to normal. It all happened so quickly that Greg had little time to be frightened. He was too fascinated by the whole thing. 'So, old Tobias made the big mouth sweat it seems,' he said, and then laughed.

The next day, the vicar contacted Greg and told him of his findings. He found an entry in the parish records about Jacob taking his own life. He had left a note that read, 'My soul is not my own. I have begged for my release but he (Tobias) is unyielding. If I am to face damnation then let it be soon. Rather this than live as a beggar.' Tobias was called before the parish to explain his part in all this. He was said to have broken down in floods of tears. He was reported to have said, 'Foolishness and the vice of gambling have caused me to lose a friend and a brother. I just wanted to teach him a lesson. I wanted to teach him the folly of his ways. We hatched a plot to have fun at his expense. I cry to the heavens that I release his spirit unto god.'

Greg felt an overwhelming sense of sadness. 'Poor, poor man,' he said.

The vicar then told him, 'It gets worse.' He went on to tell him that his wife and children consequently fell on hard times and became destitute. Tobias and the other conspirators paid towards their modest upkeep in a poorer part of town. Jacob's brewery closed and the men became unemployed. Suddenly, the whole idea of the bicentennial brew lost its lustre.

The vicar asked if Greg would like to join him in a prayer of forgiveness and reconciliation. As the two men prayed, tears were seen to fall from the eyes of the painting. They heard the plaintiff and pitiful words fill the room, 'He was my brother and my friend. Can you ever forgive me Jacob?' It was now Tobias's turn to beg for his salvation. Shortly after the words were spoken, a white rose appeared on the actual painting itself. It seemed as if an invisible hand had painted it there. A single white feather drifted down from the ceiling and nestled on top of the picture frame. 'It seems he is forgiven' the vicar said.

The bicentennial brew did go ahead. It was named 'The Two Brewers' in tribute to Tobias and Jacob. All profits from the special edition went to a children's charity. Rather than losing money, the kind gesture boosted the brewery's popularity and sales picked up. Each year they released another old recipe and donated a portion of the profits to the same charity. They also had the oil painting of Tobias professionally restored and cleaned. It hangs there still.

What Have I Done?

I had never been there before. I can say that with absolute certainty. At least, not in this life anyway. It was a three storey Georgian style country house. Not grandiose, but functionally elegant. The big, wide doors and the three steps that led up to it were meant to impress, but not intimidate. This was going to be an interesting investigation - of that I had no doubt. The remote setting added to the feeling of isolation. When darkness fell, it was going to be very dark indeed. The main feeling that I couldn't shake was the familiar one: the deja vu that I felt. It felt like I had been here many times. With the familiarity came a sense of dread. Something told me that I shouldn't be here. That I should turn upon my heels and run. My scientific mind took over and I forcibly calmed my nerves.

Ever since the renovations the house had been unsettled. There were noises, creaks, bangs and even footsteps heard. The owners weren't too concerned over these, but they were concerned about the dark figure. They presumed it to be male, and it was usually seen at the top of the stairs, but of late, it had taken to appearing in the master bedroom too. It had now started to speak, and always the same thing was said. That was 'Dear Lord help me. Oh what have I done?'

Michael and Felicity, the owners, enthusiastically greeted me. 'Call me Flick. Everyone does' Felicity said.

'If you want it to rhyme, everyone knows us as Mick 'n Flick,' Michael added.

We sat in their drawing room and sipped at our coffee. 'When did the disturbances start?' I asked them.

They both agreed that it had started when they began to renovate the old library. They wanted to restore it back to its former glory, with oak panelling and built-in bookshelves. They had seen pictures of how it used to look at the turn of the twentieth century and had fallen in love with it.

All the materials they had scraped together from salvage companies the length of the country. The treacle toffee, rich patina of the bookshelves screamed of a classical elegance that modern wood just could not provide. The room was stunning. It was adorned with a long reading table made of ancient mahogany. It mirrored the old photograph quite closely. The old library steps they had discovered in the cellar. These had been professionally restored to their former grandeur. When they discovered them, it looked like they had been used for painting walls.

'I've been doing some research,' Mick said. 'It seems there was a murder here. A servant strangled an old lady to death in this very room.'

This took me aback a little. 'When did this happen?' I asked.

'In 1816,' Mick replied.

The date hadn't passed me by idly. It was 200 years later. The bi-centenary.

'They hanged him for it,' Mick added.

My intuition and jangling nerves resurfaced. There was something so familiar about all this. Something gnawed away in the pit of my stomach. I did a preliminary examination of the property and took EMF readings in every room. Nothing seemed out of the ordinary. I made arrangements with Mick and Flick to return in four days time to do an overnight investigation. They had agreed to book into a hotel for the night.

That night, I returned home, but still couldn't shake the feeling of dread. Why on earth did I feel that way? I had investigated old hospitals, asylums, prisons and never once felt the kind of dread that I did in that house. I had a couple of whiskies and retired to my bed.

The dream I had was a nightmare of the worst kind. It was terrifying. I found myself standing on the scaffold with my hands tied behind my back and my ankles fastened with a strap. I was panting like a dog in sheer terror.

'Do you have anything to say?' the executioner said.

'I didn't do it. It was him. Him up at the big house. He killed her.' A bag was put over my head. I felt the platform drop from beneath me and I let out a small scream that was abruptly brought to a shuddering halt. I woke up covered in sweat and shaking uncontrollably. I had tears streaming down my face. I curled myself up into the foetal position and rocked from side to side. The reality of the dream had temporarily unhinged me. I fell asleep and woke to the sun streaming through the window.

The evening of the investigation arrived. I gathered together all my equipment. For some reason, this time I took along a crucifix and a copy of the Prayer of St Michael, which in itself is odd behaviour, seeing I am neither Catholic nor a believer. I met the owners at the hotel where they were staying, and they handed over the keys. Twenty minutes later I pulled up outside the forbidding edifice that was the dreaded house.

Once inside, I busied myself with the tasks in hand. I brushed all the troublesome and niggly thoughts away. I set up the remote cameras and synchronised them with the recording device on the laptop. I then set off to take EMF readings. As I entered the library, I clutched my stomach and doubled over in pain. The sweat began to pour from me and I felt nauseous. I wondered if I had eaten something that was off - but then it felt as if someone was trying to climb inside my body with me. Was this how it felt to be possessed? I dismissed this as pure nonsense. I sat down upon one of the library chairs to compose myself. It was then that I heard the voice coming from upstairs.

It said 'Dear Lord help me. Oh what have I done?'

I suddenly rose to my feet and felt a wave of anger sweep through my body. It was as if another mind had connected to mine, and all fell into perfect focus. I knew everything. The full story.

'YOU KNOW WHAT YOU HAVE DONE, YOU UNSPEAKABLE MONSTER,' I shouted. I sprinted from the library and mounted the stairs two at a time in my haste to get to this loathsome spirit. I arrived at the top of the stairs and flung open the bedroom door. There he was, the eminent professor. So beloved by his peers, but none under this roof ever saw that side of him. Wasn't it he that got poor Daisy, the scullery maid, pregnant, and then dismissed her to her fate in the workhouse? The pure hatred I felt for this slimy excuse for a man knew no compass. His mother, the owner of the property (which never sat well with him. He wanted it) threatened to tell his peers what he had done, and how abominable he was towards his own family and the servants. In a fit of rage he strangled her. He then called the magistrates and blamed it on me.

'You ask the Lord our God to help you? YOU OF ALL PEOPLE?' I hissed at him. 'It is not God who awaits your presence. You know who waits for you and the welcome he will have for you' I circled the wretched, snivelling creature like a cat around an injured mouse. 'You had me hanged in your place. You saw my wife and child forced into poverty, and eventually, the workhouse. Ask no quarter of me sir. None shall be given.'

It was then that the spirit of his mother appeared. The one he had murdered. She spoke to him and said. 'I have asked for leniency upon your soul, and it was granted.'

'WHAT!!' I shouted in defiance and disbelief.

'Hear me out,' she said. 'He is to walk this earth forever and to witness each gruesome murder that occurs. He will witness the grieving and the suffering of those left behind for all eternity. He will BEG to see the devil and pray to burn in hell.'

We both laughed until we cried. It was then everything went black.

When I came to my senses, it was daylight. I steadied my thoughts; then I remembered the CCTV cameras. They would have recorded everything. I scrolled back to the time when I mounted the stairs and flung back the bedroom door and saw a man enter the room, but the man was not me. It was a young man dressed in the garb of a footman. I had avenged a wrong and brought about justice two hundred years after it had happened. When I checked the records it was exactly two hundred years to the day when the footman was hanged.

The Surgeon's Story

It had been a very tough time, and I needed something. A spark, a vision, a direction, just something. The unfortunate part was, I had no idea what that 'something' was. I never imagined it could turn out to be what consequently happened to me.

It was a grey, autumnal day. I open an old, rusty iron gate that led into the garden of a property. The leaves blew around my feet like dead butterflies. Small fragments of death that once were full of life. The clouds threatened rain, but none had arrived thus far. It had once been an immaculately kept, formal garden, but now it was quite overgrown. It had a reputation, the house that stood in these grounds. It was early Victorian, and had once been owned by a physician and surgeon. He was known to have done experimental medical procedures on the poor. These people could never have been able to afford any medical care. They were more or less doomed and had little to lose, but everything to gain.

The property had been in the same family ever since the eminent surgeon bought it. The last family member died in her nineties, and the property had been bought by a company that was going to turn it into flats for multiple occupancy. What they found inside disturbed them. The doorway to the top floor had been boarded up. It looked like it had been that way for a very, very long time. In fact, it was later discovered, it had happened after the surgeon's untimely death at the hands of the father whose daughter had died under his knife. He had beaten the surgeon to death with a heavy walking stick. He was tried and hanged for his crime.

When they tore away the boards and opened the door, everything was exactly how it had been left after the surgeon's demise. Even his pipe was still sitting in the ashtray on his desk, and a box of matches nearby. In the next room to his study was the operating theatre. It was chilling to see. It was the stuff of nightmares. The roof had suffered some storm damage many years previously, and the damp had penetrated the room. Black mould was everywhere. The tray of instruments were rusted and corroded away in places. They sat inside a porcelain tray in about a quarter of an inch of water. The rust made it look like blood. The stench of decay was everywhere.

The builders were due in two days to tear out this scene of horror and start work on the building. I had been given the chance to see it in its raw state before it disappeared forever. It is a nightmarish scene that will be etched into my mind until my dying day. I knew the scene that awaited me, but the garishness of the equipment and the hectic patina of rust and decay made it infinitely worse than my imagination could conjure up. I couldn't wait to be out of this room and back downstairs in the parlour.

The surgeon had died in 1874. He had been attempting an appendectomy on a twelve year old girl, but the appendix had burst causing peritonitis. She died some hours later. It was a valiant attempt at saving a young girl's life, but one that he paid the ultimate price for. Her father had been consumed with grief, and in his anger, had sought out the surgeon and clubbed him to death. It was soon after that the myths and stories about his gruesome experiments began to emerge. All of them completely unfounded, but everyone loved lurid tales. The 'Penny Dreadful' mentality abounded. It was said to be haunted by the restless spirits of his patients that clamoured and howled for justice. All I had found was an eerie atmosphere and hearsay.

Later that evening I set up CCTV cameras in the surgery and his study and linked them wirelessly to a laptop that I used as a monitor. I did an initial sweep of the entire rooms with an EMF meter and, barring a few small fluctuations, all was as it should be. I sat back and prepared myself for the night ahead, but no amount of planning could have prepared me for the things that I would witness.

They say that midnight - the traditional witching hour is the time when most spirits walk; it isn't, it's three in the morning. This is known as 'dead time'. The time when most people report paranormal activity and the time when most people seem to die.

Ever since about 1 o'clock, the atmosphere had started fizzing. EMF meters started to bleep unexpectedly. Shadows moved in front of the CCTV cameras. It was as if the whole house was beginning to wake up. Gradually, I became aware of several presences encircling me. The hairs on the back of my neck began to rise. My mouth became dry.

'Is there anyone present who would like to speak to me?' I asked, whilst simultaneously switching on a digital recorder.

Slowly, as if a photograph was developing, I became aware of a circle of children sitting cross-legged on the floor. They looked as if they were in sepia tone, like an old, withered photograph. Their faces were patient and happy looking.

'Are you trapped here? Do you want to move on but someone is holding you here?' I asked.

One child spoke up and said, 'We are here because we want to be. We are here for him.'

I asked who they meant, and a tiny girl with curls in her hair said, 'The doctor. The man who tried to make us better.'

The eldest child then spoke up. 'Every one of us that he failed to save he prayed over. He prayed for our souls and wept. He gave parts of his own soul without knowing it. We want to make him whole again. We need your help.'

The wave of sorrow that swept over me was powerful and all-consuming. They say that there is no purer love than that of an innocent child. These little ones were the proof.

'How can I help you?' I asked.

'You must go to his office and sit in his chair. He will appear at the door of the operating room. He is trapped there by his own sorrow. We cannot venture into there,' the child said.

I nodded in agreement, rose from my chair and walked towards the stairs. 'Thank you, Mister,' the little girl shouted after me. I could hardly see for my tears.

Once in his office I did as I was asked, turned his chair towards the door and sat down. 'The children have a message for you,' I said.

I heard the sound of crying, followed by a voice that said, 'I tried. Please believe me I tried to make them live.'

'I know you did, and they are very grateful that you at least tried,' I answered.

He appeared at the door. A gaunt and wearied figure of a man. You could almost see the crushing weight that hung around his shoulders.

'They are still here because of you. You tried to save their little lives. It is your pain that binds them here. They love you, because you tried, and then prayed and cried over their lost souls. They only want you to be happy, then they can rest in peace too,' I told him.

'Oh thank God, oh praise be to the Lord,' he said.

It was then that the circle of children appeared, but this time around him. The little girl held his hand and said, 'Come on mister, let's all go home.'

The doctor stroked her curly locks, and said, 'Thank you.'

The whole scene began to fade away in front of my eyes, but not before the little girl smiled at me and said, 'Thank you, mister.'

It was at that very moment I realised what the spark and the direction was that I needed. I needed to start looking outwards instead of inwards. My own troubles were insignificant in comparison. It wasn't only the good doctor's soul that was saved that day.

Dark Days and Tears.

The evening sunshine stretched the shadows across the garden and exploded into a riot of colour against the red brick gable end. Something about the way the light fell and the way a light breeze shook the trees, made John feel nostalgic - yet when he tried to track down a specific memory, nothing came forward. Just more pictures from his childhood. Random and unlinked memories.

Things were a lot better these days. The counselling had done him good. He no longer hated and despised himself. He no longer punished himself by re-running memories and scenarios from his childhood. The essence of it all being, he had stopped blaming himself. It was as if he was watching The Wizard of Oz, and the black and white had given way to colour. For the first time in years he had begun to actually enjoy things.

On top of a chimney pot a starling began to sing, perfectly mimicking other birds. The perfection of it moved him. One perfectly formed tear-drop ran down his cheek. The range of notes, from warbled trills, to piping notes echoed off the wall, adding a natural echo. Then there were the other sounds it made. A mobile phone ring tone being one.

Suddenly, the temperature felt as if it had plummeted, only for it to return to normal within seconds. He involuntarily shook a little. His wife, Sally, had noticed it and said, 'Did someone walk across your grave?'

John laughed and said, 'A whole rugby team I think.'

'I'll pour us both a gin and tonic. It's too nice to go indoors yet,' his wife said. Then disappeared towards the kitchen. A couple of minutes later she returned with the drinks, and then said, 'I found this in the middle of the kitchen floor. Is it yours?'

She then handed him a gold wedding ring.

John looked at the ring and saw it had an inscription inside it. It said 'Forever yours'. 'Whoa, hang on, it can't be. It just can't,' John said. Before going on to say, 'This was my mother's wedding ring.'

'Did you mislay it or drop it?' Sally asked.

What John said next shook her to the core. 'It can't be hers. They buried her with it.'

'Perhaps you were mistaken, and they didn't,' Sally said.

'Okay, maybe I am, but how did it get in to the middle of the kitchen floor?' He went on to tell her that the last time he saw it, it was on her finger as she lay in her coffin.

'Look love, you've been through a lot of trauma,' Sally said.

John snapped back at her by saying, 'So you think I am having one of my funny turns I suppose.'

'I'm thinking no such thing, and you know it. All I was about to say is that your memory isn't what it used to be. Neither is mine.'

John apologised and blew her a kiss. They retired indoors and ate dinner.

John took the ring out of his pocket and examined it again. 'Perhaps Dad bought the ring with this already inscribed inside it. Perhaps it was a popular design back then and this is just a coincidence,' he said to Sally.

Sally then told him that when she entered the kitchen a magpie flew past her.

'Oh that's it then. Mystery solved,' John said. 'You know what thieving little sods they are. You startled it and it dropped it.'

'That will be it, there we go then. Well done Maigret,' Sally said, and then chuckled.

They watched a little TV and, as he did quite often, he drifted off to sleep.

Sally quietly slipped upstairs to bed and left him snoring on the couch. She was shaken into wakefulness by the sound of her husband screaming.

Sally ran downstairs and John was curled up into a ball on the sofa. His face was white. 'He was here. The bastard was here, standing right there and looking at me,' John said.

'Who? Who was here? Sally asked.

John looked at her with terrified eyes and said, 'It was Dad.'

Sally sat down beside him and put her arms around him. 'You were fast asleep. It was all a dream. You know your Dad has been dead thirty years and can't hurt you any more.'

John seemed to relax. Sally went on to tell him that between waking and sleeping, dreams can sort of leak into reality. 'Could you move or shout out when you first saw him?' she asked.

'No, it was like I was completely paralysed,' he said.

'That's it then. They call it a hypnagogic hallucination. It's when you are neither awake or asleep and your bad dreams and nightmares happen.' She felt John relax a little.

He then said, 'Phew... I'll tell you it felt bloody real.'

Sally smiled and said, 'If you are a good lad and come to bed, I will let you share my hot water bottle.'

John laughed and said, 'It's a deal.'

The next morning was a Sunday. The beauty of the previous day had been replaced with an overcast and grey morning. 'I'm off down to the newsagents for a paper. Do you want anything, love?' John asked.

'Get me an OK magazine and a KitKat,' Sally answered. She heard the front door close and started filling the kettle in readiness for his return. She then heard the familiar voice of John's mother say, 'Look after him Sally, love. You know he can be moody.'

Without thinking, Sally laughed and began to answer by saying, 'Don't worry Alice I will...' before realising that Alice, John's mother, had been dead over a month. Sally let out a whoop of shock and the kettle went clattering across the kitchen floor, putting a crack down the side of it.

'My god, he's got me at it now,' she said to herself.

John returned, and she explained that she had clumsily dropped the kettle and it had split, so she had put a pan of water on the stove for their cuppa.

'We can pop up town and get a new one this afternoon,' John said. Which is exactly what they did.

Sally kept the little episode to herself.

That same evening, John said to her, 'Have you moved that wedding ring? I left it on the mantelpiece.'

Sally said that she hadn't. 'Oh well, perhaps the magpie took it back,' John said.

The next day, John had to drive across the county to look at a job. He was a plumber and was going to give them a quote to fit a new bathroom suite. As it often did on such journeys, John's mind wandered idly back to his childhood. He now looked at it objectively these days. He had laid all his demons to rest. He remembered his mother trying to placate his drunken, violent father, and him being handy with his fists. He would cower underneath the kitchen table, powerless to interject. Vowing that one day, when he grew up, he would sort the bastard out for good. Then he remembered the boxing lessons, and then the day. The glorious, glorious day. The day when his father was about to hit his mother and he said, 'Keep your hands off her you piece of shit.'

His Dad turned in fury and spat at him the words, 'And who's going to stop me?'

John answered with one quietly spoken word. That word being 'Me'. He felled him with one punch and knocked him out cold.

It was that same day that his mother packed her bags and went off to live with her sister. A couple of weeks later, the police informed her that her husband had committed suicide. John happened to be there at the time. His mother's face showed no emotion at all. She merely asked one question. 'How?' The policeman informed her that he had hanged himself. She merely nodded, thanked the policeman, then closed the door. John's mother turned to John and said, 'Hanging was too good for the bastard.'

They never spoke about him again afterwards. John arrived at his destination and left them with a quotation for just the fitting, if they bought the suite themselves, or fitting and the bathroom suite included.

John arrived home to find Sally in a bit of a state. She was sitting in the garden, although there was a chill in the air. 'Are you alright, love. What's happened?' he asked.

Sally burst into tears and just shook her head. 'Nothing, I'm fine' she said.

'Well, that's obviously not the sodding case is it? Come on love. Tell me' John said.

Sally said, 'I heard your mum's voice behind me in the kitchen. That's why I dropped the kettle. Today I saw her. I saw her ghost, and your Dad was standing behind her. She looked terrified'.

John's blood ran cold. Although he had placated his reason with theories of how the ring couldn't be his mother's. In his heart of hearts, he knew it was hers.

'I've invited your cousin Janet to come round tonight,' Sally said.

John's expression changed. 'Are we now resorting to delusional mumbo-jumbo? Half-arsed supposed psychics?' he asked.

Sally looked him defiantly in the face and said, 'Do you have any better ideas?'

John admitted that he hadn't. He also knew that when he

saw his father, it was no dream.

Later that evening, Janet arrived. 'John was a little graceless with his guest by asking, 'Have you brought a proton pack like the ghostbusters?'

Janet merely gave him a sickly smile, and said, 'As charming as ever I see?' before mumbling 'Arsehole' under her breath.

'Take no notice of him,' Sally said, whilst giving John a disdainful look.

Janet then said, completely out of the blue. 'It's him isn't it? It's Alec, your Dad?'

Sally turned to John and said, 'I haven't told her a thing. Just that we had experienced a couple of things.'

John's mouth opened and moved, but no words came forth at first. He eventually stumbled out the word 'Yes.'

'Well, he's here now, and grinning like a Cheshire cat.' Janet said, before going on to say, 'Wait, your mum is telling me something.'

Janet sat with her eyes closed for what seemed like an eternity. She then opened her eyes and smiled. The story that she unfolded made John almost pass out. She told him that his father still had a hold over him. That hold being John's own fear. Not the fear that he felt for his father, for he was dead and could no longer touch him. It was the fear that it ran in the blood. That he too would turn into a violent monster.

'You had better sit down, John. Your mum has some news.'

John sat on the sofa as instructed. She then went on to tell her that his mum should have told him, but somehow the time was never right, and the longer the lie went on, the harder it would be to tell him.

'Tell me what??' John asked.

'That he wasn't really your Dad,' Janet answered.

John stared in disbelief, before saying, 'What?'

Janet told him that his mum had said that she was courting a soldier. He left to go and fight, and never came home again. Unfortunately, he had left her pregnant. His mum was something of a catch - a very beautiful woman. Alec had always liked her, and this was the ideal arrangement. He would make 'an honest woman' of her, and bring John up as their own. In her shame and her weakness, his mum had agreed to the arrangement. Janet told him that it was what he used to control her. 'Do as you are told or I tell the boy,' she said.

Janet then said, 'Your mum is asking if you can ever forgive her.'

John just burst into tears and said, 'Tell her there is nothing to forgive. What she did was a very brave thing indeed, and it makes me love her all the more. Tell her that for me, please?'

Janet smiled and said, 'No need, she heard every word.' She then said, 'He is where he should be now. He won't bother you ever again.'

John sobbed uncontrollably.

Janet put her coat on to leave. John said to her in a somewhat embarrassed voice, 'Thank you Janet, love. Thank you.'

Janet smiled, winked at Sally and said, 'Perhaps he will stop calling me witchy-poo now.'

'But how did you...?' John began to ask.

'How did I know?' Janet replied. 'Your mum told me.'

My Diana

It was a find in a million. The sort of thing that all classic and vintage car collectors dream about. It was a 1937 Riley Kestrel. An old lady had died, and the contents of her house were being auctioned off. The car had been immobilized by its owner for the duration of the war. It had been tucked away in a dry garage and under a tarpaulin since 1940. Its owner failed to return from a bomber mission over Germany in 1943. As the bidding started, his hands were clammy and his heart thudded with excitement. As the bids rose, he kept on holding up his hand. It began to climb very close to his financial limit, but with a stroke of luck, his opponent shook his head. The car was his!

Cameron was a vintage car fanatic. He would buy them to restore, and then sell them on at a profit. This one was different though. This one was a keeper! He had already cleared all the rubbish from his garage workshop, and had even swept the floors. His new mechanical love affair with this car would begin as he meant it to go on. She (all his cars were feminine) would arrive to an immaculate new home. He would have even carried it over the threshold in his arms had such a thing been humanly possible. This was the beginning of an obsessive love affair.

The car arrived on the back of a transporter. Cameron watched it being unloaded with as much emotion and attention as a father at the delivery of his first-born. His heart was in his mouth. He hopped around looking here and there and waving his arms around until his precious car was on all four wheels and on the road. With the help of the driver, they pushed and manoeuvred it manually inside the garage. He had already named her Diana, after the goddess. This was to be his goddess. His pride and joy.

The first thing he did was to show it to his somewhat unimpressed wife. 'Yes, it's lovely Darling,' she said, with as much enthusiasm as she could muster. 'Lovely... just lovely.

Is that all??' he asked.

'Okay then, it's absolutely fabulous. If I stand here any longer I will be in danger of having an orgasm. Is that better?' she asked him sarcastically.

Cameron gave her a sickly and patronising smile as an answer, then mumbled something under his breath about her and orgasms being complete strangers. He patted the bonnet of the car, as if to say, 'There there, Darling. Take no notice of the awful woman.'

He started work on the car the very next day. He decided to look the car over from top to bottom to see how formidable or otherwise the job might be. The paintwork seemed to have been covered in a light film of some kind of oily substance. The owner had obviously anticipated it being moth-balled for some time, and didn't want the bodywork to rot away. The paintwork underneath was in amazing condition. The leather seats had perished, but he knew a fantastic car upholsterer who could repair them sympathetically, whilst retaining as much of the original as possible. He opened the glove box and, to his excitement, there was quite a bit of stuff in there.

Amongst a few old garage bills and other bits and pieces, he found two tickets for a West End theatre. Plus, he also found a small box. Inside it was an engagement ring. Suddenly, the old car took on a whole different perspective. He had obviously been planning a trip to the theatre where he would probably have proposed to his love. He knew the story. The house and contents had been passed down to his sister. His sister had never married, and had probably left the car and all its contents intact as some kind of permanent memorial to her fallen brother. It occurred to him that his car, his 'Diana', had belonged to someone killed in the war. He felt it almost to be a duty to make this car 'Concours Condition'; to make every nut, bolt, engine component and bearing to be of the original manufacturer's specification. It was that very night that the dreams started.

Cameron climbed into bed and dreamt about his car. It pervaded his every thought to the exception of everything else. His wife, Jean, had once remarked, 'You think more of those bloody cars than you do of me.' Instead of doing the sensible thing and saying, 'Of course I don't darling' (even if it had been a lie), he just smiled at her. This infuriated Jean so much that she hardly spoke a word to him for three days. Such was his obsession with old cars.

Cameron's dream began to change subtly. He imagined driving down a country lane on a beautiful summer day. By his side was a beautiful young woman. She looked no older than late teens. She was immaculately dressed like something straight from the pages of Vogue. A little hat on her head coquettishly tilted to one side and held in place by a hatpin. Her perfect, red, cupid's bow lips looked full and luscious. She had perfectly formed, delicate features. Her eyes were a stunning blue. She was the sort of woman that a man could go happily to his possible death to defend from a vicious enemy. Her look told him that the love was fully reciprocated. She leaned her head against his shoulder as they drove along. His senses were caressed by the soft warmth of her body and the heady smell of her perfume. For some reason the name Joyce kept springing into his dream. He could only assume that this was her name. When Cameron awoke, he could still smell the perfume in his nostrils. It had felt so very real. He desperately wanted to see this woman again in his dreams.

Cameron's day, after the dream, was one that felt steeped in nostalgia. This was very strange, because he was feeling nostalgic for times before he was born. Times he had no right to feel nostalgic about. He had even stopped listening to his usual diet of rock and pop, as supplied by Radio 2. He had now started to tune in to classical stations, or even better, songs from the 30s and such. He had even invested in a few CD's. He had even taken to tucking himself away in the evenings in the bedroom to watch old, black and white films from the era.

His wife, Jean had started noticing the difference in him too. One day he asked her if she would mind if he started dressing in period clothing and wearing Brylcreem.

'Yes I bloody will mind. I have to own you,' she barked at him. 'When you have fixed up the bloody car, then we will go to rallies and the like and dress the part, but I married you, not my Dad.'

Cameron bristled a little. Not because she had given him a verbal bashing, but she had referred to 'Diana' as 'the bloody car'.

'For God's sake Cam, just think about what you are saying. Are you having some kind of breakdown?' Jean said.

Cameron shook his head and began to cry. He said, 'I just don't know, love. It's as if the car is talking to me.'

Things didn't improve, and Jean spoke to her friend, Eileen, about it. 'He is besotted with the car,' she said. 'It's not just the car either.'

Eileen asked what she meant by that, and she said, 'He has dreams. He shouts things. Almost as if he is talking about flying over somewhere. He sounds so scared.' Jean then told her the back-story of the car.

'Do you think it's haunted?' Eileen asked.

'Don't be ridiculous,' Jean answered, but Eileen noted the tone in her voice. It was almost as if she had hit a nerve.

'Come on, spit it out,' Eileen said.

Jean then told her that he had gone up to his bedroom to 'Watch his bloody stupid films'. She told her that he had left the garage lights on, so she popped in to turn them off. Jean then started to cry.

'Come on lovey, I'm your best mate. What's up?' Eileen asked.

Jean then said, 'He talks about a woman too. Shouts her name. Shouts out stuff like, I love you, Joyce.' She then told her, 'I went in to turn off the lights in the garage and I saw someone in his car. I thought it was him, so I walked over and looked. It was a woman in 1940s dress.'

'What?... a REAL woman?' Eileen asked.

Jean shook her head and said, 'No, I saw her for about five seconds then she just vanished. She was sobbing, and saying, Frankie, Frankie over and over.'

Eileen was wide-eyed at this news. 'You need to talk to someone. Leave this to me,' she said.

A week later, Jean and Eileen were in the study of Bob Ellwood, a local medium and historian. He told them that he had been doing some research. 'I looked at the auction address you gave me. The house was owned by the sister of the man Frank that you mentioned. He was indeed lost in a bombing mission over Germany. He was a bomb aimer,' he said. 'Seems to me a little like he isn't happy about a few things. Your Cameron seems to have almost opened up a tomb.'

Jean asked what he meant by this, and he said, 'He seems to have attached himself to Cam. Frank was robbed of his life, and now his precious car has gone too. He now wants to live his life inside Cameron.' He then went on to say to Jean, 'Stay away from that car. Joyce is also looking for a host body.'

'I want to throw up,' Jean said, and made a dash for the bathroom.

Whilst they were alone, Eileen asked Bob what could be done. 'Beyond me I am afraid, but I may know a way. I may know someone who can sort this,' he said.

Things seemed to go from bad to worse. Cameron was now totally uncommunicative. Against Jean's wishes, he had indeed taken to dressing in period clothes. His face even began to look different. Jean was now living at Eileen's as she no longer felt safe inside her own house. Bob rang Eileen and said that he had an idea, and could they both meet him outside the house that evening.

Jean and Eileen pulled up outside the house. The garage light was on and 1940s music could be heard coming from inside. It gave them both the chills. Currently, another car pulled up and Bob stepped out of the car. He was accompanied by an RAF officer. There was one distinct difference though. He also wore a clerical collar, more commonly known as a dog-collar.

'This is Ralph. He is a chaplain for the RAF.'

Ralph beamed a warm smile at the two women and said, 'Let's see what we can do shall we?' Ralph walked up to the garage door and knocked upon it. The music instantaneously ceased.

A voice from inside yelled testily, 'Who is it? What do you bloody want?'

Ralph answered with, 'How dare you address an officer in such a tone? Get out here man, NOW.' All fell quiet for a while, then slowly the garage door opened.

Jean gasped with horror. He looked so weak and gaunt. Almost a travesty against the now gleaming car. 'My God man, look at the state of you. I want you back at base now. Get your coat.'

Cameron nodded mutely, but also stood to attention. Soon he was in the car and heading off to the local base.

Ralph had obtained passes for everyone to allow them inside the camp perimeter and inside the little chapel on the base. He sat Cameron on a chair and began to talk to him. 'Who am I speaking to?' he asked.

Cameron told him his full name, rank and number. 'So, Frank. Do you know what year this is?' Ralph asked.

He told him that 'the other man' lived in that time, but he chose not to.

Ralph turned to Eileen and Jean; then said, 'It looks like he knows what he is doing. He knows he is a host in your husband's body.' He then turned to Cameron and said, 'You know this is wrong. Joyce has also passed over, so you can be with her whenever you want. You will never be reunited on this side of life.'

Cameron then looked directly at his wife, Jean, and grinned with an unnatural and malicious smirk and said, 'Is that so, chaplain. Is that so?'

Jean was furious. She screamed into Cameron's face and said, 'If you and your bloody corpse bride think you are using our bodies for your sordid little affair, I will kill him too before letting that happen.' She grabbed Cameron's face between her hands and shouted, 'We were married in a church and we made a promise in front of God. Fight man. Fight with all you have. Fight for OUR love. They are dead.'

Just then, they heard a voice behind them. 'I'm here Frankie love,' it said. A young lady in period 1940s clothing was standing there. Everyone seemed to know that this was Joyce.

'Don't you bloody come near me!' Jean shouted at her.

Joyce had tears running down her cheeks. 'I am so sorry this has happened. It all happened so quickly for him. It might be decades for you, but it feels like minutes to him.' She then went on to tell her that all she wanted was to take her Frankie across to the other side. 'It's that car that held him, and it holds him still. I have told him that I am happy on the other side and want my Frankie with me.'

Cameron's body then slumped down into the chair. It was as if he had woken from a deep sleep. 'Jean, where the bloody hell am I?' he asked.

Jean fell upon him and began to smother him in kisses. She was half laughing and half sobbing. 'Who are those two. Are they actors?' Cameron said, and nodded towards the door. Standing there was Joyce and her Frankie. He was in his full dress uniform.

'Joyce said, 'We will be going now,' and Frankie added. 'Enjoy the car, and never forget that a really good woman will always fight for your love.' They both faded out as if it was the closing titles of an old black and white movie.

Cameron did finish the car, but he sold it on at a nice profit. He took the money that he had spent on it and put it aside. All the profits he donated to charity. He donated it to the RAF Association.

Night Terrors

It was just after midnight. As Clare was drifting off to sleep, she became aware of a weight upon the bed. She opened her eyes and saw it. It was a man with a blood-stained face, and where the eyes once were, there were bleeding and raw sockets. She tried to scream but no sound came forth. She tried to move to escape this demonic presence, but was paralysed. In an instant, the man was gone and she could move again. She sat bolt upright in bed and dissolved into a flood of tears. This woke her husband, Craig. 'Was it that dream again?' he asked.

This was happening with alarming regularity. Unbeknown to Craig, Clare had booked in to see a psychologist to see if there might be some underlying reason as to why this should be happening. It wasn't that Craig would have stopped her seeing someone about it. Quite the opposite, in fact. Somehow she just felt ashamed of even admitting it was a problem. 'Everyone has bad dreams' she was fond of saying. Some bad dreams don't go away, and need winkling out and disposing with. This was one such dream.

Two days later, Clare was sitting comfortably in a chair in the office of a psychologist by the name of Tom.

'So, when did these dreams start? Can you remember?' he asked.

Clare thought back and came up with the conclusion that it was the day after the funeral of a favourite uncle of hers, by the name of Colin. It was her father's brother. She remembered this distinctly, as she thought it had been the upset of the funeral that had been playing on her mind that led to the dream.

'The face you mention. Is it a human face. It isn't like a devil's face or anything like that?' the psychologist asked.

'No, it is definitely a human face,' Clare replied.

'Do you recognise this face? Does it remind you of anyone?'

Oddly enough, this hadn't even crossed Clare's mind. She had been in such abject terror that it had never even occurred to her.

'Have a good think when you get home. It may help track down the origin of this recurrent dream' Tom said. He then went on to tell her that the feeling of paralysis and being unable to scream or shout out were quite common. 'They are called hypnagogic hallucinations, or sleep paralysis. It is a condition where the body is neither awake nor asleep, and the conscious and subconscious are operating at the same time.

Clare already knew this, but pretended that she didn't, and thanked him for the information.

'We will bring this session to a close now. I want you to relax somewhere comfortable at home. Somewhere bright and cheerful. Then try and think if the face seems somehow familiar,' Tom said. He gave her a reassuring smile and bid her farewell.

Clare felt quite positive about the whole experience. At least she was now doing something about the situation.

That afternoon, Clare sat on a sun lounger in the garden. It was a warm, sunny August day. The lightest of breezes made it pleasant to sit outside. The aroma of the nearby pine trees and the buzzing of the bees that drifted from flower to flower, made for a peaceful and tranquil atmosphere. It was an ideal time and place to think about the dark presence, her night time tormentor. It seemed like an obscene thing to do on such a beautiful day, but she knew she must. Clare closed her eyes and tried to summon up the face in her mind. She began to adopt the mental relaxation techniques that Tom had taught her. Soon the horrendous face came back into her mind. She thought she almost had it - who it was. Then suddenly she heard, 'I've poured you a nice glass of white wine.' It was her husband Craig.

Clare let out a whoop of fear, and said, 'What are you doing creeping about like that? You scared me half to death.'

Craig laughed and said that he was doing no such thing; then asked her if she wanted the wine or not. Clare smiled and said, 'Well, seeing you have already poured it.'

That night Clare prepared for bed. She did all the things that friends had suggested, such as not thinking any bad thoughts past nine o'clock at night, having a milky drink, making sure she hadn't watched any scary films. She was completely relaxed. She lay down and drifted off to sleep. Then it happened again: the familiar weight upon the bed, and then the face. The horrific and bloody face, with its raw and gaping empty eye sockets. This time though it was different. This time Clare didn't scream or try to escape. She found herself saying in her mind 'Who are you. Let me see you more clearly?'

At this, her tormentor fled the scene, but not before Clare had looked at the face more clearly. She now knew who it was. Everything began to make even less sense than before. Surely it couldn't be him? she thought to herself.

Clare was back in Tom's office. 'Now, did you think about who it might be?' Tom asked.

Clare told him about the dream recurring but how this time she confronted it.

Tom smiled gently, and said, 'I'm impressed. Well done, that took courage and strength of mind'.

Clare went on to tell him that it was, in fact, her grandfather on her mother's side. She then went on to explain that she hadn't known him for too long as he had died when she would be around nine years old. 'He was lovely. Not at all scary. Loved gardening, and used to let me pick pea pods straight off the vines and eat them. Also let me raid his strawberry patch.'

Tom nodded and scribbled down a few notes in his notepad.

The session ended a while later.

All day long, the thoughts of her grandfather had been rattling around inside her brain. She knew that he would never try and do her any harm. So why was her brain turning him into some kind of horrendous bogeyman? She found it all very puzzling. Clare decided to go to the cemetery and visit her uncle's grave. She bought some flowers from a local florist and headed off. The gravestone was kept clear of weeds and in good order, but the little stone vase was empty. It was obvious that no one had been to visit or left any flowers. This saddened her a little. Clare took out the inner container and cleaned it out at a nearby tap. She then filled it with clean water and replaced it.

She was arranging the flowers into a pleasing display, when she heard the words, 'I always find it sad when flowers are cut. They look so much prettier when they are growing in the ground.'

Clare turned around to engage in conversation with whoever was there but, to her astonishment, no one was. She then realised that she actually remembered the voice. It was her grandfather's voice.

'Yes, it really is me. This is not in your mind.' The voice had spoken again. Clare saw a shape begin to materialise in front of her. A sort of indistinct, cloudy patch. She began to back away. Her mind was in turmoil. She wondered whether she was in fact having some kind of breakdown. Then the voice spoke again, 'Don't be afraid. I need to tell you something.'

Her grandfather then went on to tell her that there was a box of papers that was still in the loft at his old house. Her uncle had inherited it after he had died. He asked if she would go round to her uncle's and ask to look at the papers. 'He will think I am mad,' Clare said.

The voice laughed and said, 'You will find a way.'

Soon after, Clare timidly knocked upon the door of her Uncle

Paul's house. He opened the door and exclaimed, 'Hello Clare love, what a surprise,' but then looked concerned, and said, 'Is everything alright?' He wondered if she was the bearer of some kind of terrible news, such as a death in the family.

'No, I just want to chat with you about something,' she said.

'Come on in then, I'll put the kettle on,' he said, then showed her through to the living room.

Clare sat on one of the easy chairs in the living room, whilst clutching her mug of tea.

'So, what's on your mind, love?' her uncle asked.

Clare fidgeted around for a while before exclaiming, 'I'm just going to have to tell you, even if you think I am bonkers, and need locking up.'

Paul laughed, then said, 'I'm sure I will think no such thing.'

Clare then relayed the whole set of events, including hearing the voice in the cemetery.

Far from thinking her mad, Paul was moved to tears. 'Before he died, he went blind with the illness. He said that it felt like someone had torn his eyes out,' he told Clare.

Paul had realised that this whole series of events was for his benefit. His father was trying to talk to him. 'I have had the same thing happen to me in the cemetery. I have heard his voice too' Paul told her. 'I don't believe in stuff like that and I just put it down to grief. In the end I stopped going, because it kept on happening.' He also told her that there was indeed a box of papers in the loft. They had glanced at them but they just seemed to be old bits of newspaper clippings, such as marriages and christenings etc. He told her to wait there whilst he went into the loft to bring down the box.

Paul dusted down the old shoebox with a cloth and placed it on the coffee table. They were indeed just old newspaper clippings, but amongst it all was a small pocket book. On closer inspection it was a diary. A diary outlining events as they had unfolded during his time as a soldier. Paul's father had never mentioned the war in any way. He always just laughed and said, 'Oh, I was just in the catering corps. I stabbed onions not Germans.'

The diary told an entirely different tale. It told about the latter days of the war. It told about the final push. It also told about the time they discovered a concentration camp by the name of Belsen. He had even made pencil sketches of some of the wretched inhabitants he had found inside the gates.

'He saw all that. He saw all that horror and never said a word,' Paul said. Then the final words in the diary made them both shudder. They said, 'Rather than witness such inhumanity that man can inflict upon his fellow man, I would rather my eyes were torn from their sockets.' He then wrote that if he had children, he would sit them on his knee and tell them never to hate anyone. To always see people as just different and not evil, and that war and killing could never be the right way.

Paul had his father's diaries printed as a book. Each member of the family received a copy.

No Tears Beyond the Grave

There was something stately and graceful about the old yew tree that stood in the church grounds. The gnarled and twisted trunk and branches gave it an elder-statesmanlike demeanour and bearing. Much beloved of our ancestors and sacred to the Druids, this tree also gave shelter and sustenance to birds such as the blackbird, the fieldfare and the thrush, who gorged themselves on its berries. The little goldcrest often made a nest in one of the nooks in its branches. This particular yew tree was also known locally as 'The Salvation Tree'.

Where this title first came from had been lost in the mists of time. Several scholars had put forth theories about it pre-dating the actual church, and sacred gatherings being held around it, but in truth, no one actually knew. The local superstition was that it was a conduit for the spirits of the departed. It was believed that, if you sat beneath its canopy at midnight on the second Sunday in the month, the spirits of your loved ones would show themselves to you. Why the exact day was so specific, and not just any Sunday at midnight, again, no one knew. As with all local myths and legends, no actual proof above that of local gossip and hearsay had ever been obtained. This was exactly why Rory was there. He wanted to be the first to offer proof.

Rory was a man in his late forties with black hair and steel-blue eyes. Many considered him attractive but a little bit off at a tangent from the norm. He was very much a believer in Wiccan and Druidic ways. His girlfriend, Hazel, was a pragmatist. They say that opposites attract. This was definitely true in the case of Hazel and Rory. Her name had helped things along, as it sounded kind of New Age. Hazel's reply to this when he first said it was, 'I was named after my auntie.'

'I have a theory about this tree thing,' Hazel said.

This irritated Rory, as calling it a 'tree thing' lent a certain sarcastic angle to her statement. 'What's that then?' he asked. She went on to explain that the Yew was a poisonous tree, and that people have suffered headaches and even hallucinations from prolonged exposure to just the aroma given off by the tree. She then went on to offer the explanation that people were unlikely to sit around under its canopy in the depths of winter, and this was most likely an activity for hot summer evenings. This would be when the tree was at its most fragrant and potent.

Begrudgingly, Rory accepted that this could be a possible explanation.

Hazel could see that he looked a little crest-fallen, so she offered up a suggestion. 'Why don't we wear respirators? That way we won't be exposed to the danger.' She went on to say, 'I can borrow a couple from my uncle who wears them when he is paint-spraying cars.'

At this, Rory cheered up considerably, and placated himself with the fact that it was useful to have a sceptic along for balance.

They had already gained permission from the vicar and the church committee who were quite agreeable to let them 'camp out' under the yew. In truth, they were a little intrigued themselves as to whether it was just nonsense or true. Christians they may have been, but they were also villagers. Scratch many a Christian, rural dweller and you will find a Pagan beneath. So all was set and in place for the night.

Rory and Hazel arrived around ten at night. They made themselves comfortable beneath the canopy of the tree. It was a warm evening with hardly a breath of wind. The tree was on the far side of the church, away from the road. There was the back of a barn to one side, a tall stone wall to another, and the back of the church, making a natural, sheltered arbour. Hazel smiled to herself and remembered another time beneath the canopy of a tree. Their intentions that night were of a completely different nature. She desperately wanted to kiss him and lay him down on the soft ground, but wearing a respirator made this something of a non-starter.

'Sodding druids,' she said under her breath. When Rory asked her what she said, she just replied, 'Oh nothing. Just thinking aloud.'

Hazel began to feel drowsy. She told Rory that she was going to get her head down and have a nap. Rory nodded in agreement. He was far from tired and his belief that something really would happen was quite strong. He was running on pure adrenaline. Eventually, by about 12:45, he decided on a nap too. Nothing had happened and the designated hour had been and gone. He lay down beside Hazel and put his arm around her. She subconsciously responded and snuggled against him.

They were awoken around 1:30 by a booming voice saying, 'What are you doing here?'

Rory shouted a four letter word in shock and surprise and grabbed his torch as the nearest available weapon.

'Don't swear in this place. Remember where you are,' the stranger said.

Rory replied by saying that he would swear wherever the fancy took him, and asked the stranger what he was doing creeping around a churchyard in the early hours of the morning. He shone the torch to discover that it was a man in what appeared to be his late sixties or early seventies. A man with a grey beard who looked as if he lived on the streets.

'We have permission to be here - not that it's any of your business,' Hazel said.

The old man went on to explain that his name was Jeremiah Puddifoot and he was a guardian of the tree.

'Guardian in what way?' Rory asked.

The stranger went on to tell them that he was something of a spiritual guardian. He told them that many young people found the lore irresistible, and would find their way into the churchyard to the tree, then get up to no good. Some would even try and damage the tree. The tree was central to his own pagan belief system, and so he voluntarily kept an eye on the place. The church didn't recognise his right to do this, but turned a blind eye to it, as it meant they didn't have to patrol it themselves.

'Why didn't they tell us this then?' Rory asked.

Jeremiah just shrugged.

'So, is it true that the spirits of the departed come to visit?' Hazel asked.

Jeremiah smiled and said, 'Only those who crave forgiveness. That is why it is called The Salvation Tree.'

Hazel told him that she didn't quite understand what he meant by that. What he then said took her breath away.

'I think you *do* understand. You hoped against hope that it really was true, as you need forgiveness from your father - don't you?'

Hazel just stared at him with her mouth wide open. The words were unable to leave her mouth.

'You are thinking how I know. Your father told me. He tells me that you believed your mother's stories about him being a bad man, and that is why you refused to speak to him or go to visit him.'

Hazel dissolved into floods of tears and said over and over, 'Sorry Daddy, so, so sorry Daddy.'

Jeremiah smiled softly and said, 'Don't tell me, tell him.'

Hazel's father walked out of the shadows from beside the tree and said, 'Hello Poppet'.

It was at this time that Hazel's pragmatism kicked in. She said 'This is hysteria. I don't know how you know my story, but I want it so much that I am seeing things.'

It was then that Rory said, 'Then how come I can see him too. He just said hello Poppet.'

Hazel and her father talked briefly. He told her many things; he told her that her mother had apologised to him when she passed over too. He said that he had watched her grow into a fine woman, and that he was so very proud of her. His parting words to her were, 'All that is behind us now, and there never was anything to need forgiveness for. Your mother and I will be waiting when your time comes.' He also told her to love and look after Rory, as he was a very devoted and loving man.

It was quite a night for Hazel and also for Rory. Rory's beliefs had been affirmed and Hazel had been converted towards believing. The sun was just beginning to break over the horizon and flood the churchyard with its amber glow.

As they were packing up to go, Hazel said, 'Rory, come and look at this.' She pointed at a gravestone. The inscription read: 'Jeremiah Puddifoot. Beloved churchwarden of this parish. Born 1831 - Died July 28th 1902'.

Rory looked at Hazel and said, 'That's today's date.'

The Ancestors

The lights in the sky had been witnessed by several people and many theories had been put forward as to what they were. Some said that they were part of the Aurora Borealis; some said it was some kind of laser projector; the truth was no one knew. No one apart from one person, a man by the name of Ian. He had decided to jump off the merry-go-round of life and live rough in the woods. His shelter was made up of anything that he could lay his hands on. He wasn't poor, and actually owned the woods in which he had set up camp. He had built himself a comfortable dwelling out of several different materials. It was a ramshackle affair and partly beneath ground, but it was warm, dry, and heated by a pot-bellied stove he had rescued from a salvage yard. His lighting was provided by car headlights attached to a bank of car batteries. He had crafted a windmill out of an old lorry alternator, and this recharged the batteries. Most times he just used paraffin lamps.

Ian was adept at trapping rabbits and living off the land in general, but did purchase, milk, bread and vegetables from the village store. Everyone knew and loved Ian. He was also lucky enough to have a trout stream running by his property. The fish also supplemented his diet.

Ian had been foraging for fungi when he spotted the corner of something that looked metallic poking out of the ground. He began to dig away at the object, but found that it was part of something much larger. He also found it weird, because it was obviously metallic, but was also slightly warm. It was more or less at skin temperature. It also seemed to be vibrating ever so slightly.

Ian was aware of the fact that there was a military research facility just a few miles away. This angered him. How dare they bury some piece of apparatus on my land without asking me, he thought to himself. He did wonder just how hazardous touching this thing would be. He was at a loss as to what to do next. Was he in danger of radio-active contamination? This really had upset him greatly. Then he heard the words: the words that seemed to be spoken almost inside his head. 'Do not be afraid. It will do you no harm.'

Ian turned around and saw what he took to be a human being. He was alarmed when he realised that the creature's eyes were far larger than most humans, and jet black. His ears were also tiny. Just mere flaps. His skin was flesh coloured, but very pale.

Ian wasn't sure whether he was rooted to the spot in sheer panic, or this creature had in some way paralysed him. Either way, he didn't move.

'It is a Genesis Switch. It is difficult to explain, but it works across several different time planes and also controls what you know as dark matter,' the creature explained.

Ian stumbled out the words, 'Who are you... WHAT are you?'

The creature never changed from its expressionless countenance and said, 'I am an ancestor.'

'A WHAT?' Ian asked.

The creature sat upon the floor and beckoned Ian to do the same.

'I'll stay standing if it's alright by you,' Ian said.

'As you wish,' the ancestor replied.

'You look like no ancestor of mine,' Ian said.

'But I am,' the creature replied. 'I am one of twelve original ancestors. I am the last one. My time is limited to mere centuries now, so this is the Genesis Switch. This summons forth replacements for the next stage of evolution.'

'Genesis? Like the book in the bible?' Ian asked.

The creature nodded.

Ian found himself feeling quite relaxed, which was surprising as he was in the presence of an alien being. 'So, you took the name from the bible?' Ian asked.

The creature told him that it was the other way around.

'Your religions, your beliefs, the beliefs of all the peoples of the earth stem from the Ancestors. I believe your religion calls us Apostles. Twelve is a very important number. It is the number that rules all nature. Twelve apostles, twelve months of the year. This is no accident. You have twenty three pairs of chromosomes. In the next and forthcoming evolution, you will have twenty-four. This will be the final evolution. Forty-eight is divisible by twelve. Four quarters, which matches four seasons. This also gives you your symbol. The cross. The crucifix. To die and to rise again,' the Ancestor said. He then told him to watch for the night-time rainbow. He told him to watch for the rain that falls upwards. He told him to look for the star in the east, as this would be the beginning. 'I believe you know this as the return of the great one,' he said. Seconds later, he disappeared from sight. It was almost as if someone had switched off a hologram.

Ian slumped to the ground and seriously questioned his sanity, and what he had just seen. Genesis, Apostles, what is all this? he thought to himself. He had never been in the least bit religious - quite the opposite, in fact. If anything, his leanings were more towards Wiccan beliefs. It was then that he felt the fracture in time. It felt like an interruption, or a flicker in a television programme: a stutter in time. Everything seemed to end.

Ian awoke, and was back in his own bed. He sat bolt upright; he was covered in sweat. He wondered whether he had made a mistake with some of the fungi he had eaten in the previous meal and was relieved that it had all been a weird dream. Then he heard the humming noise. He looked through his window and saw a glow in the woods. It was roughly where, in his supposed dream, he had met the Ancestor. Suddenly, Ian began to realise that it hadn't been a dream at all. He put on his boots and coat and walked towards the shining.

When he was within feet of the area, he could see that the buried object was now a solid sphere, and was hovering some ten feet above the ground. Coming from the object looked like drops of molten metal. But instead of falling to the ground, they were levitating upwards. 'Look for the rain that falls upwards,' Ian said to himself. When he looked upwards he saw a smear of colour across the sky. It seemed to be every colour in the entire spectrum. Amidst it seemed to be a craft of some kind.

Ian was one of the first to be genetically modified. His recall was astoundingly good. He could remember every word of every book he had ever read. His head was filled with facts, figures and knowledge that had previously been well beyond his comprehension. It was then that he noticed the Ancestor again. He was standing beside the orb and he seemed to have aged. He approached Ian and, almost without needing to be asked, Ian extended his arms to embrace him. The Ancestor informed him that his earthly name was Andrew. Ian immediately understood the religious significance of this.

There seemed to pass a sort of light between them, but a cold and icy light, not a warmth. At this, Andrew's body melted into his own.

Within days of the lights in the forest, the whole of the earth fell unexpectedly into peace. People just seemed to have lost the appetite for it. No one wanted revenge, or any kind of reckoning. Scientists pooled all their resources into renewable energy sources and the advancement of medicine. Boundaries seemed to just disappear. Strangely though, religion seemed to perpetuate, but this also fundamentally changed. People began to borrow from other religions and assimilate it into their own. A phrase began to appear. Written by millions of hands, 'Let the little children come to me and do not hinder them, for to such belongs the kingdom of heaven.'

Everyone realised a new kind of truth, that they were indeed all children, because within children lies the uncorrupted spark of pure love. Peace became not a word, but a fact.

Thoughts of Home

The scrape of wood upon stone as the chair is pulled away from the table. I had been drawn in by the aroma of baking bread and fresh coffee. A wooden table that has been scrubbed clean to within an inch of its life, adorned with everything that is needed. Salt, pepper, a bowl of lump sugar, various sauces and ketchups and a sparse menu upon a card in a small, chrome stand. No self-service here. A petite waitress with fascinating eyes and a disarming smile approached the table. The white pinafore over the top of a black dress looked perfect. 'Just a latte please,' I said.

She smiled and thanked me. The shape of her from the back as she walked away, I could have watched all day. I suddenly felt so very old.

This could have been anywhere in the world. It just happened to be around half an hour drive from where I lived. It was late summer and a weekday. All the children were at school and everywhere was quiet and peaceful. I had visited a small, independent bookshop: the kind that you so rarely see these days. Racks and displays containing new releases by popular authors, but alongside these were bookcases filled with selected, secondhand books. The shop was deceptively large. A small frontage, but it went back for yards and yards.

As I sipped at my coffee, I took one of the books that I had bought out of my bag and opened the hardback cover. Inside was a handwritten inscription. It said, 'To Christine. My inspiration and my heart. All my love, Robert. August 1941'. A million visions and ideas flooded into my mind. It was a book of love poems, so I guessed that it wasn't a gift to a favourite aunt. It would be a love token from one to another. My mind rambled, and ideas tumbled around inside my head. Was he going away to war? If so, did he ever return, and if he did, was he the same man that she had known? The book had cost me pennies, but the intrigue, the romance and the undying love inside the cover was priceless.

The book naturally fell open to a specific page. I love this about old books. They tell you the favourite thoughts and passages of the previous reader. It fell open at a love poem by Keats.

It was a poem of loss and of yearning. It told of a deep and intimate love between two people who were very much in love, and probably far apart. I pondered over how many tears had spattered upon these pages. Had Christine held this to her heart and shouted out his name as she was alone in her lonely bedroom? Was Robert somewhere dark and dangerous, clinging on to the hopes and visions of home, and the soft, remembered arms of his Christine? I could only guess!

I finished my coffee and put away the book. Somewhere outside, a group of sparrows squabbled like annoyed children. The sun appeared and highlighted the semi-clad and russet trees. 'Just perfect' I whispered under my breath.

Then I heard the words, whispered in a woman's voice, 'Yes... it's exquisite isn't it?' They seemed to come from somewhere behind me. I turned to look but the café was empty. I chuckled to myself and put it down to the atmosphere and the images from the book that were still lying easily inside my mind, like a curled up dog upon a fireside rug. I felt wistful, but filled with hope and warmed by the words and inscription inside the little, second-hand tome.

As I walked back towards the car, I was catapulted back into the present day. A screech of tyres and a blaring car horn, as a car had pulled out from a side street. This was closely followed by a string of rude words from the offended driver's window. It was as if someone had thrown cold water on a fire. It was almost an obscenity. The wistfulness had been dispelled like dried leaves in a gale. The taste of the coffee upon my lips and tongue soon brought me back to thoughts of the café, and the waitress with the delightful little bottom and fabulous eyes. I smiled and forgave their impatience, and blessed the fact that I was in no hurry. I was in absolutely no hurry at all.

I opened the car door and sat behind the wheel. I gently placed the bag containing the books on the passenger's seat beside me. The inscription inside the book still made me smile. 'Time we were heading off home, Christine,' I said to the book, then started the engine. Almost instantly, I could smell the faintest aroma of perfume. It was gone almost as quickly as it had arrived. I put it down to imagination and the perfection of the day. This turned out to be my first mistake.

Once home, I attended to the mundane jobs. I checked the mail box to see if it contained any post - it didn't. I went to my computer and checked my email. As I flicked through the emails and deleted all the spam, I caught a whiff of perfume again. The same perfume that I could briefly smell inside the car. Again, it disappeared within seconds. This began to mildly bother me. Did I have something physically or mentally wrong with me? Was it a sign of the onset of some illness, experiencing anomalous smells? Something else was also troubling me. It was a feeling that something slightly creepy was happening. I couldn't quite put my finger on it. Like my spider senses were tingling.

I put it all to the back of my mind and busied myself around the house. Evening was drawing in. I glanced in the mirror for some reason. Behind me was the living room window, reflected there, but for a brief moment, I saw white crosses across the windowpanes. I had seen such things in photographs where people had stuck masking tape to the windows to stop the glass flying around in the case of an explosion. I spun round upon my heels but the windows were completely normal. I looked back in the mirror and could no longer see the illusion. Then I could smell the perfume again, but this time quite strongly. I turned towards the mirror again, and reflected in the glass I saw a lady with blonde hair, and upon her head was a sort of brown coloured trilby style hat. She was also wearing overalls. She was in the uniform of a land girl. I let out a whoop of surprise, expecting it to all be imagination again, but when I turned around, I could still see her. I lurched backwards into the cabinet, almost knocking over a cut glass decanter.

'Tell George, tell George that I didn't mean it. It just happened,' she said, and then disappeared.

I was now in full scale panic mode and seriously wondering if I was having some kind of psychotic episode. 'That just didn't happen. It didn't fucking happen. It's too daft,' I said to myself. Nervously, I glanced towards the mirror again. My heart almost stopped when I saw the unmistakable shape of lips, as if someone had kissed the mirror whilst wearing pillar-box red lipstick. I leapt back away from it as if it would somehow attack me. My body was now tingling all over with the panic and the adrenaline. Somehow I knew that the book that I had bought had something to do with this. It was just too much of a coincidence, the spirit asking me to 'Tell George'. If proof was needed it was there in plain view on the mirror. I examined it more closely, and it was real lipstick.

I poured myself a glass of scotch to calm my nerves. My hand was shaking quite violently. Some of the scotch splashed onto the table as I poured. I drank the glass dry in one hit. 'Okay, let's examine the facts. All that has happened is that the spirit of an attractive lady has kissed your mirror and told you to give a message to someone called George,' I said to myself. 'Hardly a gothic novel is it?' I continued. I wasn't convincing myself in the very least. The inner voice inside my head was screaming, 'What in holy fuck are you saying? Are you mad?'

The rest of the evening was spent looking at the television set. I wouldn't say that I was watching it. It was more like background noise. Something of this era to drive away the demons. I was still quite jumpy. I had goose-pimples that you could have struck matches on. It ran through my mind to open the back door and throw the book in the bin, but something told me that this wouldn't be a good idea. This turned out to be my second mistake.

That night, I went to bed, but left the bedside lamp lit. I fell into a fitful sleep that was plagued with strange dreams, and all of them about wartime. One dream I had was so very vivid. There was a band of us running through a vineyard. The staccato sound of automatic weapons in the distance. The 'zip' sound as the bullets flew through the vines and rattled the leaves. I woke up in a complete panic. My body soaked in sweat. I glanced at the bedside clock. It showed 3:20 in the morning. I pondered upon the idea of going downstairs and making a cup of tea, when I heard raised voices. Faint at first, but becoming louder. At first I thought they were outside, but discovered that they seemed to be coming from downstairs. I tip-toed onto the landing to hear what was being said. I already had my mobile phone in my hand to call the police. It was then that I heard the woman's voice from earlier. The one that spoke to me by the mirror. 'It meant nothing, George. Nothing at all. It was a dance, and we had been drinking,' she said.

Then came an unfamiliar male voice who shouted, 'Nothing? NOTHING? - he meant enough to get you in the family way - DIDN'T HE?'

I then heard the back door slam. then a woman sobbing - and then silence. I had absolutely no intention whatsoever of going downstairs to look. At least not before it was broad daylight. I stood on the landing for three hours before carefully creeping downstairs.

Once downstairs, the house was completely normal. I looked at the mirror and the lipstick had gone. I began to wonder if it had all been a dream. That was when I spotted the teacup and saucer on the coffee table. On the rim of the cup was the familiar shade of lipstick.

'Oh will you just fuck OFF!' I shouted into the empty room. Something told me that this would have no effect whatsoever. Beside the teacup I spotted something. It was a book. It looked brand new, with a clean book sleeve. To my amazement, it was the poetry book. I opened the cover to see the familiar inscription, but the ink looked vibrant and strong, and not faded as before. 'This goes straight in the fucking bin,' I said to myself. Then I heard a familiar voice say, 'No, please... don't'.

The sensuous but terrifying silhouette of a woman began to take shape. Within moments, she was there once again. This time dressed in an elegant and figure-hugging satin dress.

I stood open-mouthed and stared at the woman. She seemed solid. Flesh and blood. 'Please may I sit down?' she asked. Her voice tinged with sadness.

I nodded my head and gestured towards an armchair. This was my third mistake.

She told me that she had been at a harvest dance in the village. The land army girls from the farm had gone along. They had been drinking, and she had been dancing with a young, Canadian airman, and one thing led to another. 'So now I am in the family way, as George puts it,' she told me, before bursting into tears. 'I have no idea what to do. I can't go home in this condition, I just can't,' she said, then she disappeared.

It turned out that she and George were to be married, but he had told her that he wouldn't 'Bring up another man's bastard'. So he called off the marriage and had headed back to base.

George was a Dunkirk survivor, and my imagination had proved right. He had been in some dark and scary places, and one of the things that pulled him through was the thought of returning to his 'Chrissie'.

I began to wonder if it wasn't my imagination at all, but some form of intuition. 'Maybe I have psychic gifts?' I thought. The vivid dream made sense all of a sudden. Running through a vineyard with bullets flying around my ears. They were in full retreat. They were heading for the beach and Dunkirk. I shuddered at the thought of both having this gift, if a gift it was, and not a curse, and the events as they unfolded. I noticed that the teacup had gone from the coffee table, and the poetry book was old and weathered again. 'I'll keep that book. If I see that it is new again, I will know that one of them is around. This was my fourth and final mistake.

I emailed an old friend. I hadn't spoken to her in a couple of years and felt that I had no right to ask for her help. We had worked together and had become friends. Actually that isn't strictly true. We had later become 'friends with benefits', to use the modern parlance. Spookily, her name was also Christine, but everyone knew her as Izzy. Apparently, as a toddler, her dad would call her Chrissy, but she couldn't pronounce it properly, so said Izzy instead. It had stayed with her throughout life.

In the email I told her everything that had happened so far. I knew that she was a gifted psychic. She had the disturbing habit of repeating things that you happened to be thinking - including some of the rude ones! Around ten minutes after sending the email, my mobile phone rang. It made me jump with fright. My nerve-ends must have looked like celery that had been hit with a hammer. I answered the call, and Izzy's chirpy little voice greeted me. 'SWEETIE,' she squealed excitedly at me 'It's me, Izzy. What the hell is going on darling man?'

I told her that everything was in the email.

'Can I pop round, lovey?' she asked.

I chuckled, and said, 'I rather hoped you would. That's why I sent the email. We haven't spoken in years. I feel almost like I am using you,'.

She responded with the delicious, earthy, dirty laugh that I remembered so well, and adored 'Oooooo, you know how to charm a girl out of her pants don't you?' she replied.

'No, I meant... no I wasn't,' I stuttered back at her.

She laughed, and said, 'Only teasing sweetie. Don't worry, your little soldier is safe,' She told me that she would be arriving in approximately ten minutes. It turned out to be half an hour.

There was a knock at the door. I opened it to find the sweet little bundle of fun that was Izzy. 'Stopped at the off-licence on the way for supplies,' she said, whilst waving a bottle of Chablis.

She then leapt upon me and smothered me in kisses. 'Get two glasses and let the dog see the rabbit. Let's see what I pick up,' she said.

I poured the wine and she sat beside me on the couch. 'That book, hand it to me,' she said, whilst pointing at the book of love poems.

As soon as she touched the book, she gasped as if she had stepped into icy waters. 'Oh, this isn't good. This isn't good at all,' she said, before going on to say, 'This is a portal, sweetie. This is how they got in. You are now in their triangle. She has feelings for you, and this angry spirit, this man, wants to kill you.' She went on to tell me that the angry spirit thought that I was the lover,. The Canadian airman. 'He is just a huge ball of hate, of pain and of regret. He knows that the Canadian was killed on a bombing mission, but now he sees that she has feelings for you,' Izzy told me.

She sat slightly apart from me and closed her eyes. I could hear her regulating her breathing. The room began to feel cold. I could actually see her breath.

'She's here,' Izzy said.

Again, I saw the shimmering outline before me, but it never fully materialised. I didn't know it at the time, but Izzy was controlling the entire situation and keeping her at a distance.

'Oh, poor, sweet thing. She hanged herself. She didn't do a good job of it and choked to death,' Izzy told me.

Quite suddenly, the temperature plummeted. I heard an angry, male voice shout the words 'It might as well have been me that kicked away the chair. I drove her to it.' It was George.

Izzy then spoke calmly to the angry spirit, and said, 'You are her one true love. She wants only two things. Your forgiveness and your love.' A picture flew off the wall and hit the opposite wall with some force, smashing the glass and destroying the frame. Again, Izzy spoke calmly, and repeated her words. You are her one true love. She wants only two things. Your forgiveness and your love.'

Then, the shimmering outline of Christine materialised again. There was an intense flash of blue light, and the room felt instantly warmer. Izzy let out a sigh of relief, and said, 'He has forgiven her, and they have crossed over.' She then took the book of poems, showed it to me one last time, opened the door of the wood-burning stove and threw it inside. I didn't try and stop her. At last, I had stopped making mistakes.

'The answer to your question is 'yes'. You do have psychic abilities. I knew it as soon as we met. You are also like an open book to me. How ironic eh?' she said.

I knew exactly what she meant.

'Izzy smiled, and said, 'I have packed my toothbrush as well. I will let you decide on the sleeping arrangements.'

She then winked and blew me a kiss.

Printed in Great Britain
by Amazon